Time to Play

K.A. Richardson

K.A. Richardson

Printed and bound in Great Britain by Clays Ltd, St Ives plc.

ISBN: 978-0-9955111-8-7

For my best friend, Claire – for keeping me grounded and always believing.

Prologue

6th June, 1994 – Foster Home, Ryhope, Sunderland.

It was cold and cramped. The young girl shifted position, trying to stop the spade digging into her back.

She shivered, pulling her dressing gown tighter. Tears filled her eyes.

It was her own fault anyway. She could have been sleeping in the nice bed with the floral bedding, and her pretty white furniture that held all her new clothes. She could have been warm inside the house rather than cramped in the shed out of sight.

But she wasn't. Because she knew if she'd stayed in the house he would have come for her. And he would have done far more than just touch her leg this time.

She'd been in the foster home now for the total of three weeks and four days – the longest she'd ever been in one place that wasn't a group home. If she told on her foster mother's boyfriend then that's where she'd end up again. The four-to-a-room home where the noise never stopped. Surely this was preferable? Even with Chris's roaming hands and his gravelly voice giving evidence of his thirty-a-day habit.

The tears fell down her cheeks.

She really couldn't cope with him touching her.

It was how she'd ended up in the shed with the woodlice and spiders.

She stared through the open shed door at the kitchen window. It felt like she'd been in there for ages. In reality it hadn't even been half an hour. How was she supposed to sleep here? There was nowhere to lie down. *Can you even sleep sitting up?*

1

She wiped the tears away with the back of her hand. This was her decision. She'd just have to be grown up and deal with it. Just like she dealt with everything else. She was eleven now. As of today she was practically an adult. Ann had even been nice and made a party tea with a birthday cake – her first ever cake. She had presents too.

She should have been happy.

But Chris's wandering hands had made her so upset she'd thrown up all the nice cake and sandwiches. She'd made a decision when she was in the bathroom that if that's what birthdays were about then she didn't want any more.

Her eyes narrowed as a flash of orange appeared in the kitchen window. The lights danced and moved and it took her a moment to realise that the kitchen was on fire.

Oh my God. That was me. I left the candle burning near the window so I could still see it from out here. Ann will get hurt. It's all my fault.

The candle was Chris's rule – no wandering in the house putting lights on at night.

The girl got to her feet and stood in the shed and stared as the flames started burning harder. What should she do? What *could* she do?

Taking a deep breath she ran to the back door, and flung it open, intending to run past the fire and shout for Ann. The flames flew towards her with a `whoosh' and she knew she wouldn't get past.

She was going to run to the front of the house but the fire alarm suddenly started squealing.

That would alert Ann. She knew that.

So she backed away, and curled up on the floor of the shed with tears streaming down her face.

She'd done this. It was her fault.

Chapter One

Present Day
1ˢᵗ November, 2125 hours – Ryhope, Sunderland
He bent down at the cage door and glanced inside.

The girl was curled up in a ball, her eyes closed. He knew it had taken her a while to fall asleep, her belly was empty of food and fear inhibited the natural instinct to rest. He purposely hadn't fed her much in the two days she'd been his.

He smiled because he knew hunger gave them an edge, kept them more alert. And when they were alert the pain they felt became more acute.

Normally they lasted a few months in his care, each experiment different to the last. Their eyes, so terrified to start with, slowly grew accustomed to the tests and they eventually became accepting. To a point anyway. Their screams lessened, the pain grew less acute, but eventually he pushed them too far and they died.

Such is life. Everything dies.

Once their screams lessened, he started to get bored, began looking for the next experiment. The lack of screams meaning they were finally becoming accustomed to the pain, which was, after all, the whole purpose of the experiment.

It wasn't that time yet, though, this one still had plenty of fight in her. Plenty of time to realise he was trying to teach her that life was pain, and to accept the fact.

Standing upright, he reached for the metal bar that was sitting on top of the cage. He felt his heart quicken as he ran the bar across the cage loudly.

'Time to play,' he said softly, as the girl jerked awake with a gasp. She shot to her knees, huddled in the furthest corner from the cage door, and started begging. Her native tongue made no sense to him.

He slipped the bolt to one side, reached in and grabbed her arm, tugging hard until her body followed. She was crying now, and she tugged back from his grasp.

His anger simmered. He would make her understand that pulling wasn't allowed.

Forcibly, he placed her into the chair in the centre of the room and secured her hands and feet silently. Placing a section of material over her mouth, he tightened it and knotted it at the back. Then he stood back and stared.

This one was a beauty.

He hoped she would last.

Depressing the record button on the camera set up on a tripod in the far corner, he began to speak. 'Subject six. Day three. The bruising from day one's injuries is starting to yellow at the edges. When ejected from the cage today, the subject has been reluctant and screamed. She sits before me now, shaking but still somewhat defiant. She doesn't understand the rules of the game yet. Today I will break three bones. She will receive minimal pain relief and then will be fed this evening for the second time.'

Turning towards the girl, he grabbed the thumb on her left hand and forced it backwards, waiting for the crack to reverberate around the room. As it sounded, the girl screamed loudly through the gag, her breath laboured and staggered as she gasped through the pain he knew was now shooting up her arm.

Time for break number two.

He liked doing them quickly, before the body had time to adjust to the pain sensations and become accepting. Clenching his fist, he slammed it hard into her nose, listening as it crunched and blood spurted forth from the girl's nostrils.

Her eyes lolled back in her head as a steady stream of the red liquid fell from her nose. She was almost unconscious.

'Last one,' he whispered, his hand stroking the back of her hair gently.

Kneeling down, he took hold of her left ankle and gave it a sharp twist. It was too much for the girl, whose body went limp and sagged in the chair.

The third one always made them pass out.

Untying the restraints, he placed her back inside the cage, put a sandwich and a bottle of water, and a strip of paracetamol beside her, and locked the cage door.

'I'll be back in two days, sweetness. Then it'll be time to play again.'

2nd November, 0225 hours – Shincliffe, County Durham

It had been a good night.

Grant Cooper, or GC as he was known to his friends, had been out since early afternoon. He'd managed to drink his weight in alcohol, draining dregs from half-empty glasses and swiping drinks when people weren't looking. What little money he'd had had been spent on some E tablets. At some point during the evening he'd even managed to slip a pair into the drinks of a couple of lasses. He'd laughed hysterically from his perch in the corner of the bar as the effects had set in and the girls had gotten high.

Now though, he wished he hadn't wasted the pills on girls he didn't even know. It felt like he'd been walking forever. The city centre of Durham seemed so far back it might as well have been in another country. The winding road to Shincliffe was like a marathon tonight. And he was tired.

The effects of the drugs and alcohol were wearing off, not that it was obvious as he stumbled his way down the road towards the lights of the village ahead.

He finally made it to the edge, then veered left into one of the side streets. As he neared his destination he felt anger bubble to the surface. *Who the hell does she think she is, dumping me? Stupid bitch even phoned the cops on me last week.* He chose to ignore the fact the police had also told him to stay away from the address or risk getting locked up again. *What the hell do they know anyway?*

He couldn't stay away. Stevie-Lea *owed* him an explanation. It wasn't even that she was good in the sack; he'd told her she was every time they'd had sex, knowing in his wise nineteen-year-old heart girls needed to be told all the time. It was that she was *his*. The few times he'd lost his temper and lashed out at her were her fault anyway; she'd always taunted him and pushed his buttons.

He stumbled up the path and started banging loudly on the door. 'Stevie-Lea, open the door. It's me, GC, Stevie!'

He heard her open the bedroom window, and she leaned out and yelled, 'What the fuck are you doing, GC? Go the fuck away.'

'Stevie, please. You owe me an explanation,' whined GC, looking up at her.

'I owe you fuck all. Now naff off. You'll wake the whole bloody village.'

She slammed the window shut and GC felt his rage burn. He hadn't heard the whisperings she shared with her new boyfriend upstairs – there was no way he could have – but he was fuming. How dare she just dismiss him like that?

He lost his temper, slamming his fists on the front door and screaming her name over and over. *Wake the whole village? I'll wake the whole bloody city, you selfish cow.*

As the front door opened suddenly, GC tipped forward and almost lost his balance. He grabbed the side of the door and stood slowly, plastering a grin on his face. 'Knew you'd come round.'

As GC's eyes connected with the man at the door they widened in shock, realisation taking a moment to dawn.

'Name's Kyle. Stevie-Lea told you to fuck off. Now I'm telling you. And I'll say it real slow so you can understand. FUCK … OFF.'

'And who are you? Man-fucking-mountain?' GC squared up to the male in the doorway, his chest stuck out as he waited for a reply.

The man didn't speak, he moved quickly instead, his fist connecting with the side of GC's jaw like a bumper car at the fairground. GC felt his head spin around and his legs go beneath him as he flew backwards and landed hard on his backside. He heard the door slam as he lay there looking up at the stars above.

It took him a few minutes to clamber to his feet, and when he did, he grabbed the nearest thing he could in temper. The rock impacted with the bedroom window; the bang echoed around the street. Glass sprinkled over the garden, and GC heard the roar of man-mountain inside, and realised he didn't want to face that wrath twice, so he turned tail and ran.

It felt like his feet were pounding for hours as the path changed from paved to undergrowth. But he kept running, convinced the big man was right on his heels. Tree branches slapped him in the face as he ran, and he registered how much his jaw hurt. He could still taste the metallic tang of blood around his back teeth and for a moment he wondered whether something was broken.

When the ground slipped away beneath his feet, he felt his arms flail outwards as a scream escaped and he fell forwards. The freezing cold water was like another slap to his face and he inhaled sharply as his body went into shock and froze momentarily. It was long enough for the water to take him, though.

It had been raining persistently for two weeks now, and yesterday had been especially heavy. The River Wear had risen, bursting its banks in places and fast whirling rapids were now in places that had been calm previously. The flow carried GC away quickly, and he opened his mouth to yell for help. Seeing his weakness, the dark river sent a wave crashing into his mouth, the water filling it instantly and making him gag in response as it hit his throat. He felt himself cough and splutter, and panic set in.

Any remnant of alcohol and drug stupor fled from his mind as he fought the water, trying to stay afloat. He tried to swim, flapping his arms hard and wishing he had paid more attention in his PE lessons at school.

His teeth chattered as the water dragged him further towards the city. He opened his mouth to scream again, and was suddenly pulled underneath the surface as his foot snagged on something unseen. Struggling, he kicked his other leg at whatever it was and tried to free himself. But the river had other ideas and the tree gripping his foot held steady.

The waves shifted suddenly as a large branch interrupted the flow. GC felt the cold air on his face and gasped in a few eager breaths, shuddering breaths as he tried not to cry in fear. He tugged hard at his leg, his tears clogging his throat. But the tree held fast.

His movement did dislodge the large branch behind him though, and the end swung round suddenly and connected with the side of his head. The impact was hard enough to make him see black curtains closing in, and there was nothing he could do to stop them. His eyes fluttered closed, and the river pulled him back down.

GC didn't feel the water replace the air in his lungs, he didn't feel the tree release his ankle, and he didn't feel the river carry him further into oblivion.

2nd November, 0240 hours – container on a truck, southern England.

The steady drone of the diesel engines was a constant. Elvie Aquino was sitting huddled in a corner of the container. Her knees were pulled up to her chest and she was doing her best to ignore the strong smell of urine from the bottom end of her nightie. Sweat from the start of her journey had dried and set, making her clothes stiff. Her dark hair was no longer shiny; it hung in limp strands around her face. She couldn't stop shaking and her teeth chattered loudly together whenever she unclamped her jaw.

She felt a tear escape and roll down her cheek.

It wasn't supposed to be like this.

When her grandmother, Noni, had died a couple of weeks ago, she was supposed to inherit the lean-to and the people of the village were supposed to look after her until she was deemed able to do it herself. That's how it was done in her village.

She'd been asleep when the men had come. They had put a hand over her mouth and carried her out to a car, a knife sticking against her ribs warning her to be quiet. From the car she had been put into a van, driven for a long time and then placed inside the container with nineteen other women. They were all older than her, though. Elvie was only fifteen.

Nita Thress, another girl in the container had quickly befriended Elvie, talking to her and telling her it would all be alright. Nita was older than her, and Elvie had happily let her take charge. But Nita was now ill. A lot of the women were.

Elvie didn't know how long they had been inside the container, but it had been long enough for the women to drink almost all the water, and empty the tubs of rice and vegetables, even after they had gone slimy and started to smell. Now the container was starting to smell like death. There were no blankets to keep the girls warm in the decreasing temperature, no fresh water to keep them hydrated, and no toilet. They had all been defecating and urinating, and it had gotten to the point where it was no longer confined to one specific area.

Hearing Nita moan for water, Elvie climbed to her feet, ignoring the pins and needles in her legs from being pulled up to her chin for so long. She grabbed one of the few cups and went to the last bucket with water inside. It held about an inch at the bottom and Elvie had to use her hand to scoop a little into the cup. She took a small sip for herself, then walked back over to Nita. She picked up the girl's head, and held the cup to her parched lips, allowing her friend to drink the last dribble.

Elvie placed her hand on Nita's head, checking for a temperature as her grandmother had done when she was small. Nita's head felt hot and sweaty as she thrashed beneath Elvie's touch.

The fear she had felt at the start had faded. Now Elvie just wanted to get to wherever she was going. She had an ache in her head that had been a constant for days. Her hunger had eased today and she felt tired. Whatever was coming she would deal with when she got there. She missed her Noni terribly. Her gran would never have let anything happen to her. Laying her head on top of her knees, she started to cry silently.

2nd *November, 0610 hours – footpath along the* *River Wear, Durham*

Wallace Pemberton was following his normal route. He'd been to the corner shop to pick up his newspaper, as he did every day, and had progressed down the road and onto the footpath that ran alongside the river. His west highland terrier, Poppet, was eagerly sniffing every plant and bush as they made their way leisurely along.

It was still dark, and the path was deserted: the joggers and dog walkers not yet braving the early morning. But Wallace liked the dark, and the walk kept his ageing muscles from seizing up. At almost ninety years old, his hearing was starting to fail and his eye sight wasn't the best, but he was definitely fitter than your average old man.

He had his paper tucked under one arm, his jacket collar was pulled up around his neck and the flat cap sat perched on his balding head keeping the skin warm. Poppet's lead hung loosely beside him, not that she would ever run off even without the lead. The dog was almost as old as he was, in dog years at least.

The sun was just starting to think about rising, and the sky to the east changed from black to blue slowly; Wallace was just approaching the cathedral. It stood on the opposite side of the bank to the path, lights illuminating the walls and turrets. It had stood for nearly a thousand years, and was one of the main tourist attractions in Durham. He had visited once as a young man, trying to impress his latest flame. They had walked all the way along to the lovers' chair and shared their first kiss. So long ago he couldn't even remember when. Her name had been Lacey, and she'd ended up his wife so his wooing had obviously done the trick. Lacey had passed on several years before, but Wallace always thought about her when he passed the Cathedral. He missed her a lot.

'Love you, Lacey,' he whispered with a nod as he passed.

The route Wallace took wasn't short; it was probably five times longer than just using the normal streets to get home. But it was a nice walk, the odours of wild garlic and aniseed ripe in the spring and summer, and the crisp smell of winter approaching at this time of year. The leaves had started falling from the trees the month before, and Wallace trod carefully, mindful that he might slip.

He was just walking past the weir, when something caught his eye. It was trapped in the tumultuous water rolling at the weir itself, and it looked like clothing. Wallace pulled the hard glasses case from his inside pocket and placed the lenses over his eyes. The water ragged the object about a little more and suddenly, Wallace realised it wasn't just clothing. It was a dead man. He should know; he'd seen enough of them during the war.

Wallace felt a pain start in his chest and move down his arm. He struggled to draw breath and the pain increased. He tried not to panic, he'd had a heart attack a few months back and had ended up being fine. His legs gave way and he sank to the ground with a soft sigh. Remembering what he'd been told last time, he coughed hard. Drawing in a shaky breath, he coughed a few more times. His newspaper floated off in the morning breeze as he freed the new-fangled mobile phone from his pocket. His grandson had insisted he carry it with him on his walks. Now he just had to remember how to use it.

The pain intensified and he coughed again. Pushing 999 and the green call button, he steadied his breathing to respond as the operator asked which service.

'Police and ambulance, please,' he gasped.

'This is the police, sir, how can I help?'

'Dead body ... weir near the cathedral ... need help.' Wallace was trying his best to stay conscious, and he forced another cough from his tired lungs.

'Sorry, sir, did you say there's a dead body in the weir near the cathedral?'

Wallace grunted in reply, 'send police ... and ambulance.'

The call handler must have known something was wrong and asked, 'is the ambulance for you, sir. Do you need help? You sound very breathless.'

'Heart ... attack.'

Wallace couldn't say any more. The phone slipped from his grip and hit the concrete floor with a clatter. The call handler was still calling 'sir' as Wallace finally succumbed and slid backwards, his eyes closing and his head lolling to the side, his breathing raspy and shallow.

Poppet knew something was wrong; she had sat down beside him the minute he'd fallen. Now, she threw her head back and howled mournfully.

Chapter Two

2nd November, 0620 hours – Marlo's flat, Sunderland

The heavy buzzing from the bedside table invaded Marlo Buchanan's sleep and tried to pull her into the land of the living. Doing her best to ignore it, she pulled the pillow round to cover her ears and tried to force her mind back into the dream she'd been having. But the buzzing persisted.

Groaning, she reached an arm from the warm confines of the duvet and blindly felt around for her mobile phone. *It seriously cannot be time to get up. I've been in bed like ten minutes. There's no way that's my alarm.*

Finally finding the phone, she pulled it towards her and cracked open one eye to glance at the caller ID. Seeing who it was, she swiped across the screen and mumbled, 'Go away. I'm sleeping,' before hanging up. She hadn't even had chance to put the phone down when the knocking at the door started, softly at first but then louder. She would swear she could hear someone talking through the letterbox too.

'Christ what's a girl gotta do to get some sleep around here. I get in at 2 a.m. and I'm getting knocked up at just after six? Jesus Christ, I'm actually gunna kill her,' grumbled Marlo as she pushed the duvet off and got to her feet. She grabbed the hair bobble off her bedside cabinet and tied her dark hair in a loose bun as she walked through the flat.

She unlocked the front door and opened it slightly before turning and heading towards the kitchen.

'You forgot,' accused Deena Davis, her hands on her hips in mock anger.

'Obviously,' said Marlo with an eye roll at her friend. Then realising she might actually be offended, Marlo added, 'Sorry, I was out late at a search last night and our jog just slipped my mind. I'll make you a special coffee on my machine to make it up.'

Marlo's eyes narrowed in on her friend, then widened suddenly. 'Bitch! You're not even dressed for a run. You weren't going anyway!'

'Wondered how long it'd take you. Where's my coffee?'

Marlo made it and the pair made their way through to the living room.

'So, if we weren't running, why on earth were you banging at my door at this ungodly hour?'

'I wasn't banging. And it's not ungodly, it's almost 7 a.m. You'd have been up soon anyway. I'm on 8 a.m. start today.'

Marlo acknowledged the statement with a nod and took a sip of the hot coffee, sighing as she savoured the sweet caramel hit. That coffee machine was one of the best things she'd ever bought.

'We still on for trying that new cocktail bar tonight?' asked Marlo, suddenly remembering what day it was.

'All being well. I'm due to get off at four but have a dentist appointment scheduled in at five. Then have to go home and put my face on, so say meet there about sevenish? That's provided I don't wind up being kept on of course. The dentist must think I'm a complete piss-taker. I've rescheduled the appointment twice already; once more and he'll probably take me off the books. You know what the dentists are like nowadays.'

'Yeah it is hard to get in. But you need to. No putting it off this time. That tooth needs pulling! How is it today, anyway?'

'The same. Took some codeine this morning to ease it off. Hopefully the doc's gunna just whip it out and save me more misery. What're your plans for the day?'

'At work 'til five. We've got a buyer coming to look at the boat. Wish the force weren't selling it, it's a lush machine. Shame we don't get much opportunity to use it. All this cost cutting's a nightmare. Did you see the briefing the other day about the potential cuts? I thought this was all over and done with a couple of years ago but we still have to lose another five million over the next year.'

'Yeah, they've put us all on the "at risk register" again. Crime scene investigators are still not classed as frontline staff, which is ridiculous. Half the time we're at the scene before the cop gets there these days. It sucks.'

'Sorry, honey. Am sure you'll be fine though, you're an old hand now. Hasn't Cass put you forward for the crime scene manager training?'

'Yeah, she's fab bless her. There's four of us been put forward. I'm just keeping my fingers crossed. Johnny got accepted for the Arson Investigation course last month so hopefully he'll be out of the running for the CSM one; but you never know. You know what Hartside's like. He's a complete prick.'

'Hate to say it, but bosses usually are. Especially one's like him with their head so far up their own arse they can practically see daylight.'

Marlo's phone interrupted their conversation with a loud buzz. Seeing it was her sergeant, she swiped and answered.

'Buchanan ... yup, OK, Sharpie. See you in a bit.'

She didn't even need to explain. Hanging up the phone, she watched Deena curl her legs up underneath her.

'Yes I'll lock up when I leave, and no I won't forget to wash the cups. Go to work, Marlo.'

Marlo grinned at her friend and made her way to the bathroom. *At least it's a late call in.*

2nd *November, 0625 hours – Container on truck,* **Washington Industrial Park**

The truck braked hard, jolting Elvie from a disturbed sleep. She rubbed her eyes, trying to rid them of that feeling of sandiness. She glanced down at Nita who was laid beside her. Nita's skin was pale and clammy and there was a thin sheen of sweat over the girl's forehead. She occasionally whimpered as the fever tried to tear her body apart.

There was no water left now. Elvie's tongue felt swollen and cracked inside her mouth. The initial gnawing of hunger that had started when the food had run out was now nothing more than a dull ache. Her eyes were heavy and hot; she really didn't feel too good.

The smell in the container had intensified overnight and Elvie suddenly leaned over herself and heaved. There was nothing to come up, but her body kept heaving. When she sat back up, her eyes were glassy with tears. She hated being sick.

Elvie knew that some of the other girls had died, releasing their weak hold on whatever life they were heading into. She envied them in some ways. They were free, not cooped up in the stinking container where the only light was artificial and the only warmth was each other. She cocked her head to the side, listening. The truck was no longer moving.

There was a loud clatter as the container doors were suddenly wrenched open. Two men leapt inside and started kicking at the girls on the floor.

'*Pataas*,' they said as their toes connected with ribs and legs. The men obviously didn't know much Filipino; their pronunciation was all wrong, but '*pataas*' was up, and '*puminta*' was go. It was all they needed, they weren't paid to chat.

The girls who didn't move, whether through illness or death, were left behind. They would be dealt with later.

Elvie was more scared than she had ever been. She had to get Nita up. She moved to her knees and shook her friend hard. Eventually, Nita opened her eyes, struggling to focus. She felt rather than saw Elvie's fear, and turned to pull herself to her knees. Elvie helped her up, taking pretty much her full weight as Nita leaned into her.

'*Puminta*,' said one of the men, nudging them towards the open doors.

The security cameras that should have been watching the industrial estate had been disabled earlier in the night.

16

There was no one to see or hear as the girls were herded from the container into nearby vans in the car park of the abandoned factory. Years ago, it had been one of the most productive factories in Washington. Now though, the only thing it was used by was the rats and pigeons.

Elvie clutched Nita tightly, knowing if she let go then her friend would fall. There was no one to help them to the ground. Elvie leaned her friend against the side of the container and clambered down, wincing as the glass shards on the tarmac cut into the soles of her bare feet. She reached up and helped Nita to the ground, flinching as the men jumped down beside them.

'These two aren't bad. I can put up with the stink if there's a nice warm mouth round my cock,' said one with a sneer.

'Boss lady said no touching,' said the other one, looking bored. He put up with the same or similar on every transportation.

'Come on, no one would even have to know,' whined the first man. He wasn't well built, verged on skinny in fact. He was well dressed in a white shirt and black trousers, his hair neatly styled. In contrast, the other was well built and muscular, also dressed in the same uniform of sorts. He lost his temper suddenly, one hand wrapped around the skinny man's throat and he threw him against the back of the truck.

'No ... Fucking ... Touching.'

The skinny man gasped and nodded, trying to catch his breath. As he was released his hands instinctively touched his neck, almost as if he were checking it was still there. He watched the other man make his way to the driver's side of the transit van, and only able to vent his frustration one way, he gave Elvie a sharp kick.

Elvie gasped as hot pain seared up her thigh. *Why did he do that? I didn't do anything.* Tugging Nita alongside, she climbed into the back of the van. Only one of the other girls from the container was inside, huddled in the far

17

corner, looking as afraid as Elvie felt. The doors slammed shut behind them, and within seconds the van left the car park.

2nd *November, 0710 hours – Dive Team HQ, South Shields*

By the time Marlo arrived at the dive team's headquarters, her appearance had changed completely. The dishevelled, just-got-out-of-bed look had been banished and replaced with something more functional. Her hair was swept up in a tight bun, and her figure disguised with the loose folds of the non-descript black t-shirt and combat pants that made up her work uniform. The coffee had kicked in making her look like she'd been awake for hours.

She made her way down the stairs to the wet room at the base of the stairs. The room wasn't actually wet, it had a waterproof coating all over the floor, and drains strategically placed around. When the team came back from a dive, this was where the equipment was stored and cleaned. It was also where the team would congregate.

True to form, the dive team sergeant, Colin Sharp, looked up as she entered.

'Hey, Marlo. Since you're first here you're lead diver. Check your gear. We're taking the small RIB,' he said, referring to one of the rigid inflatable boats used by the team for rescues. 'It should be big enough. The body's in the weir at Durham Cathedral. River's high 'cos of the rain. Body's probably snagged as the report from the cop on scene is that it's not moving from the weir.'

'Have we got a rendezvous point?' asked Marlo, as she checked her mask and lines.

'Yeah, the RVP is at the small car park next to the cathedral. DI Ali McKay is running point. The guy who handled that murder in Sunderland a few months ago, the one that got away?'

'Oh great, so we've landed some tit who probably doesn't know his arse from his elbow?'

'Now that's no way to talk about Mac,' joked Doc entering the room and receiving a punch to the arm from Mac in response. Mac and Doc were like chalk and cheese. Complete polar opposites but they got on like a house on fire. Mac aptly nicknamed from a shortening of his surname, MacDonagh, and Doc after an incident involving the rescue of a dog from a pond whilst he was walking the beat. He'd given the dog mouth to nose resuscitation and the nickname Doc Dolittle had been his reward.

All the team had nicknames. Marlo's was Buck, a shortening of her own surname, though some of the cops would dispute that if asked. The sergeant was known as Sharpie. The only member of the team that didn't have a nickname was Connor Maynard, the crew's youngest member at only twenty-seven years. He'd transferred into the force a couple of months before with full qualifications and breezed through his entrance interview. Once in, he'd been seconded to the dive team when a spot became available.

Sharpie stopped the comments about the DI with one look at Marlo. His mouth set in a line, he told Mac and Doc to go and prepare the RIB, before turning towards her.

'Buck, you know what I'm going to say. You don't even know the guy, and he out-ranks you. Bite your tongue.'

Marlo had the grace to blush slightly, knowing her mouth often spoke before her thoughts had caught up. 'Sorry. I'll rein it in. Won't happen again.'

Sharpie nodded and went back to lining up the oxygen tanks ready for removal into the vehicle.

With all of them working together, they were briefed and ready to leave inside of half an hour.

2nd *November, 0720 hours – detached house, outskirts of Hetton-Le-Hole*

Elvie was terrified. She and Nita had been herded out of the van and in through the front door of a house. They'd been shepherded upstairs to a tiny room, thrown inside and a key had been turned. There were two single beds and a lamp on a small table. The walls were bare and the only other thing present was a tray containing a large jug of water and a plate with some dry sandwiches on.

Elvie had never really eaten bread. She knew what it was but was more used to the flat breads her Noni had made, or, of course, rice. But her hunger and thirst won over any doubts she had. She pushed her fear to one side, helped Nita to the bed, and slowly held a plastic cup to her friend's lips.

'*Mabagal,*' she whispered as Nita tried to gulp the water. Nita nodded and slowed down as ordered. After Nita finished downing the water, Elvie handed her a piece of sandwich. Slowly Nita took a bite of the strange food, and chewed. Cheese. She'd had that before. Nodding at Elvie, she took the sandwich and took another bite leaving her friend free to eat too.

From the language of the men at the car park, Elvie presumed they were either in the United Kingdom or America. For a moment emotion clogged her throat as she silently thanked her Noni.

Noni had taught her to speak, read and write English. When Noni had been young, she'd fallen head over heels in love with a British soldier, stationed at one of the nearby camps. The soldier had fallen for Noni too; his name had been William Grant. William and Noni had begun a relationship. He had wanted her to come and live with him in Suffolk, England. But Noni's parents had been unhappy with the relationship. They had kept Noni inside and after a few weeks, William had had to leave to return with his platoon. Only days after he had left, Noni had discovered she was carrying his child, Elvie's mother, Myrna. Luckily for Noni, her parents supported her throughout. They'd had no idea that Noni had kept in touch with William, who went on to marry and have his own children. The letters between the two continued, until a few years ago they had stopped coming. And when they stopped both Noni and her granddaughter presumed that William had passed away.

Elvie had fond memories of sitting on her Noni's lap reading all of William's letters. She hadn't let on she knew English to the men, of course, and there were some words she hadn't understood. But, she understood the gist of it. She knew what was implied and was grateful the big one had stopped the thin one from forcing them to do something they wouldn't want to do.

Whatever this place was, it wasn't a good place to be. They had to find a way out.

Elvie felt her eyes grow heavier, her legs felt like weights. She looked at Nita, confused at the depth of her tiredness. But Nita was already laid out on the bed with her eyes closed, breathing deeply. Elvie had nothing left to fight with; she sank back onto the bed and let the darkness take her away.

Neither girl noticed the bedroom door open or saw the two males enter with two other young girls. Between them they picked Nita and Elvie up, and took them to another room.

2nd November, 0740 hours – Car Park, next to Durham Cathedral, Durham City

Marlo jumped out of the 4x4 used to tow the RIB and made her way with Sharpie over to the melee of cops stood around an unmarked vehicle. The dawn had just broken and the cathedral loomed in the background, ominous yet protective. It had seen its fair share of war and was still standing, though some of it had been rebuilt and restored over the years. Marlo shifted her attention to the conversation as they reached the man who was obviously the DI.

'DI McKay? Sergeant Colin Sharp, dive team. This is my lead diver, Marlo Buchanan.'

'Just Ali is fine. Thanks for getting here so quickly. Don't envy you the job of getting in the water on a day like this. It's bloody freezing. Guess winter's definitely on its way.'

'The suit keeps me warm enough,' replied Marlo, making eye contact with him. His suit jacket was fastened over his shirt, and his dark hair moved with the wind. His grey eyes held her gaze and her cheeks flushed again as she remembered her comments of earlier. She really needed to learn when to shut up. 'Show us the body?' she added.

The river was high, not far from the top of the bank and almost at breaking point. Any more rain and the river would flood the nearby cricket field, not to mention immerse the 'Lovers chair' that sat not too far away on the footpath. The chair had been there for a long time. It was made of stone and from the front looked like a normal chair, but the back had gargoyles pulling from the stone as if trying to escape.

Marlo and Sharpie glanced at each other as the body came into sight.

It was still in the same place, caught in the water tumbling at the base of the weir. The body was being battered but held solid in place. It had to be snagged; otherwise the river would have carried him off towards the ocean at Sunderland.

Sharpie frowned, 'I don't like the sheer volume of water here. Getting you in the water, even with the lines, wouldn't be safe. We'll try and do a snag and bag. We can reassess once we're in the RIB if need be.'

Marlo nodded. When the water was that bad it made sense to reduce the risk as much as possible.

'Go suit up and help the team,' said Sharpie with a nod. He turned back towards Ali and added, 'Are we thinking murder?'

'Won't know 'til we get the body out. There's a couple of missing persons outstanding but I think he's too old; they're both just teenagers. Maybe he's a jumper. The sooner we get him out and make an ID the better. It's getting later anyway. The last thing we need is more people having a heart attack.'

Sharpie looked at him, puzzled.

'Sorry. The old boy that found him had a heart attack. He managed to get it rang in to the control room but then passed out. Doesn't look good for him but he's at the hospital now.'

'Jesus. Poor fella.'

'Are you wanting me on the RIB or the bank?' asked Ali.

Sharpie raised an eyebrow – the DI knew boats? 'Bank is fine. I'm gunna go brief my team.'

Ali watched as he walked off. He had noticed the look of surprise. No one down here knew he'd worked the dive team in Edinburgh years before. There'd never been any need to tell them. His heart filled with sorrow as he remembered his reason for leaving. *You'll never catch me diving again.* Turning, he made his way back to the car.

2nd November, 0800 hours – River Wear, near Durham Cathedral, Durham

The engine of the RIB hummed loudly as it came to a stop in front of the weir. The body was more in view now with the sun rising and banishing the darkness. Marlo could see the male was in his early twenties, and a jagged gash was visible against the pale skin of his forehead. It didn't look good: wounds like that usually came from being clocked round the head with something hard. Marlo glanced at Sharpie and he nodded almost imperceptibly. This was potentially a murder.

She held the pole steady as she tried to hook the body to pull it towards the RIB. Sharpie was at her side, acting as the stand-by diver. Mac and Doc were both working on the tanks in case Marlo had to go in the water, and Connor stood at the engine trying to maintain position against the heavy flow of water. Marlo managed to hook the body and tugged, trying to free it from the hold of the weir.

A tree branch hit the RIB causing it to jerk suddenly, and Marlo felt herself pitch forwards. She inhaled a sharp breath in anticipation of the blast of cold water that she was about to hit, but her body jerked backwards. Sharpie had grabbed her utility belt and heaved her back.

'Intent on taking a dip today, Buck?' he joked.

'Just making sure you're awake.' She yanked the pole again, firmer this time and the jolt was enough to free the body from the water's grip. They pulled the male towards the RIB and grabbed his clothing, pulling him over the inflated edge and onto the base of the boat. Working quickly, they manoeuvred him inside a mesh-sided bag. The mesh allowed any residual water to drain off, whilst holding any potential forensic evidence inside.

As Connor navigated the RIB back to shore, Marlo cupped her hands to her mouth and blew hard, trying to warm them up. The Kevlar gloves were great for preventing injuries but they didn't stop the cold seeping through into finger joints.

'What have we got then?' asked Ali as the team pulled the RIB up the bank.

Marlo opened the zip fastening at the top of the bag, peeling it down so Ali could see the male's face, watching as Ali frowned.

Kneeling down for a closer look, he said, 'I know this lad. We had him in not so long back for domestic assault, I'm sure we did. Charlie handled the interview. He bashed his missus round the head with an ornament. Maybe this is her way of striking back. Is there any ID on him?'

'We haven't looked. We pull 'em out. You can put your hands in his pockets, gov.' Connor's voice was sarcastic as he stood beside Marlo glaring at Ali. She shot him a warning look. *What the hell is his problem?*

Ali looked suitably shocked at Connor's tone. 'Problem?' He queried, his eyebrows raised.

Connor looked ready to respond with anger, so Marlo quickly interrupted. 'No, no problem. I'll check for ID now.' She patted the male's pockets and found his wallet tucked in his jeans at the front. Pulling it free, she flicked it open. 'Grant Cooper?'

She handed Ali the wallet so he could look at the picture on the provisional driving licence card.

'Aye, that's him.' Ali put the wallet into a small evidence bag, sealed the open end and turned back towards his team. Remembering his manners, he turned back. 'Thanks, Marlo.'

'What the hell was that?' hissed Marlo in Connor's direction.

'What was what?' he asked, looking confused, 'I just told him to do it himself.'

'He's a DI, Connor. Checking the pockets wouldn't have killed you.'

'Cops like that do my head in, waltzing in like they own the place and taking over. Besides, he's a knob. It's his fault that guy escaped the other month. Proper risk assessments weren't carried out. Because of him, a prison guard was killed. That guard was my cousin, Billy. No way Billy deserved to die like that. His deaths on *his* shoulders.' Connor jerked his head towards Ali.

'I'm sorry about your cousin. But I'm sure the prison does their own risk assessments. I don't know much about the case so can't really comment, but –'

'Well keep your comments to yourself then,' snapped Connor before marching off towards the van.

Marlo stared after him. *Jesus, overreaction much. Though I guess I'm one to talk. It was only this morning I was bitching about Ali. Pot. Kettle.*

2nd November, 0825 hours – River Wear, near Durham Cathedral, Durham

Connor stopped beside the van, immediately regretting his harsh words to Marlo. She wasn't to know Billy had been his cousin. To be fair, Connor had often wished he and Billy hadn't shared familial ties anyway; his cousin had been a tosser for the most part, always had multiple women on the go and treated people like shite. Connor knew Billy had been responsible for half the drugs going into the prison, but it was just one thing on a list of many that he couldn't prove. And regardless of his faults, he was still family.

He sighed deeply.

His family really were the bane of his life. He was convinced he'd been born into the wrong body. He tried his damndest to stay on the right side of the law, despite every opportunity placed in his path by his uncle. He had always been in the picture looking after Connor and his sister, and Connor had always been expected to enter the family business. If racketeering and smuggling could be called a business. Instead he'd stuck to his guns, kept his nose clean, even moved to the Midlands and joined the force.

The rumour mill however, had closely followed him, eventually forcing him into the transfer to the North East Police.

His new colleagues knew nothing of his family, despite the fact that Uncle Fred had soon moved up to the North East himself. To help his parents he'd said. Lord knew his mum and dad needed the help. His mum had early onset Alzheimer's, and his dad struggled daily with looking after her. His uncle made sure the mortgage was paid, and visited every day – always making sure Connor never forgot just how much he had to be grateful for.

And his Uncle Fred rang him every day when he was at work, fishing for goings on and information. Which Connor had to provide, or his mum and dad would end up homeless. His wage, though decent, wasn't enough to pay their mortgage as well as his own. Not to mention the cost of putting his sister, Marie, through university. Uncle Fred took care of it all, and if all he wanted in exchange was snippets of information, then Connor really didn't have it in him to say no.

Connor was smart though, at least he thought he was. The information was only ever minor – drugs raids going down, whispers of searches heard in the bait room. He'd never accessed the force systems purposefully for intel, but it was still bad enough. He knew if he ever got found out, it wouldn't be something he could just explain away. Professional standards would have his job.

And now he'd snapped at one of his colleagues and made himself look like a prat.

Sighing deeply, he shoved his hands in his pockets and frowned. *When on earth will this all end? When will I be able to dig myself out of this shit-pit? When will I be able to make amends for all the bad things I've done.*

He knew there was no excuse. One day fate would come knocking, and then what would he do?

Putting his face straight, he turned and walked back to the team. They could never know. He needed to get Marlo alone and apologise.

2nd November, 1105 hours – detached house, outskirts of Hetton-Le-Hole

Elvie felt consciousness try and tug at her mind. She tried her best to resist, wanting to stay in the dream world where she was safe and nothing could touch her. But a voice invaded her subconscious, prompting her to become more aware. The voice was female, nasal, and spoke English with a Filipino accent.

'The youngest one stays. She is pure. She will bring much money. The other goes. Tonight. Take her to Rocko on Wear Street. He will teach her how to be a good girl.'

Elvie heard a male voice give confirmation, 'Yes, boss. Make sure she's drugged. The last one used her teeth on me, the bitch. I've still got the scars.' It was the same skinny man who had kicked her.

'She was punished. The only thing she bites now is the pillow in the bed of the man who owns her.' The woman cackled as she and the man left the room, closing the door and clicking the lock into place.

Elvie opened her eyes, carefully in case she had been wrong about the door closing. She saw Nita on the bed opposite; her hair was damp and she had different clothes on. Putting a hand to her own head, she realised her own hair was damp. She had been washed and changed also.

'Pure?' she muttered the word to herself. *What does that mean?*

She tried to sit up, but the room spun making her feel sick. Placing her head back down on the pillow, she closed her eyes. *Just for a minute, I'll get up and...* Darkness dragged her back down and she fell back into slumber.

2nd *November, 1540 hours – Dive Team HQ, South Shields*

Marlo stood in the doorway to the sergeant's office. 'Hey, Sharpie. Everything's sorted in the kit room. Am I OK to get away?'

'Yeah sure, Buck. You're at HQ tomorrow, right? The professional standards hearing?' said Sharpie glancing up.

'Yeah at 1 p.m. I'll pop here in the morning. If we don't get a shout I was thinking I might do some practice dives. It's chilly but the water's supposed to be calm tomorrow.'

'That's a good idea. Connor can join you. He hasn't had much chance to get in the water with being the new guy. In fact, we'll all pitch out. It's been a while since we used the Delta RIB: it could use the run out. Can you tell the team to report in at 7 a.m. and we'll get started immediately.'

'Sure. I'll need to be out and dry for about twelvish though. Give me enough time to drive back down to Sunderland. Glad this is the final hearing, like.'

'Well, you paid for the phone. There's no other issue really. I'd have reacted the same in your shoes.'

'Yeah, this meeting's just a formality now. Even so, I'll be pleased when it's over.' The incident they referred to had happened a couple of months ago. The team had just finished pulling a body out of a lake in Washington. A woman had been walking with her three-year old daughter on the path that ran alongside the man-made bank. The mother had been busy playing on her mobile phone, too engrossed to notice the child walk to the edge to look at the ducks. Marlo had happened to look up as the child pitched forward over the edge and landed headfirst into the water. She'd jumped back in and grabbed the child, pulling her to the surface. The mother hadn't even heard the splash as her eyes were still fixed on the phone screen.

In a fit of temper, Marlo had grabbed the phone out of the woman's hand and thrown it towards the centre of the lake. A complaint had been lodged the next day demanding payment for the phone, and demanding the force address Marlo's 'attitude problem'. Professional standards had told Marlo to pay for a replacement out of her own money and the meeting tomorrow would put the matter to rest.

'Last day in tomorrow then rest days. I need 'em like, am shattered this week. Don't ever have kids,' warned Sharpie with a shrug of his shoulders.

'Do I look like the kind of girl to settle down and want a family?' joked Marlo. 'I can barely look after myself. Besides if I had kids, I wouldn't have time to dive. I'm heading up to the Farne Islands on my rest days. Bit of solo diving with my camera. I'm hoping to get some decent shots of what's left of the wrecks up there. Last time I went there was too much sediment. I couldn't see naff all.'

'You're the only person I know who dives at work, then goes home to dive on her own time too. Have fun though, and be careful. You know how I feel about solo diving. Something can ...'

'... always go wrong,' finished Marlo. 'I'll be careful don't worry. I'd better run if I'm gunna catch the guys before they leave. See you in the morning.'

'Bright and early,' replied Sharpie turning back to the computer.

Chapter Three

2ⁿᵈ November, 2320 hours – detached house, outskirts of Hetton-Le-Hole

Muffled sounds invaded Elvie's sleep – a whimper, the sound of feet scuffling on carpet. She remembered a hint of a thought from earlier; something bad was going to happen but it stayed just out of her mind's reach.

Forcing her eyes open, she gasped as she saw the two men from the truck half-carrying, half-dragging Nita between them. Elvie couldn't understand why Nita didn't even struggle. She looked fast asleep.

Elvie pulled herself to her feet and launched herself at the man nearest to her. It was the skinny one who had kicked her, and she grabbed his face with her fingernails and scraped them down his cheek.

'Argh,' he grunted, dropping Nita's shoulder and turning to face Elvie. He was angry, and she saw his eyes glint with evil as he came towards her. She took a step backwards, terrified. The back of her knees connected with the edge of the bed and she couldn't go any further. She whimpered as the man raised his arm and smacked her in the face, hard.

The force of the blow flung Elvie backwards and onto the mattress. Her face burned and she felt tears fill her eyes. No one had ever hit her before.

'Maybe I'll show you just how pissed off I am,' growled the man, reaching to unbuckle the belt around his waist.

'Gaz. Leave it.' The warning came from the other man, the one holding Nita up. 'Boss said no touching.'

The man in front of her leaned forward until he was so close she could feel his breath on her lips. She couldn't have moved if she tried, terror had her paralysed. *What's he going to do? Why did he unhook his belt?*

'One day, I'm going to have you. And fat boy over there ain't gunna be here to stop me,' he whispered.

Elvie didn't follow all of his words, but she understood the meaning.

Her breath whooshed out as he stood and strode to the door, slamming it shut behind him with such force that it rattled the tiny window built into the roof. The lock clicked into place and Elvie was alone.

It took a few minutes before she could move again, and she put her hand to her face. She winced as her fingers found the area he had struck her. It throbbed painfully and felt warm to the touch. Tears filled her eyes again but this time she fought them back. It was time to stop being a child. Crying was pointless. She needed to figure a way out of this room to start with and then she needed to get some help.

But who will help me? The police? They'll be the same here as they are at home, anything overlooked for the right price. Who will help me, Noni?

Her brow furrowed in concentration as she considered what to do. *If only Noni hadn't died then none of this would be happening.*

Sitting back against the wall, she pulled her knees to her chest and hugged herself tightly. *How will I get out of this?*

3rd November, 0005 hours – Wear Street, Sunderland

Gaz and the other man, Danny, held Nita between them and made their way quickly from the van through the faded front door to the terraced house on Wear Street. Nobody would notice them, even if it was daylight; the area was rough and there was a code, a form of honour amongst those destined to live on the other side of the law. No one would tell, even if they knew what was happening inside the dingy house.

They dragged Nita through the porch and into the hall. Wallpaper hung off the walls, peeling and damp-smelling. A small table had been placed at the foot of the stairs and a Filipino woman sat filing her nails. She glanced up as they approached.

'Attic. Rocko want her there for training.' She pointed towards the stairs, needle scars evident along the pale inside of her arm. If you looked closely you'd see the pin prick of her pupils; if she'd opened her mouth her teeth would have been discoloured and missing in places. She looked about fifty years old, but she was only twenty-one. She'd lived in houses like this one since she had been fourteen. Then, she hadn't been allowed to leave. Now, she chose to stay because they fed her habit.

Gaz and Danny pretty much carried Nita up the bare stairs to the room right at the top. The other doors in the house were all closed. Muffled sounds came from behind some of the doors. The rest were silent.

The attic walls were covered in thick grey material, the kind used to soundproof music studios. There was a chair with straps on in the centre of the room, and a computer desk in the corner. A small unit was beside one wall, and it was stiflingly warm. The men dropped Nita onto the chair and Gaz applied the straps, then turned towards the man who was seated at the desk.

Rocko.

His very name brought about shivers of fear in the circles they ran. He was a hard-arse, took no shit from anyone, and was rumoured to have killed men just for looking at him wrong.

'Is she ready for me?' he asked, without turning around.

'She's still out cold,' said Danny, suppressing a shudder. He hated what Rocko did in here, how he 'taught' the girls he was brought. His methods were hands on, and Danny had no inclination to stay. He'd stayed just once, and it was enough to make him sick to his stomach. He wouldn't want to be the girl right now. Taking debts with the wrong people meant he had to transport the girls; that was his repayment.

And it didn't matter how far away he tried to run, there was always someone waiting to bring him back.

Danny sighed and turned to leave.

'You not gunna stay and watch? It cracks me up,' Gaz nudged Danny in the ribs as he spoke, an evil leer passing over his face as he nodded towards Rocko.

'No,' said Danny curtly, leaving the room and clicking the door shut. His partner was a dick, a complete and utter jerk. Danny had to practically lift Gaz's jaw off the floor every time they picked girls up, and every time he wanted to punch his lights out. The girls didn't deserve the lives they were brought into the country to lead. But what could he do about it? He owed the bosses, and they knew everything about him.

The last time he'd tried to leave the fold, they'd kidnapped his girlfriend. She'd been seven months pregnant at the time. They'd threatened to cut the baby out of her and put her to work in a house just like this one if he ever tried to leave again.

So he stayed. Because he had to.

Sighing again, he hung his head and made his way back outside to the van.

3rd November, 0007 hours – Wear Street, Sunderland

Back in the attic, Rocko finally looked up from his computer. 'You staying?' he asked Gaz who nodded silently. 'Good, then wake the bitch up.'

He watched as Gaz moved to the side of the bed and flattened his palm. It connected with the side of Nita's face with a resounding slap, causing her to gasp in shock. As she saw the two men in the room, she opened her mouth to scream. Moving like lightening, Rocko put a hand over her face, squeezing hard.

'One sound from you, bitch, and I will cut your tongue out.'

There was no way Nita could understand his words, they were in English, but he saw the fearful acceptance in her eyes. Rocko eyed Gaz thoughtfully. One of the two delivery men would go far in the organisation, and Rocko knew it would be Gaz. It was obvious he got off on the pain, and they needed loyal people.

Deciding it wouldn't hurt to get started, Rocko said, 'Hold her arm out for me. She needs her first dose of brown sugar.' He checked the tension and deftly tied a piece of elastic round the top of her arm. 'First we get her high, then she'll start to learn the trade for which she has been employed.' He pushed the needle into the vein in Nita's arm, and loosened the elastic. Stepping back, he watched as her pupils dilated and her mind floated elsewhere.

'Fill your boots,' he said to Gaz, nodding towards Nita's spaced-out body. 'Nothing too kinky, and don't mark her.' Leaving Gaz in the attic, Rocko left the room. He wasn't in the mood anyway; fucking the new girls was often best left to other staff. And he had several he knew would get the job done. He partook occasionally, but only with the extra special ones. The one's that still had the spark of fight left in them. And they only came along once in a blue moon.

He left the building by the back door, climbed into the red Shogun and left the alley with a squeal of rubber.

Chapter Four

3rd November, 0620 hours – Connor's parent's house, Sunderland

'Come on, Mum. It's time to get dressed then we'll get you into your chair by the window and you can watch for the postman. You like that, don't you?' Connor spoke softly to his mum who was laid on the bed facing the window.

His dad had called him in a panic saying she wouldn't get up and she was having an episode. He'd cried on the phone, breaking Connor's heart. And Connor, ever the dutiful son, had gone round to his parents' to help.

He sighed as he watched his mother turn her head towards him, suspicion in her eyes as she snapped, 'Who are you? I'm not getting up and dressed in front of some stinking man I don't even know, I'll call my son, he's a policeman you know. Now GET OUT!'

Her shrill voice turned to a scream as she launched herself off the bed and went for his face with her nails outstretched.

'Mum, please. Stop. It's me, it's Connor.'

He gripped her wrists less gently than he would have liked, knowing her to be stronger than her slim frame suggested.

Eventually she stilled and her eyes cleared, gazing at him. 'There's my boy,' she whispered, giving him a watery smile, 'So grown up. Where's your dress up box? Let's see my handsome man in his police uniform.'

Connor swallowed at the lump in his throat. His mum would jump from one memory to the next in the blink of an eye. Just once, he wished she'd jump back into the present.

Without further incident, he managed to get her dressed and seated in her favourite armchair, which was inside the bay window of the front room. His feet heavy, he wandered into the kitchen to see his dad.

'Sorry, Son, some days it's all I can do not to walk out of that door. She hit me. She always has to hit me.'

His father sounded so desperately sad as he rubbed his hand subconsciously over the bruise to his cheek.

'Maybe it's time to think about a home again, I mean she's not getting any better, Dad, and –'

'No. Whatever she did, she's still my wife. In sickness and in health. That's what I promised. She'll be fine tomorrow.'

Connor shook his head in frustration, 'No she won't. She'll never be fine, Dad. There are homes where people are trained to take care of people as ill as she is, nice ones where she'd be looked after and –'

'I said NO!' shouted his dad, 'And that's the end of it. I will not put my wife in a damn home to rot away with people who don't know her. Besides, Fred is coming round soon. She's always better when Fred's here.'

Sadness threatened to overwhelm Connor. He hated seeing his mum this way, and hated how his dad refused to listen to reason. But while his mother was ill, his father certainly was not. It didn't matter how many times Connor broached the subject of a home, the answer was always the same.

Sighing, he said, 'I've gotta get to work, Dad. I'll see you soon, OK?'

He saw his dad nod once, then Connor turned and left the room. He planted a kiss on his mother's forehead as he walked past, and with his shoulders drooping, he made his way to the car.

Life sucks.

3rd November, 1410 hours – Sunderland City Police HQ

'Damn and blasted file boxes in this day and age. I thought everything was supposed to be computerised,' grumbled Ali as he carried three boxes, all balanced precariously one on top of the next. 'Trust the maintenance men to take the lift offline today of all bloody days.' He couldn't even see over the top box, and made his way cautiously up the stairs, keeping his left shoulder to the wall to keep him steady.

He made it to the top of the stairs without incident, and used his hip to wedge open the door to the corridor. A little wobbly, he managed to navigate through, though the top box was threatening to make the long jump to the carpeted floor. Feeling it start to slip, Ali jolted his body to the opposite side, hoping to right the balance. He had no way of seeing Marlo heading down the corridor, or the mobile phone in her hand that held her attention.

The sudden impact was swift, and the top box fell to the ground with a clatter, spreading case files and crime scene photos across the carpet. The middle box teetered as Ali peered over the top and saw Marlo on the floor.

'Shit, Marlo, are you OK?' He put the other two boxes down and held out a hand to help her up.

'Jesus, why don't you watch where you're going you clumsy –' Ali watched as her cheeks grew pink and her blue eyes sparkled, initially angry but then easing off.

'Sorry, I erm, wasn't watching where I was going.' He pulled his hand back as she hauled herself to her knees, ignoring him, and started scooping up his files. 'I don't know what order they were in but I'm sure you can put them right. That's everything I think.'

He grinned at her, somewhat amused as she haphazardly plonked everything inside the box and picked it up to hand it to him.

'Actually, would you mind carrying it to the Major Incident Team office? I'd rather not have any more accidents.' She nodded, and Ali turned and picked up the other two boxes. Making general conversation he added, 'They're files from a murder a few months back. We've had an enquiry from Hertfordshire Police about a rape with similar MO in their area. Might be the same guy.'

His face took on a pained expression, but Marlo was in front of him and didn't notice. 'Ah, the one that got away. Bit of a mess that.' She pushed open the office door and held it for him to pass through.

Ali saw her shoulders tense as she said the second sentence, and intuitively knew she hadn't meant it to sound so flippant. Even so, his reply was curt. 'Just put the box on the table.'

Without saying a word, Marlo put the box down and turned to leave. Ali felt like an idiot. Her lips were pursed as she strode past him into the corridor.

'First class jerk,' he muttered to himself as he watched her walk back into the corridor. He could almost hear his mother's voice in his head, echoes of a conversation they'd had some weeks ago.

'Ye need to learn not to take everything to heart. Ye'll ne'er find a girl if you dinnut start accepting that not everything's gunna go yer way, Son. Ye're more like yer father than ye know. He held it all in, too, overreacted at wee things. His shoulders would've taken the weight of the world. As would yers. Let things go.'

It had pleased him that she thought he was like his dad, even if she had meant the comments as a negative trait.

'It's why ye're single,' she'd said. *'Women know when men are hiding somethin'. What happened up here wasnae' yer fault.'*

'Nope, not going there, Mum. Get out of my head.' Ali purposefully put his mother's words to the back of his mind and turned his attention back to the file boxes. He had a job to do and brooding would not get it done.

3rd November, 1415 hours – Sunderland City Police HQ

Marlo had paused outside the MIT office door, listening as Ali had called her a jerk. She tried not to feel hurt. Maybe Connor was right; maybe Ali was a tosser. *Or maybe it's you. You did almost call him a clumsy oaf. He's not exactly gunna thank you for it, is he?*

Huffing to herself, she made her way to the nearest stairs, and headed back down to the car park. Time to get back to the office. She still had her statement to finish up from the incident the day before. The rumour mill had already spread the word that it wasn't thought to be murder. Grant's ex-girlfriend had reported that he'd been to her house, got into an argument with her current boyfriend then smashed a window before running off through the woods opposite. The woods led straight to the River Wear, and it had been dark. The post mortem had been scheduled for that afternoon, so no doubt the dive team would hear the outcome through the grapevine.

As she drove back to the dive centre, she let her mind wander to the training exercise that morning. The water had been brisk, and there was low visibility due to the weather churning the sea bed which had been an issue. She hadn't even been able to see her hand in front of her mask. Connor had been stand-by diver, and Sharpie had sunk a reflective weight for her to recover. She'd used the jackstay search technique, a method of searching across a given line then a diagonal direction. It made for an efficient search and she had eventually pulled the weight to the surface. Methodically they'd worked through each team member diving and recovering until it had been time for Marlo to return to shore for the meeting.

Turning the tunes on the radio up loud, she slowed down a little, and sang along to Sweet Dreams by the Eurythmics. There was something about eighties music that called to her soul.

3rd November, 1615 hours – Wear Street, Sunderland

Nita couldn't stop shaking. She didn't know what was wrong with her. She kept having flashbacks of bad things; things she didn't want to believe could have happened to her. But she knew they had. Her dress had been torn, she had bruising to the sides of her breasts and she had a burning sensation between her legs.

She could only remember the person responsible as a monster. Whatever they'd injected into her had numbed any pain, but she remembered his eyes, dark like a sharks, as he grunted above her. She'd been floating on clouds, seeing things that couldn't possibly be there but at the same time, she saw things she knew were real. Her sense of time had altered and it had felt like he had kept her pinned to the bed forever. He'd forced her to drink salt water, slapped her face and said something to her, 'whore' she thought it was, though she didn't know what it meant.

And now she'd been put in a different room. Another girl was laid on the bed next to her. Her eyes had rolled back in her head and there was vomit at the side of her mouth. It smelled like she had soiled herself and Nita crinkled her nose.

She wished the shaking would stop. She yearned for something but it wasn't food or water; she'd already eaten the sandwich that had been left for her. *More bread. Didn't they eat anything normal in this country? Wherever she was.* She started to cry as memories of the evil shark filled her mind. Curling into a ball, she sobbed until there were no more tears. And even then she rocked, the movement oddly comforting to her. Nita wondered where Elvie was. Had the same thing happened to her friend? Was she even alive?

Suddenly the door opened, and the evil shark entered. Shaking her head fast from side to side, she scooted to the back of the bed, praying if she pushed into the wall hard enough then she would go right through it.

It didn't work.

She watched as he checked on the girl on the other bed, tilting her head sideways so she didn't choke on her vomit. Slowly he turned back towards Nita, and her shakes turned to terrified shudders as the shark seemed to swim towards her.

'Shhh. I've got a little something to make you feel better,' he said, grabbing her arm. The syringe only had a small amount of brown liquid inside, but as soon as it entered her system, Nita felt like she was swimming with the evil shark. She couldn't stop him now if she tried.

And she did try.

'Noh,' she muttered, flailing her arms in his direction. But he pinned her beneath him easily. He held her still with one arm, and used his other to pull down the zipper on his trousers. Nita tried to wiggle from his grasp but this made him angry. His hand around her throat made her gag, she couldn't breathe. Her small hands grabbed at the hand round her throat, and even through the drug-induced haze, she felt searing pain as he pushed into her. Nita was seeing flecks of black in her vision; tears fell from her eyes as he pounded at her mercilessly. He grunted loudly, his hands squeezing her throat even tighter as he suddenly stilled and juddered with a cry.

Unable to fight the black spots any more, Nita sank into unconsciousness.

Chapter Five

3rd November, 2045 hours – Ryhope, Sunderland
As he opened the door to the room, he could hear her crying. That would stop soon, usually within the first couple of weeks the girls cried less. He would be glad when she did: he hated people crying. It always reminded him of *her*. The one he tried his best to forget when he was in this room. The one that had caused him all the pain he felt then, and still felt now. The one who made him do what he did.

He watched as the girl looked up, her face swollen and bruised with blood crusted down her chin and onto her neck. She held her left hand to her chest as she watched him warily, and he knew she was silently begging him to leave her alone.

He couldn't though.

It was how it was. *'C'est la vie,'* as his dearly departed mum used to say.

It was almost as if he had woken up one day a completely different person. One minute he had been normal, then the next he had been... this.

He had a compulsion to find out what made people tick, to help them become immune to the pain of life so they wouldn't have to suffer like he had. So they wouldn't have to make the choices he had to make.

Frowning, he realised the girl had defecated in the cage, and there was a strong smell of urine.

She would have to clean that up. He wouldn't tolerate a dirty cage.

Unbolting the cage door, he reached inside and grabbed her spindly arm. The right one, not the left. She whimpered, but allowed him to pull her forward, and he heard the scrape of her backside on the bottom grate of the cage.

His thoughts wandered, and he didn't take the care he should, startled as she let out an agonised scream. Glancing down he realised her injured foot had caught on the side of the cage. She turned to a lead weight in his arms, and he felt his back twinge in response as he struggled to hold onto her.

Half-dragging, half-lifting, he pulled her from the confines, and placed her into the chair. Her ankle was now bent at an odd angle: bent like that it would catch every time he needed to move her. Making sure she was unconscious, he pushed it back into place and methodically tied a bandage round to hold it in position. He felt it crunch under his fingers, and heard the fluid built up inside squelch.

Going to the workbench, he placed a few drops of antiseptic into a bowl and filled it with cold water. Turning the camera on, he turned to face her.

Taking great care, he said 'It's time to play,' and proceeded to wash the dried blood from her face and neck before continuing. 'Day five. Subject six passed out today. This is the fourth time a subject has fainted after catching the broken foot on the cage. It may be time to review my storage methods. She is still being resistant and vocal, though less today than on day three. Today I will give her pain relief, the next stage will occur after the weekend.'

He felt her start to stir as the cold cloth caressed her face, and slowly she opened her eyes. He watched as confusion turned to terror as she registered him close to her. 'Shhh, it's time to play,' he soothed.

He felt an intense pain surge through his groin as the girl's knee connected with as much force as she could muster. Belatedly, he realised he had forgotten the restraints.

Tears pricked at his eyes as he dropped to his knees, his hand cupping himself as he struggled to breathe through the melee of stars now invading his vision.

He felt more than saw the girl get off the chair and hop towards the door, and pushing his pain to one side, he leapt to his feet and grabbed her by the hair, dragging her head backwards with a hard yank. She screamed as her weight adjusted and she landed on her bad ankle.

No longer gentle, he shoved her back into the chair and deftly applied the restraints.

What girl wants to escape playtime? Doesn't she realise I'm trying to help her? She needs to be able to cope with the pain.

He was confused, he'd been nice. He'd been washing her face ever so gently when she'd come around. Now she would have to be punished.

As her eyes finally focussed on him, he said, 'I don't tolerate naughtiness. Escaping is naughty. Now you will have to be punished.'

He unclipped his belt buckle and pulled the leather free from his trousers. Seeing her eyes widen and her head shake, he understood what she thought. It was what she knew after all, all the girls in the brothel he'd got her from did.

But raping her wasn't his intent.

Twisting the buckle end of the belt around his hand, he extended his arm and swung it round with force. The leather strap connected with her thigh with a resounding slap and she gasped loudly. He repeated the motion another four times, surprised that the most noise she made was a whimper.

That's good, she's learning to cope with it.

Finally, he removed her from the chair and put her back in the cage, putting a couple of sandwiches inside, along with a bottle of bleach and a cloth.

Happy she would be fine, at least for now, he locked the cage door and replaced his belt before leaving the room with a smile.

4th November, 0620 hours – Ryhope, Sunderland

He had just enough time for a quick check on her before he had to leave the house. Normally he would leave it longer, but there was a bad feeling burning in his stomach that no amount of Alka-Seltzer was settling.

45

He knew the minute he entered that something was wrong.

She wasn't crying, and the smell of bleach was so powerful it almost overwhelmed him. Pulling the neck of his jumper over his mouth, he walked further into the room.

The girl was inside the cage, her red eyes open and glassy, obvious burn marks to her mouth and around her nose. Her head sat in a pool of vomit and her skin had blistered on her arm where it had been laid. The screw top from the bleach bottle was clutched inside her hand, and the bottle lay on its side next to her, obviously empty.

I can't believe she did this. She's a coward. After a week of teaching, I thought she was stronger than this.

As he made his way closer to her, he realised she had also managed to get a tool off the workbench. The screwdriver was tucked under her, the open wounds on her arm congealed with blood as it had seeped from her.

She was definitely determined. What a waste.

He didn't understand. Why would anyone choose this option? He was teaching her how to deal with life, that it was painful but that she could become immune, and this was how she repaid him? By killing herself in his room, with his bleach?

Now he would have to clean up, find another girl, start from scratch. He sighed loudly. *Why does everything I touch turn to shit?*

He felt himself drift off in his mind, trying to remember when everything actually had turned to shit.

It had been years.

He barely even recalled the exact moment. Not anymore.

Slowly he hung his head, and just for a moment he muttered a quick prayer for the girl. However she had chosen to die, it probably would have been the end result anyway. He had helped her all he could.

He glanced at the clock on the wall; he'd have to deal with the mess and the body later. For now, it was time to leave or he'd be late.

4th November, 0645 hours – Car park, Dive Team HQ, South Shields

'Marlo, wait up,' came Connor's voice from behind her as she made her way towards the front entrance of the building.

For a moment she was tempted to just ignore him, but that wasn't her style. Hopefully he'd pulled his head out of his arse now anyway. He'd been quiet as a mouse the day before during the training exercise, and had been gone by the time she made it back to the office from the nick in Sunderland.

She was already beginning to regret her decision to pop into the centre on her rest day to grab her kit bag. She'd left it there accidentally last night and it had her personal dry suit in, which she needed for the day's dive. She'd fully expected to pop in without seeing another soul.

'Connor,' she greeted coolly, turning to acknowledge him. Immediately though, she felt guilty. The lad looked torn up and guilty as hell. Not one for prolonging torture, she added, 'You OK? What're you doing here today?'

'Left my mobile last night. Thought I'd grab it before Bravo Team came in. Need it in case something happens to my mum. She's erm… well, she's not too good. You OK?'

Marlo noticed him falter when he mentioned his mum, but she didn't ask about it. It was obviously something he wasn't keen on talking about. 'Am fine, just picking up my kitbag. I'm off up to the Farne Islands to do some diving. You ever been up there?'

'Once, years ago. Listen, Marlo. About the other day –'

'It's fine, we all have bad days. Don't worry about it.' Apologies always made her uncomfortable, and she knew that's where the conversation was headed. She held the door open for him and motioned him through.

47

'OK, thanks,' he nodded at her. 'If you ever want a dive partner, I wouldn't mind diving up that way. Heard the wrecks are amazing on a good day.'

'There's not much of them left to be honest. On a good day you can see a few joists and belly rails in the sediment, but it's been a while since it's been clear enough for good views. I'll get my shot one day. You're welcome to come next time I go if you like though.'

'Great thanks, Marlo. And I really am sorry for snapping. I'll see you Monday.'

She watched after him thoughtfully as he made his way up the stairs towards the locker room. *He's a funny soul that one, young in age, but he has old eyes.*

Reading people was something she did well; she'd grown up having to be able to read the moods of others and understand things children shouldn't need to know. Foster homes and care homes had a tendency to do that, you practically slept with one eye open. She knew Connor had been genuinely sorry, but she also knew he'd been hiding something. *Hate it when people do that. Why can't they just be honest and say what's bugging them.*

Her mind taunted her with its reply, 'You should know. You do it.'

Guilt flashed over her: yes, she did hide things. Every day, in fact. Things no one on her team knew about. *What right do I have to judge Connor when I hide something so awful?* Jutting her chin outwards in defiance, she retrieved her kitbag from the wet room, got back into her car, and turned the music up loud.

Anything to drown out the screaming.

4th November, 0905 hours – detached house, outskirts of Hetton-Le-Hole

Elvie strained, her ear to the door, listening. She had heard voices outside her room a few minutes before and wondered what was going on.

Suddenly the key turned in the lock, and she leapt backwards to the bed, curling her knees to her chest as the woman entered.

Elvie sat silently. She knew the woman was from her home land, could tell by looking at her. The man who had kicked her was there also, following the woman inside. The other driver was there too, his face looking shameful as he glanced up at her and shuffled on his feet.

'She needs to be taken to Wear Street. Rocko has man there wanting to pay for this one. He pay much. He come at ten o'clock. She must be there before then and she must remain pure.' The woman sidled a hateful glance at the man who had kicked Elvie.

The woman walked to the bed and sat down beside Elvie, not suspecting for one moment that the girl had understood every word she had said. Reverting to Filipino now, she spoke to Elvie. '*Shhh, child, it's OK. These men will take you to your new home. You will meet your husband there. He will teach you to be a woman and take care of you.*'

Elvie knew a response was required, and she knew there was no way in hell she was going home with a man to be his wife. She was only fifteen; even at home it wouldn't be forced on her like this. But this woman couldn't know that Elvie knew what she'd said to the men. Forcing tears to her eyes, she nodded slowly at the woman. '*But why must I go, I want to stay here? This room is bigger than my whole house was at home. Can't you look after me?*'

'*No, child. But you will be fine, I will check on you.*'

As the woman stood to leave, Elvie heard one of the men snigger. They didn't have a clue what the woman had said, that much was obvious. But they knew it was a lie.

Wherever they were going to take Elvie, it wasn't going to be a good place. Suddenly she remembered that they'd mentioned the street before; it was where they had taken Nita. She would get to see her friend again. Nita would help her. She just knew she would.

Chapter Six

4th November, 0840 hours – Connor's parent's residence, Sunderland

Connor had been sitting in the car for almost half an hour. He'd purposely parked behind the hedge that surrounded his parent's property so he could take a minute to prepare himself. But the minute had turned into more before he even realised.

He loved his parents, he really did. And he felt so guilty over what his mum was going through that it tore him apart at times.

Like today.

He sat in the car not wanting to go in and face his mother, or his dad for that matter. His dad had called him half an hour ago. *I can't even spend an hour in the gym without interruption. This sucks. Why won't Dad just let me put her in a home? I'd choose a nice one, she'd be way better off. Hell, I'd be better off.*

Frowning, he realised how selfish he sounded. His mother had carried him, cared for him and raised him into a good man, despite the family trying to intervene. Who was he *not* to want to care for her now she needed it. *But she would be better off; that's not selfish if it's true.*

Shaking his head he pulled the car key from the ignition. He'd been battling with himself over this for months now and half an hour in the car wasn't going to make it any clearer, or easier. Sighing, he got out of the car and carefully shut the door, knowing if he didn't concentrate on it, then his mood would cause him to slam it out of frustration.

When he entered the house, all seemed calm. There was no screaming, no shouting. Just peaceful quiet.

His suspicions instantly aroused, he yelled out, 'Dad? I'm here.'

The kitchen was empty so he made his way upstairs.

This is weird; he called me cos she was kicking off. Doesn't sound like she's kicking off.

He thought he heard something and cocked his head to one side, listening. Eventually the sound came again, a whimper or soft cry. Focussing on the sound, he made his way towards the bathroom.

'Dad? Mum?' he said when he reached the door. He heard the sound again, but this time it sounded more like a groan than a whimper. Reaching for the handle, he twisted it and pushed the door open, not quite knowing what to expect.

His father was lying on the floor by the bath, a towel draped over his shoulder and a large cut and bruise to the side of the head.

'Shit. Dad? Are you OK?' His first aid training kicked in and he checked his dad's vitals while pulling his mobile phone from his pocket and dialling 999.

'Ambulance please, 41 Wainwright Grove, Sunderland. Adult male with suspected head injury, breathing but not conscious.' Connor hit the loud speaker button and put the phone down beside him.

It must have been a relatively quiet day, as the ambulance arrived within minutes, by which time his dad had started coming around. The crew took him to the hospital, but Connor had to stay at the house, he had bigger problems. *Where the hell is Mum?*

His dad had babbled about his mum hitting him over the head with a vase before the ambulance crew had arrived, and stoically remained silent whilst the crew asked him the relevant questions. The only thing he told them was that he'd slipped on the bathroom floor.

Connor did a quick house search, room by room. He was sure she wasn't inside. He made his way out into the rear garden. The large shed at the bottom was locked, and she wasn't seated on the decked section.

Why didn't I just get out of the car? Instead of sitting there like some kind of loser while my mum hits my dad then runs off. I'm such a bloody coward.

A noise sounded from inside the house, and turning he ran back inside.

'Mum,' he yelled loudly, 'You here?'

He pushed open the kitchen door and made his way into the hall, then paused, his mouth dropping open slightly.

His mum stood before him, wearing only her nightie, and next to her stood a cop.

'Mum,' he said, making his way towards her. 'Are you OK?'

'Where's my son? He's a police man you know. He'll arrest you both for being in my house without permission.' Her voice sounded shaky, scared even.

Connor walked until he was right in front of her, 'Mum, it's me, Connor. You remember me, right?'

Narrowing her eyes at him, she screamed in his face. 'You're not my boy, you're not my boy…' She reached out her hand and went to slap him, but the police officer beside her caught her wrist and stopped the motion.

Connor knew he must look desperate. *I don't even know what to do now. This is ridiculous.*

'Connor? I'm Harry Green, the sergeant off D-Relief. We've met briefly. Is there somewhere she'll calm down?'

'Yeah, sorry, the chair in the living room window. She loves sitting there. It might help.'

Sheila pulled back against both of them as they manoeuvred her to the chair and sat her down. She had tears streaking down her cheeks and her screams slowly dulled to hiccups as she sat.

Connor and Harry sat on the sofa behind her.

'Must be hard. We found her wandering down near the shops. Said she was looking for Marie and that she hadn't come back with the milk?'

'Marie's my sister. She's twenty-five, and lives away at uni. She hasn't been back in a month. Mum has Alzheimer's.'

'Figured as much, my granddad had it. Could barely remember his name most of the time. Is there someone to take care of your mum or do you live with her?'

Connor looked up. 'My Dad takes care of her, but it turns out he slipped this morning in the bathroom. He's at hospital getting checked over, I'll stay with her until he gets out, don't worry.'

'OK, no problem. I just happened to be near the shops. The shop owner told me where your mum lived. There isn't any job on or anything. Can I suggest, though, that you have a chat with the social? See if they can offer any support?'

'Yeah thanks, sarge. I'll give them a call later when Dad gets back.'

'OK, Son. I'll leave you to your day.'

As Harry stood to leave, Sheila turned around. 'Connor, baby, I didn't realise you were here. Go make your old mum a nice cup of tea will you?'

Connor walked over to his mum, planted a kiss on her head, and sighed before adding, 'Course I will, Mum. Stay here.'

As he walked Harry to the door, he heard the sergeant's radio come to life in a burst of static. 'Yeah go ahead LV,' he said to the dispatcher as he gave a wave to Connor and made his way down the path.

4th November, 0950 hours – Wear Street, Sunderland

The van pulled up outside the house on Wear Street. Elvie looked out of the window and shuddered, it looked dilapidated, in need of repair, and just plain dirty. *This* was where they had taken Nita? Elvie felt a sense of foreboding as the skinny man opened the door and roughly pulled her out.

The street was by no means busy, but a few people were milling about. *Maybe someone will help me.* Elvie opened her mouth to scream but gasped instead as she felt the tip of a knife dig into her ribs.

'Scream and you die,' hissed Gaz pushing her towards the front door.

The other man pushed open the door and led the way inside.

The same scrawny girl glanced up from her perch in the hallway.

'Upstairs, second on right. Will send man up when he arrive.'

Her job done, she turned back to picking her nail varnish off with her teeth.

Gaz pushed Elvie up the stairs, pausing at the door on the left not the right.

'Danny, take her in there,' he said, nodding his head towards the right hand side. 'I'm going to go and pay a visit to my friend in here.'

Elvie watched as he opened the door wide. She saw Nita lying on the bed, her dress torn and ragged and her friend gazed at her with glazed eyes, not recognising her.

'Nita?' she said, pulling Danny towards the door.

'Trust me, sweetheart, you don't wanna go in there.' He pulled at her arm, trying to navigate towards the room where they were supposed to be waiting. But Elvie resisted. The man holding her didn't scare her, not as much as the other one anyway.

Tugging hard, she entered the room.

She watched as Gaz undid his belt, and realising his intent, she cried out. 'Noh!' She pulled hard at Danny's hand, imploring him to let her go and to help her friend. But he just hung his head in shame.

Elvie tugged again as Nita licked her lips, obviously knowing what was coming. Gaz pulled a needle from his pocket and stabbed it into Nita's outstretched arm. Elvie saw the moment her friend floated off into another world, and pulled at Danny's arm again.

This time though he was more firm. He pulled her back and shoved her out of the room and into the one opposite.

'You can't help her, not now.'

'Please,' begged Elvie, pulling back towards the door, forgetting for a moment that she wasn't supposed to know English. Belatedly, she remembered, and turned back towards Danny with wide eyes. He stood with his head cocked to one side.

'You understand me, don't you?'

Elvie paused. If she admitted it he would no doubt tell on her and she would end up in trouble. If she didn't he might turn nasty and beat her like the other man would.

'It's OK, I'm not going to hurt you.'

'Yes, I speak little. Understand more.'

'Then listen carefully. There's a man coming here who wants to take you away. He's an evil man. He wants to make you his wife and will hurt you. He wants a virgin. Do you know what that is?'

Elvie nodded, fear gnawing at her stomach.

'Unless you want him to take you home and rape you, then continue to do that for many years then you need to do something. When the man comes in, you need to look like you're not a virgin. Do you know how you can do that?'

Elvie shook her head, tears pricking her eyes.

'I don't want you to get hurt. I won't hurt you I promise. But if you kiss me when he comes in then he might leave without you. I'll take you back to the big house then. I promise I won't hurt you. I want to help you but this is the only way I can think to do that. Understand?'

Elvie nodded slowly. *I don't want to kiss him. What if he wants more? Like the other one would?* But what if he's right? She argued with herself until suddenly, footsteps could be heard coming up the wooden stair case outside.

'Well?' asked Danny, moving closer to her.

Elvie nodded almost imperceptibly and had to stop herself backing away as his lips met hers. He was gentle, and as the door opened, he whispered against her mouth, 'Look like you're enjoying it.' He pulled the zip on the back of her dress down and slipped one sleeve further down her arm, stopping to protect her modesty.

Nervously, Elvie put her arms around his neck and pushed her body into his, deepening the kiss. It wasn't like this was her first kiss. Before Noni had died she had been getting friendly with a boy from her village. She was shaking as Danny moved his hand down and cupped her behind, bunching the bottom of her dress upwards, whispering 'sorry,' as he lifted her slightly. She was close to panic as the footsteps finally entered the room.

'What the fuck?' snarled the man, entering the room and grabbing Danny's arm, yanking him away from Elvie. She gasped as the man pulled his fist round and connected with Danny's jaw. As Danny stumbled, she grabbed his arm and held on tightly.

Danny stood and put his arm round her protectively, glaring at the other man. 'You're too late; I've already had her twice today. Sorry, bud. Couldn't resist this sweet piece of arse.' He squeezed her behind, pulling her even closer to him, and she leaned in, knowing how important it was that the other man believe she was no longer a virgin.

Elvie slid her hand across his chest, 'You want that I go with him now? I please him too?'

She watched out of lidded eyes as the other man wrinkled his nose in disgust, turning and slamming the door with such force that it reverberated around the whole house.

Danny stepped away from her, and she knew instantly he meant what he had said, he had no intention of hurting her. She was just about to speak, when the door flung open and Gaz entered, fastening his belt as he walked in.

'What the holy fuck? How come he didn't want her?'

Elvie saw him look at the strap of her dress hanging off her shoulder, and watched his eyes bulge as he realised what he was sure had happened.

'Jesus, Danny. You must have a death wish. Boss lady's gunna kick your arse from here to kingdom come. What was she like though? Bet she was as tight as a ducks arse? Maybe later I'll dip my wick, huh?'

'Don't think so, Gaz. This one's mine. I'll deal with the old bat when we get back to the house.'

Danny took hold of Elvie's hand and led her from the room. Pausing outside the door behind which her friend was, she pulled him to a stop, begging him silently to let her see her friend.

He nodded, and Elvie pushed open the door.

Nita lay on the bed, in the same position she had been before. Her dress had been disturbed but otherwise she looked like she was sleeping. Elvie knelt beside her and saw the prick of blood on her arm, next to the few dots that were dried and crusting. She frowned as she realised her friend had been injected several times. Gently, Elvie placed a hand on her friends face. Nita didn't stir, she was deep asleep.

'Come on, time to go,' said Danny, pulling her to her feet.

Elvie knew she couldn't fight, not right now. She would plan her escape then come back for her friend. She allowed Danny to lead her out to the van.

Chapter Seven

Ali glared at the computer screen in front of him. Sometimes days just sucked, and this was one of those days. It had started when he arrived at work to a note on his desk from the chief superintendent requesting his attendance at a meeting at 10 a.m. – a meeting he had just got out of and was still reeling from.

He'd been brought into the force as a secondment almost a year ago, and had initially been based out of Newcastle. Then changes had been brought forth due to budget cuts and what not, and he had been transferred to Sunderland to provide cover. The chief super had disclosed that morning that the force may not be able to justify him being in position and were considering terminating his secondment and sending him back to Police Scotland.

To say he was fuming was an understatement. He'd uprooted his whole life to move down to the North East of England, on the proviso that the secondment would be two years in length and may lead to permanent employment. It had been somewhat easier because his brother Alex was living in Sunderland, but it had still been a hell of a decision to make, leaving his home in Edinburgh and relocating, renting out his flat, leaving his family behind. Ali was the second oldest of eight siblings, Alex being the oldest. It had been hard to walk away, even knowing they were only a few hours over the border.

He'd really only just started settling in, had decorated the flat he rented and was just becoming comfortable with the people he worked with. To be told 'thanks for your service but you're not needed' was a kick in the teeth. He wondered if it had to do with the prisoner that had escaped. Deep down he knew it hadn't been his fault. The offender hadn't even been in police custody at the time, but he knew people blamed him. If he was honest with himself, even knowing he couldn't have stopped what happened, he still blamed himself. Setting his chin in determination, he resolved to speak with the Federation rep later.

After the meeting he'd returned to his desk to find the system offline, meaning he couldn't update Holmes on the latest spate running through Sunderland. People were doing those stupid Neknomination contests: drinking a lot of alcohol in one go then tagging a friend via social media to continue the trend. So far he'd dealt with one death from the contest and a couple of very near misses where the persons concerned had been assaulted and robbed in the street without being able to remember a thing. It was a ridiculous trend; one he hoped would peter out soon.

With a sigh, he pushed the file to one side and reached for the next on the pile to his left. Opening it, he realised it was the Grant Cooper case. There wasn't much to do on that one: the post mortem had ruled accidental death by drowning. The family already had the body back and were arranging the funeral. He was lucky really as the Coroner's Office had dealt with pretty much everything, and was speedy on providing him with updates. It all just needed finishing off on the system then the file could be archived.

Ali felt grit in his eyes and tried to remember when he'd last had a good night's sleep. It felt like it had been ages. He was well over-due some annual leave. With everything going on it could be the perfect time to head home for some relaxation. The thought of a week of being pampered by his mum was appealing. She loved it when he or Alex went home: the house became filled with smells of baking, and the cups of coffee were endless. He knew if he went home now, the family would all rally round for tea and his mum would cook a huge roast. His mouth salivated at the thought of a full dinner with all the trimmings.

'Hey, bro,' greeted Alex suddenly, pulling Ali from his day-dream.

'Hey,' he replied. 'Sorry, I was away with the fairies.'

'No problem. You OK? You look tired?'

'Not been sleeping great. It'll ease off. Just been hauled in by the boss. Apparently there's a chance my secondment will end shortly as the force are running low on the funds with which to pay me.'

'You're kidding? They can't do that, can they? You signed a two-year contract, right?'

'Yeah. I'm gunna speak to the Fed later and see what they advise, just in case. You up for a drink tonight?'

'I can't, bro, I'm on backs tonight down in Durham. They're short in the south so the super asked if I wouldn't mind working. Another time though. Anyway, that's kinda what am here for, bro. Would you mind covering my shifts over the weekend? Thought Cass, Izzy and I might nip up and see Mum and co. We've not been up in months.'

Ali resisted sighing out loud, or pointing out that he hadn't been home in ages either. 'No problem. It's just the two back-shifts you mean?'

Alex nodded, 'Thanks, bro, right I'm gunna head off. Gym now then kip before my shift tonight with any luck. I'll give mum a hug from you.'

Ali watched as Alex walked out of the office. His stride was always confident. Ali compared it unfavourably to his own gait. His mum always said he walked as if he had the weight of the world on his shoulders. And he wouldn't lie; sometimes it felt that way, too.

He reached for the coffee at his side and took a slurp, then grimaced as the lukewarm liquid coated his mouth. *Definitely need a caffeine hit today.* He stood up, made his way to the kitchen and poured another. The files would still be there in five minutes.

4th November, 1110 hours - detached house, outskirts of Hetton-Le-Hole

Elvie felt tears prick her eyes. The woman who had been in her room the day before was screaming at Danny. She cringed as the woman's palm had hit his face with a loud slap, and now she cowered as the woman turned towards her.

Yolanda Bamba was not a nice lady. She had been in the human trafficking trade for many years, learning her craft and becoming one of the most trusted in the organisation she worked for. Elvie didn't know, but Yolanda herself had been trafficked in when she was a young girl. From the start she'd had the forethought and gumption to be nice to the right people, and had managed to manipulate her way up the chain of command. Her actions had afforded her luxuries such as the large detached house and the brand new BMW that sat on the driveway; and her temper ensured she didn't lose any of it.

Elvie put her hand up to block Yolanda's slap, and knew instantly that this was a mistake. Danny had already been ordered out of the room, the other driver dragging him by the arm as Yolanda had approached Elvie. The young girl stared into the eyes of the older woman, and knew whatever happened next, it was going to hurt.

She pulled herself tighter into a ball on the bed, hoping that the smaller she was, the less area Yolanda would hurt.

It didn't work.

Elvie cried out as Yolanda grabbed her hair and pulled her from the bed with a jolt. She felt her knees buckle and collapse slightly, causing the woman's hold to pull at her hair even harder. Her scalp felt as though it was burning, and she felt tears in her eyes. When the pressure released suddenly, Elvie glanced up, unwittingly giving the woman the perfect opportunity from which to strike. The impact of the fist to her cheek was enough to knock Elvie sideways, sending her crashing side-first into the bedside cabinet. Pain burst into life across her chest and she gasped, trying to inhale, but it felt like she had been stabbed to her core. The impact had broken at least one of her ribs.

The woman grabbed her hair again and pulled Elvie's face closer to her own. 'You lost me big money. I will send you back to house. You will work this debt off by laying on your back. You good enough for driver man then you good enough for other men. Especially those who like to hurt, yes?'

Yolanda hit Elvie again, causing her lip to split and swell instantly. 'You are dirty bitch. You will learn the hard way.' She flung Elvie in the direction of the bed and left the room, slamming the door so hard that the whole room shook.

Elvie tried to steady her breathing. The whole of her right hand side felt like it was on fire, and slowly she pulled herself to her feet. She lifted her dress to examine her ribs, and wasn't surprised to see them turning a dark shade of purple already. Her breath felt shallow, and her face pulsed with her heartbeat where Yolanda had hit her.

I need to get out of here. I cannot be here when she comes to send me back to that house.

Elvie made her way to the window, and fiddled with the catch. She was surprised to feel it open and pushed the window upwards. It screeched loudly, paint on paint, and she paused, hoping that no-one had heard. Shoving with all her might, she pushed the window up until it locked in position – a mere couple of inches from the bottom. Definitely not enough for her to crawl through.

Tears threatened as she looked around the room, searching for something, anything that could help her force the window open.

But there was nothing to find in the sparse room. The beds had metal frames that required dismantling with a screwdriver. There was nothing else other than the bedside table and the lamp.

She stared at the lamp for a moment.

Elvie smiled as she suddenly realised something. When the bedroom door was opened by Yolanda or whoever, it wasn't locked. They always left it ajar while they were in the room. The lamp could prove to be a useful weapon.

She pulled the plug from the wall and placed it behind the door, so it was ready for her to pick up when she heard someone coming. She allowed herself to slip down the wall beside the door to a sitting position, ignoring the pain from her side.

And she waited.

4th November, 1120 hours – Farne Islands, Northumberland

Marlo made sure her tank was secure and double checked the oxygen pressure. She dipped her mask into the salty sea water, then spat in it and rubbed her fingers around before giving it another quick rinse. She didn't know what it was about spit that stopped the mask steaming up, but it worked and that was what mattered. Popping the mask over her eyes and nose, she put the respirator into her mouth and tested it by inhaling.

She was set.

Sitting on the edge of the boat, she leant backwards and let her body fall into the water. Kicking her legs powerfully, she swam deeper.

The boat had been coming out with a group of students and a small dive team, and she'd managed to hitch a ride. They were doing some kind of ecological survey, looking at the silt around the wrecks and checking it for nutrients to compare to other areas of the sea bed. Or so she'd been told anyway. The two divers were students doing their final degree year.

Either way she was pleased to see them. It had saved hiring her own boat to take out. She'd contemplated buying her own several times, but she'd have to pay for storage, maintenance and everything else; sometimes it was just easier to hire.

Before entering the water she'd set her underwater watch on countdown so she wouldn't miss her ride back. It'd be a long swim if she did. Her camera was round her neck and hooked to her vest so it didn't stray whilst she swam.

She spent a minute taking in the surroundings. Marlo had dived there several times, but the thing she loved about the sea was that it was always changing. You could dive the same place twice in two days and something would be different. The only thing that she didn't like was the silence. A girl could really hear her thoughts when she was submerged under tonnes of water.

When she'd first started diving, the silence had been the thing that put her off the most. All that time lost in her own thoughts had been a bad thing when she was younger. It had let her dwell on the dark stuff too much. But now it was more like a form of meditation. She could force her mind to empty and her body to relax.

She swam to the north east, keeping her eyes peeled for the underwater landmarks she knew were there. Marlo jumped as a seal suddenly swam past her at eye level. It half-turned back, its black eyes glinting as her torch light flashed over them, then turned back and continued with its search for dinner. She refocused on the rocks in front of her, and veered slightly to the left.

Then she saw them.

From the depths of the silt on the sea floor, rose several pieces of curved wood. Grabbing her camera, she unhooked it and checked the digital screen at the back. The image was as clear as a bell. Snapping away as she swam around the remains of the wreck, Marlo gave the job her full attention.

She didn't see the other diver swimming up frantically behind her until he grabbed her leg to get her attention.

Marlo jumped and kicked back instinctively, using the force to push off and turn. She'd already grabbed for the knife she kept on her belt and her heart was pounding so loud it could have been hooked up to an amplifier.

The other diver waved his hands at her, silently telling her he was no threat. He used hand signals to beckon her to follow him, and even through his mask, Marlo could see he looked afraid.

She hooked her camera back onto her chest, placed her knife back in its holster and followed rapidly.

As soon as she arrived she saw the source of his panic. One of the other students had become entangled in fishing net and was struggling to get free.

Bloody kids. They should both know to carry a dive knife with them, and not to panic if they get trapped. Jesus, the way she's flailing about I'll be lucky if she doesn't rip my mouthpiece out.

Despite her thoughts, Marlo knew what to do. She grabbed the male diver's arm and pointed upwards, silently telling him to head to the surface and let the boat know to expect them. He swam towards the light shimmering above.

Turning back to the female diver, Marlo realised the girl had dislodged her own mouthpiece and was panicking as water threatened to enter her lungs. The struggling caused the mouthpiece to get caught up in the net also and the girl was unable to pull it free. Her eyes were wild, helpless as she fought against the net.

Marlo approached, took a deep breath and put her own mouthpiece in her hand, motioning with her other hand for the girl to take two breaths. She knew how hard it would be for someone in panic mode to hand it back so kept hold of it as the girl took in two long breaths. Marlo replaced the mouthpiece in her own mouth, not having time to think about potential germs, something that normally bothered her greatly, and pulled the knife from her belt. Working methodically, she cut through the netting, freeing the girls own mouthpiece and placing it in her hand.

Then she bent double and started cutting through the rest of the netting to get the girl free. It seemed like it took forever but finally Marlo cut through the last piece that held the diver in place, and glanced up, wondering why she wasn't swimming to the surface.

The diver's mouthpiece hung limply by her side, and Marlo realised she had been too scared to put it in her mouth when Marlo had handed it to her.

Damn it, come on lovely, let's get you to the boat so we can get you breathing again.

Swimming with urgency, Marlo swam powerfully towards the surface, her arms securing the girl to her chest. As her head burst free of the water, Marlo pulled the mouthpiece from her mouth and took in a deep breath before pinching the diver's nose, and exhaling into her mouth. She breathed another breath into the girl before turning to the boat and passing her to the other students who were waiting with arms stretched out.

Give them their due, they all looked petrified, but there were no tears. The male diver pulled Marlo's outstretched arm, helping her into the boat.

Marlo laid the girl flat and tilted her head back, checking her pulse whilst she used her cheek to feel for breath. There was nothing.

Breathing two long breaths into the girl, Marlo started chest compressions. Counting the compressions out loud, she got to thirty and leaned to give the girl oxygen again.

Suddenly, the girl coughed, and Marlo turned her head to the side so she didn't choke on the sea water.

'Easy love, you're alright now. Just try and breathe.' Turning to the other kids, she added, 'I need something to warm her up. Blankets, jackets, whatever?'

The boat was already cutting through the waves on its way back to shore. The male diver handed Marlo a couple of blankets, and knelt beside his friend.

'You OK, Gemma?' his hand stroked hers softly and Marlo realised the pair were a couple. Gemma nodded back at him, tears glistening in her eyes. Twisting to face Marlo, she said, 'Thank you.'

'Next time you guys go diving, remember your diving knives. When did you do your qualifications?'

'We did the PADI course when we were in college. This was our first dive in three years.'

'Didn't you do a refresher dive?' At his head shake, Marlo added, 'Book in for some practice sessions if you're planning on diving again. You need to be prepared under the water. Gemma very nearly died. She'll be OK but she'll need checking out at hospital.' Marlo left them together and sat back on one of the benches, finally unhooking her tank and pushing it off her shoulders. *Some days are good dive days, some days not so much. At least she's OK, though.* She shuddered as she thought of what would have happened if she hadn't been there. Not for the first time, she appreciated Sharpie's words of advice when it came to experience.

Chapter Eight

4th November, 2025 hours — Wear Street, Sunderland

He parked the car in the alley to the rear of the house. Like he always did. He knew no one would look twice even if he parked right out front. Nothing was ever noticed in this part of town, but he still knew he needed to be safe.

Rocko had told him to be there before nine-thirty. It made him happy, the knowledge that this man would always make sure he was taken care of, and let him choose a girl who suited. Sometimes the girls even came with recommendations. Rocko didn't ask what he did with the girls. It was part of what made good business. As long as he paid the set fee then he could choose whichever girl he wanted and no questions were ever asked.

He silently fingered the wad of cash in his inside pocket as he walked round the street to the front door. Momentarily, he felt guilty. This money wasn't really his. His own funds had run out some time ago. But he knew she wouldn't mind. She would understand that he had been trying to help someone in need. He had to believe that she would understand or he'd go nuts. Besides, a grand was nothing in this day and age. It would barely even be missed, he was certain.

He pushed open the door with the faded peeling paint and stepped inside. His nose wrinkled automatically, he couldn't stop it. It happened every time he walked in here. The smell of piss and shit with the sweet overtones of sweat and drugs, and the utter stench of desperation assaulted his nostrils but he stoically marched into the hall.

He was here to do a service, to find a girl and help her. And no smell was going to stop him.

He nodded at the girl sat at the table in the hall, and she barely acknowledged him. He'd been there more times than enough now. There was no need for her to respond.

His shoes clattered on the bare staircase as he made his way up to the attic. The room always made him cringe. Horrid things happened to the girls in there. He knew Rocko hooked them on heroin there, he also knew Rocko and the other men did things to the girls that he would never consider doing.

But he couldn't help them all.

He picked only the ones that looked like they had fight, the ones that hadn't been there all that long. Rocko nodded at him as he entered.

'First floor, first door on the left of the stair case. You'll find her suitable I think.'

As Rocko held out his hand for payment, he pressed the money in with a soft smile. 'Thanks Rocko.'

The rule was never to use real names in the house, and it was a rule that he obeyed easily. Rocko and the person he knew Rocko as outside of the house were very different people. He had never confused the two, and he never would.

He closed the door and made his way back down to the first floor. The door was a little stiff, but he pushed harder and it opened, letting out a creak that was worthy of any haunted house.

Stepping inside, he turned his nose up again. There were two girls inside, one on the left hand side bunk who was conscious and obviously looking for her next fix, and another who was quite possibly dead. Her head had lolled backwards, and he could see vomit in her mouth. Her chest was still.

Ignoring the dead one, he walked over to the bed and sat down.

'I'm here to save you. Come with me and I'll teach you how to deal with all this pain and misery. It's what I do.'

He held his hand out to the girl, taking hers in his and stood, pulling her to her feet. She didn't fight, she followed as he led her down the stairs and out of the door to his car. He knew she understood what he said, for all her olive skin and dark hair pointed to her being foreign. They all understood that leaving the hell hole he took them from would be preferable to staying. She was number seven, and not one had ever refused to go with him.

4th November, 2105 hours - detached house, outskirts of Hetton-Le-Hole

Elvie had been sat by the door all day. She had dozed off at one point and woken with a jump thinking someone was in the room with her, but it had been a dream. Her whole body ached now. Breathing was like having someone stick a shard of glass deep into her side, and her face throbbed with every minute movement.

She stretched slightly and pulled herself to her knees, intending to stand.

Suddenly she heard it. Footsteps coming up the carpeted stairs to the room she was being held in. Moving quicker now, she stood, wincing as her body protested. She grabbed the lamp and raised it high above her head. Whoever came through that door was going to get it.

The door opened quietly, and she saw trouser legs in the light from the landing.

A man then, no doubt the nasty one.

She tensed as she waited for him to come further into the room. And the second she saw his face, she swung the lamp with all her might. It shattered as it connected with the man's face and he collapsed with a loud 'oomph'.

Elvie didn't stop to see who it was. She snuck past him, and crept down the stairs. She was petite anyway, and her feet made no sound on the carpeted steps. As she rounded the corner and found herself at another staircase, she paused, listening.

It was faint but she could hear the sound of people talking, a television maybe.

Silently, she crept further down until she found herself in the hallway.

The front door loomed in front of her.

Elvie went to step forward but a hand suddenly appeared round her mouth and she was pulled backwards. She struggled, trying to kick at whoever held her steady. The pressure on her mouth was hard and she could barely even express a whimper.

'Shhh,' whispered a male voice. 'It's Danny. Don't scream.'

He turned her around so she could see his face, and she had to stop herself gasping when she realised he had blood running down the left side of his face.

'I'm fine,' he said, seeing her expression. 'Come with me, I'll get you out.'

Elvie nodded silently. He had helped her before; there was no reason for her not to trust him. He led her through the kitchen at the rear of the house, and out of the back door to a large concrete section where several vehicles were parked, including the van she had been brought to the house in.

'You see that red car over there? You need to go and hide on the back seat, there's a blanket you can cover yourself with. If you don't hide they will catch you. You're miles away from anywhere. Do you understand?'

Elvie grasped most of what he said, though some words escaped her. She nodded, fear tightening in her chest. When he pushed her towards the car, she didn't hesitate. She climbed in and peeked through the window as he made his way back inside.

Maybe he's going to tell them where I am? Maybe he's gone to get the woman and she's going to beat me again.

She heard shouts from inside the house and ducked down as the back door was flung open. Crouching low in the foot-wells, she pulled the blanket over her and lay still, her heart pounding in her chest as shouting sounded all around the car. She couldn't get out now even if she wanted to.

4th November, 2110 hours – Ryhope, Sunderland

Nita felt ill. Her nose was running and her body ached and shivered with cold but at the same time she was sweating. It felt like she was back in the container again.

She didn't know where she was, but it wasn't home.

Nita didn't know what it was they had been injecting into her, but it made everything OK, at least until it wore off. When that happened it was like raw hunger that wouldn't go away, and coupled with the horrible flu she seemed to have caught, she felt like death warmed up. In the room she'd been in, they kept the drugs coming fairly regularly so her withdrawal hadn't progressed beyond that and she wondered when this man would give her the injection her body craved.

She glanced down at her arm, and without realising what she was doing, she started scratching at the tiny scabs left behind from the needles, her nails ripping into her skin and causing red welts to appear. It gave her a focus, and she could feel the pain. In an effort to stop the shaking, she scratched harder.

The car she was in suddenly pulled to a stop and the man got out. He opened the door for her and she took the hand he offered. *He's going to hurt me, like the other man.*

But even that thought didn't make her stay in the car. She knew that however he hurt her, he would give her the drugs first. And that was what she needed. Anything else she could handle.

The man led her down a path to a building and silently pushed her through the door.

A sudden prick of fear invaded her senses, this room didn't feel right. It smelt like bleach and the walls were covered in grey material. She racked her brains to try and remember where she had seen similar material before, but the location eluded her. She saw the cage, the line of tools hanging on the wall, and the chair with wrist and ankle ties standing in the middle of the room, and knew she had made a mistake.

Wherever here was, it was no better than the last place. If anything it was worse.

Nita cried out, and pulled back towards the door.

She hadn't even noticed the man locking it as they entered.

She opened her mouth to scream but gasped as he suddenly pulled her close and clamped a hand over her mouth.

'Shhh, it's time to play,' he whispered in her ear.

Nita whimpered, the shaking stopping momentarily as panic threatened to overwhelm her. She struggled against his hold, but she was weak from lack of food. There was no chance of her escaping his grasp.

He manoeuvred her towards a metal framed cage that lay in the corner and she felt the hot tears start to fall down her cheeks. *What is going on? What does he want?*

She tried to stop him pushing her through the cage door, but he roughly rammed her through the door. Nita cried out in pain as her arm caught on the side but he ignored her and slammed the door shut with her inside.

Shaking the cage door, she screamed, her tears running freely down her face. He had turned away, but hearing her shaking the cage, he faced her once more. He was angry, and Nita was afraid. She backed away from the cage door and stopped when her back hit the rear frame.

She watched as he lowered a flap on the cage and pushed a couple of sandwiches and bottles of water inside. They would satiate her, but they wouldn't even touch the hunger she knew wasn't for food. Deciding to change her tactics, she approached the door more calmly.

'*Paki usap po*,' said Nita, trying to show the man a shaky smile. It meant please. Please anything. Please let me out, please give me a needle, please don't hurt me, just please.

But he didn't understand.

4th November, 2114 hours – Ryhope, Sunderland

He hadn't understood the mutterings from her mouth, but he knew the meaning. She was begging. Pleading with him in her own language not to hurt her. For a moment, he felt compassion. He knew how she felt, she was trapped. She couldn't get out. She was scared. But his compassion faded. The only way for her to deal with the pain life would throw at her was to learn now.

And he was the one to teach her. He had to be.

He picked up the large, wrapped piece of polythene from the corner of the room, adjusting to accommodate the weight of the dead girl now in his arms. He grunted as her arm slipped free of the polythene wrapping, and hearing a loud gasp from the cage, he knew the latest girl had seen.

Oh well, by the time I'm through she'll be able to cope with anything. She'll get through life and never have to worry about anything. Not like me.

He lugged the heavy wrap out to his car and shoved her into the boot.

It was too early yet. If he left now he would be seen. And he didn't have time today to travel to the place he normally placed his girls.

He could go later – no one would see. But he didn't think he would be able to. He had a new girl to look after now.

Suddenly he realised he knew just the place for this girl. Humming to himself, he turned and went back into the house. It was time for supper.

Chapter Nine

5th November, 0640 hours - Detached house, outskirts of Hetton-Le-Hole

Elvie heard a noise outside the car and stilled, holding her breath in case someone opened the car door. She was bitterly cold, the thin blanket doing little to warm her up, and she was shivering so hard she thought her teeth were coming loose. It hurt to breath so she inhaled in short bursts in an effort to ease the pain in her chest.

It felt like she'd been hiding in the foot well of the car for days. She'd fallen asleep at one point, her body doing what it could to help her escape the confines of the cold car, but her dreams had been filled with monsters.

The night had turned to early morning, and still she hadn't moved, not daring to even lift her head.

Danny had told her to hide. She presumed he would come looking for her when it was clear to run.

But so far, he hadn't.

She wondered whether he was alright, and had almost gone to get out of the car on at least four separate occasions, but she was too afraid. She knew what would happen if they found her now.

They would kill her. There was no doubt in her mind.

But she knew she couldn't stay in the car much longer. As well as the gripping pain she felt, her whole body was going into cramp. She ached in places she didn't even know she had, and her fingers had turned blue from the cold. Her tongue was swollen in her mouth, reminding her it had been hours since she had last had a drink, but despite this her aching stomach told her she was desperate for the toilet.

Pushing the blanket off her head, she pulled herself round slightly so she could peer over the bottom lip to the window. Agony ripped through her side and she gasped loudly, then bit her bottom lip trying to silence herself.

Someone might hear.

Peeking out of the window, the compound appeared to be in complete silence. There was no one milling around, no sign of anything except the lonely rabbit that hopped across the grass to her right. Turning, she glanced out of the other side and realised there really was no one around.

Where is Danny? Why hasn't he come?

She knew he wouldn't betray her, if he was going to he would've told the woman where she was hiding, but Elvie wondered where he was. He hadn't owed her anything, but he had helped her now on two occasions, and she trusted him.

Deciding she really couldn't stay in the car any longer, Elvie reached for the door handle. The sound of the latch opening was as loud as a gunshot to her mind, and she paused, stricken with terror that someone might have heard.

But there were no shouts, no one came running.

She pushed the door open, and climbed out of the car, her left arm holding her sore ribs as she leaned into the sharpness. It seemed to help a little and the searing pain eased to an ache that spread around her side.

Outside of the car was just as cold, and she felt her teeth start to chatter as she glanced around. Grabbing the blanket off the back seat, she wrapped it round herself. She had no idea which way to go but instinctively drew back from the house and its large hedge and made her way down the garden to the fence at the rear.

The garden backed onto fields and trees, and it was all she could see, but she knew she'd have a better chance of getting away that way than through the house.

She wished she had something warmer on. Noni had told her that the UK was nothing like the Philippines for weather, but she hadn't really believed anywhere could be quite so bitterly cold.

Climbing the fence, she glanced up at the stars but they were different from how she'd been taught. Instead, hoping it was the right choice; she picked the brightest star and headed in that direction. She didn't know it was north – one direction was as good as the next but at least she could maintain a straight line if she went that way.

5th *November, 0805 hours – Dive team HQ, South Shields*

'Morning, campers. Hope your single rest day didn't tire you out too much and that you're all raring to go.' Sharpie sat at the front of the briefing room and glanced around with a grin. Beside him sat Andy Chapman, the sergeant of Bravo Team. The two teams rarely worked together, and Marlo wondered what it was for.

Glancing at her own team, she noticed Doc looking a little green around the gills. He'd obviously had a good day off and was suffering now. Grinning, she turned her attention back to Sharpie.

'… be a long set. The next five days will be filled with our favourite people,' his smile was sarcastic. 'Providing we don't get called out we have six, yes six different groups coming through our doors for a chat and wander around this inspiring facility. Of these six groups, four are kids aged between eleven and sixteen, our absolute favourite age group. One is a writer wanting an inside look into the dive team, and the final group is the management team who are coming to see where they can shaft us financially. It'll be fun-filled people, trust me, and no doubt by the end of just today we will all be longing for rest days. But, crack on we shall. We will all be pitching in with the tours, no excuses. Doc, you're handling the group today from Thornhill Comprehensive. The writer is due in at 2 p.m. and she'll be with me.'

Marlo saw Doc drop his head to the desk top and groan loudly before mumbling, 'Aw come on Sharpie, the little shits will eat me alive. I'm under the weather today: can't Mac do it?'

She tried to hide her smirk as Mac thumped Doc on the arm, but she knew Sharpie had seen it: he was on top form today.

'Marlo will give you a hand, Doc. There's no way they'll eat you alive with her there. Hell, she might just need you to stop her eating them alive. Or at least from grabbing their phones and launching them into the bay, huh, Marlo? Connor, you and Mac are on equipment checks. The 4x4 needs taking over to fleet management at HQ for its MOT at 10 a.m. My astute team may have noticed Bravo Team sitting quietly in the wings. They're here on a training day, they'll be using the Delta RIB. Play nice boys and girl.'

He stood, effectively ending the briefing, but turned back just as everyone started getting to their feet. 'The kids will be here in an hour; you might wanna get a cuppa first.' His grin stretched widely and Marlo sighed. Bravo Team filtered out, taking the piss as they headed for the stairs, and Connor and Mac practically ran from the room, obviously raring to get stuck into the equipment checks. The whole team would prefer to chew off their own arm off than entertain a bunch of school kids, but the tours were good for PR and Sharpie rarely refused visitors.

'Blurgh,' muttered Doc, lifting his head from the desk. 'I think I may actually die. I am never drinking again.'

'Aye, 'til next time. Come on, old man, let's get some caffeine down your neck.'

Marlo walked to the door, knowing Doc would follow her to the kitchen.

5th November, 0810 hours – Sunderland City Police HQ

The pile of files on Ali's desk was finally dwindling to a more manageable level. He had a steaming cup of coffee at his side, and a hot bacon butty had just been placed on the keyboard in front of him.

Any morning that began with rocket fuel and food from heaven was bound to be a good one.

He unfolded the foil, inhaling deeply as his mouth started to water at the smell. There really was nothing quite like it. Grinning like an idiot, he closed his teeth over the bread and bit down, sighing as he tasted the tang of brown sauce under the meaty strips.

'Crap,' he muttered, his mouth full as the phone rang on the desk beside him. Glaring at it, he chewed and grabbed the receiver. 'McKay.' Listening, he finished the bite and sat back in his chair.

'Gov, it's Inspector Monaghan from the control room. The call handler's still taking the details but it looks like we have a murder coming in. It'll be log... 331 when you have a second. As I say it's still being updated. The caller's said the victim is a foreign woman. She's in the river not far from the big pond at the Washington Water Fowl Park. I've got a colleague on with Sergeant Sharp from the dive team. He's assessing the log. Can I put you down as attending?'

'Yeah, no problem. Where's the RV point? '

'I've tagged the car park near the visitor centre. Looking on the mapping at the location, there's only access to the river either on foot or via a 4x4 vehicle. I've got marked units travelling with blues and twos. First on scene will set the cordons.'

'Thanks, oh and make sure Sharpie has my mobile number.'

Replacing the receiver, Ali brought up the log on the system. It was pointless leaving until he knew what was happening. He remembered a case when he had not long been qualified as a detective, and a call had come in from a hysterical woman screaming that she had found a head in a bag. He had raced down to the scene, only to find it was the head off a mannequin. Now, he waited.

God only knew when he'd be back in the office so he picked up his sandwich and took another bite. But it felt like cardboard on his tongue. Silently he wrapped it back up and dumped it in the bin beside him.

5th November, 0820 hours – Dive Team HQ, South Shields

'OK guys, the body's in the river to the rear of a pond in the waterfowl park at Washington. Just like the one at Durham the other day, it's caught in the debris from the flood in a small weir. Bravo Team have been called off their training to assist down near Tees Barrage in Darlington with a search so this one's all ours. I want us geared up and on the road asap. Mac, you're lead diver. Marlo, you're standby. Connor, Doc, you're on the tanks. Let's go,' said Sharpie.

Once at the park, they exited the van and Sharpie was pulled aside by Mac. After nodding his head, he motioned Marlo over to listen.

'Can I swap with Marlo? My chest feels tight today. Don't know if I'm coming down with something.'

Sharpie glanced at Marlo who nodded her agreement. They both watched as Mac hung his head slightly, and went to help Connor with the equipment.

'He OK?' asked Marlo.

'Not sure, he looks pale. Could just be the hangover, like. Him and Doc hit the bottle last night. I'll keep an eye on him. Go suit up.'

Sharpie made his way over to Ali who was also just walking up the footpath back to the car park.

'What've we got, boss?'

'Can't see clearly from the bank. Looks like a female, naked.'

'Second water recovery in a few days. Gotta love this weather, definitely makes people act nuttier.'

'Aye you're not wrong. You guys ready to go in?'

Sharpie looked back at the 4x4 which was just starting to manoeuvre with the RIB towards the water. 'Yup. Hope the weather holds out 'til we're done. Those black clouds don't look too friendly.'

'You're not wrong. The temperature's dropping too. Winter's definitely on its way.'

'God I hope not! It's only just November. I'll let you crack on.'

5ᵗʰ *November, 0935 hours – River Wear, Washington Wildfowl Park*

'Mac, steady off and hold. We're close enough,' said Marlo, leaning over the RIB and looking at the female.

She was almost fully immersed, her head face up into the water with her dark hair spread around her like a large feather. She was petite, very young, and the bumps of her ribs were visible just below the water's rim. Her torso was caught under a thick branch, and it was the tree that held her in place. The girl's face was bruised, her nose bent at an awkward angle. Her glassy eyes stared up at Marlo.

The girl's left leg floated on the surface of the water, being buffeted by the flowing river. It was completely bare, the same as the rest of her body. A dirty bandage was wrapped around the ankle but Marlo could see the bruising at the top.

It didn't look good.

'Doubt we can free her from the branches without you going in the water. You ready?' asked Sharpie from beside her.

Marlo nodded, and moved position so she could enter the water. Because the body was on the surface, she didn't need the air hoses or her breathing gear. Sharpie followed suit and they both lowered themselves into the brisk cold of the river. They pulled themselves to the body using the tree and pulled her free from its grasp. Working together, they manoeuvred her into the body bag. Marlo pulled her glove off with her teeth so she could get a grip on the zipper and fastened it quickly.

They then swam, dragging the body bag between them, towards the waiting RIB.

Suddenly, it pitched and veered sharply, the hull swinging round and narrowly missing hitting Marlo on the head.

'What the hell, Mac?' she yelled. Both she and Sharpie paused in their movement towards the RIB, waiting for one of the team to tell them what the hell had happened.

Connor's face appeared over the side, 'It's Mac, Sharpie, he's collapsed. Doc's checking him now.'

'Can you hold the body?' Sharpie asked Marlo. She nodded, and watched as he swam to the side. Connor pulled him over the edge, and he vanished from view.

Seconds later, Connor jumped into the water beside Marlo. She heard Doc shout to the shore from the RIB, 'Call an ambulance!'

Connor sounded shaky as he spoke, 'Doc doesn't know what's wrong. His pulse is thready and he's not breathing right. Sharpie says can we tow the body to the bank.'

It seemed like hours before they made the riverbank, but in reality it was only a few minutes. The RIB had already arrived, and as eager hands from Ali and Charlie, one of the detectives, pulled the bag up onto the grass, Marlo dragged herself from the water. Ignoring the shooting pains in her fingers from the cold, she looked at Ali. 'One sec.'

She jogged over to where Sharpie and Doc were leaning over Mac's inert form.

'He's OK,' said Sharpie, 'He's breathing and his hearts still going. Ambulance is en route. We'll stay with him. Go deal with Ali.'

Marlo nodded, emotion clogging her throat. They were a close-knit team, and when a strong ox like Mac went down it was harrowing. Pushing it back, though, she turned back to Ali.

'Sorry, Ali. I had to –'

'Say no more, I understand.'

Ali's hand on her arm made her pause momentarily and she glanced at him. Breaking contact, she knelt down beside the body, fiddling with the zip in an attempt to open it. *My fingers are bloody freezing. Stupid Kevlar gloves. They should invent heat-giving gloves for when you're in the water.* Grumbling to herself, she put her fingers to her mouth and blew hard, before rubbing them together vigorously.

'I'll get the zip,' said Ali, kneeling down and opening the top of the bag so the girls face was on view. 'Put your fingers under your armpits, it's warmer there.'

Marlo glanced at him in surprise. She knew that but it wasn't the normal kind of thing a cop would say. Most of them would wait until she'd warmed her hands up to see what was inside the bag. Shrugging slightly, she did as ordered.

'She's a kid, Ali,' said Marlo. 'No more than about sixteen I'd say. From her bone structure, I'd say she's Asian. East of here but not as far as China. Completely naked, bruising to her face and ankle. Looks like burn marks around her mouth too. There's nothing in the river that would cause those kind of burns. They look chemical.'

Ali leaned in, and she watched him frown. 'Pathologist will be here shortly, maybe he can shed some light on it. She is just a kid; I'd be surprised if no one's missing her. Bonnie wee lass too.'

Marlo saw Ali's eyes become haunted, and she wondered what demons he saw when he did it. She'd noticed him do it at the last water body too. *None of my business. But whatever it is, it hurts him.*

'You OK?' she asked, putting her hand on his arm this time.

But he didn't reply. He got to his feet and walked back towards his team silently.

'He just blanked you completely,' said Connor, suddenly appearing beside her as she re-zipped the bag.

'He's got stuff on his mind, is all.'

Marlo didn't even realise she'd spoken aloud until Connor said, 'Oo aye, and you'd know that how?' He nudged her with his hip, 'You and him an item?'

'What? No. Bog off, Connor,' said Marlo with a grin that didn't quite reach her eyes. She turned towards the place where Mac had been lying just in time to see the paramedics wheel him off on top of the trolley.

Chapter Ten

5th November, 1055 hours - River Wear, Washington Wildfowl Park

Elvie felt like she had been walking for days. Her feet ached, the thin plimsolls doing little to prevent the undergrowth from feeling as hard as large rocks. Her side was a constant throb that pulsed with every step she took, and the cold had seeped through to her bones. Several times she had stopped, wanting nothing more than to lie down and sleep, but she pushed herself on.

She had found a small stream and taken a long drink of the icy cold water, splashing a little on her face. And had then started walking again. The stream had joined a river, one too wild to even consider crossing. So she walked alongside it instead, hoping it would lead her into civilisation.

Though what she would do when she got there she didn't know.

A noise caught her attention, something drifting down in the wind. It sounded like people talking faintly somewhere in the distance.

Maybe it's them. Maybe they've found me.

She was almost tempted to turn and go the other way, but she knew she wouldn't be able to walk forever. Noni had always said to face her demons head on, as the only way to fight a demon was not to show fear.

Determined now, she cautiously moved closer to the noise.

People were milling on the river bank. There was a boat hooked up to a large car, and slowly she realised the people were police officers. Her heart thudded in her chest.

They'll send me back, they'll give me to her and then she'll kill me. Or worse they'll send me home. And the men will come and take me in the middle of the night again. Why didn't the village help me, Noni? Why did you leave me and let them take me?

She held a hand over her mouth as an anguished cry threatened to escape. She'd barely had time to even begin to cope with grandmother passing on and so much had happened to her in the short time since. Her senses were on overdrive, her emotions acutely honed to the verge of absolute panic.

But she managed to rein it in just enough to function. Even if they couldn't help her, she was sure they would be heading to the nearest town; she could hitch a ride and get out there.

She edged closer to the people and then suddenly saw her opportunity. Creeping forward, she pulled herself onto the boat, crept underneath a large piece of tarpaulin, and lay as silent as a mouse.

The tarp acted like a blanket, the plastic trapping heat from her own body and breath. Unable to help herself, Elvie fell asleep.

5th November, 1220 hours - Dive Team HQ, South Shields

Marlo and Connor put the last of the equipment away in silence, both lost in their thoughts. Sharpie had gone to the hospital with Mac and Doc, leaving them to drive back and unload. They hadn't heard from them yet so were both worried about Mac's condition. At the time the paramedics took him off in the ambulance they suspected a heart attack, but he had been breathing. That was at least a small mercy.

A sudden burst of static in the radio hooked to Marlo's belt made them both jump, and it rapidly turned to the beeping sound that indicated a private call. The radios were primarily used by the dispatch controllers to deploy but if they needed a private conversation that didn't tie up the network, then they gave the handset a private call as if it were a mobile phone.

'Hello.'

'Buck, it's Sharpie. You with Connor?'

'Yeah. How's Mac?'

'Conscious and feeling a bit of a prick. It's not a heart attack. Mac is suffering from a case of alcohol poisoning.'

'Sorry, did you say alcohol poisoning?'

'Apparently so. Him and Doc were shooting straight vodka last night. Turns out Mac's body doesn't like vodka. He'll be fine in a few days. They're keeping him in for obs. We're heading back to HQ now. Everything OK?'

'Yeah we've just finished getting everything put back. Tell Mac I said to get well soon. About time for lunch, like.'

'He can have hospital food. Me and Doc will grab lunch on our way back if you're OK to wait for us?'

'Yeah sounds good to me. See you in a bit.'

She clicked the radio back onto her belt and turned to Connor. 'Alcohol poisoning. Just wait 'til he comes back. I'm gunna put him on granny watch! Who knew vodka would react that way. You OK going and putting the kettle on? I'll go park, cover the RIB then I'll be up.'

Connor nodded and headed towards the stairs.

Marlo made her way outside to the 4x4 and climbed inside. Sometimes, on days like this, she used the vehicle as a safe haven. Somewhere she could go to just be alone. Mac collapsing had scared her. The team was essentially her family, and for all she would poke fun at Mac when he came back to work, she was pleased he was going to be OK. She took her phone out of her pocket and sent a quick text to Deena asking if she wanted to go out for tea after work. Marlo didn't fancy being in her own tonight, it would give her too much time to dwell on what ifs and maybes.

The screams in her head started like a whisper, gaining more momentum as she tried to push them back. They got louder and louder, and she put her fists to her head. 'No. Please go away. It wasn't my fault, I didn't know.'

But her mind didn't listen. The silent noise echoed round the vehicle until she thought the only way for her to stop it was to remember.

I can't – I don't want to. It wasn't my fault.

But deep inside she believed it was. That deep dark secret that no one knew, not even her best friend, was what kept her awake at night and caused her mind to scream at her. She tried not to let it, and mostly she succeeded, but when she was stressed or had time to spend with herself, it always came back. Reminding her what an awful person she was, pushing her to do everything in her power to atone for her sins every day of her life, and screaming to remind her that she wasn't done.

She was on the verge of tears, when Sharpie suddenly opened the car door.

'You OK, kiddo? You look upset?'

'Am OK, sorry. Was just thinking about Mac.'

'He's fine, hon. Pop up and see for yourself this afternoon. Feeling sorry for himself but otherwise he's OK. The doc said he was lucky he got to the hospital when he did. He's been banned from drinking alcohol again at least for the foreseeable future until they've done whatever tests they need to do so he's grumpy, but otherwise the same old Mac. Doc chose lunch, I'm afraid. KFC buckets. Guess his hangover's kicked in. You ready to eat?'

Marlo nodded, and jumped out of the car locking it behind her. She ignored the shaking in her hands as she swiped her ID card over the reader and pulled open the door, motioning for Sharpie to go ahead of her. It was a slow-close security door, the type that closed on a spring then clicked as it locked.

They were half way up the stairs within seconds, neither noticing the lack of click to their rear. Nor did they notice the young girl creep through behind them, and huddle in the gap under the stairs.

5th *November, 1610 hours - Ryhope, Sunderland*

Nita was struggling. She felt like she was in an emotional roller coaster. One minute she felt like giggling furiously, and the next she felt so low she could die. The sandwiches had both been eaten, though she still had some water left. Her body felt like it was on fire, she was sweating profusely. Her shakes had abated but now she was aching so much her bones felt like they would crack under the pressure.

She couldn't stop the tears from arriving.

Please God, just kill me. I can't bear this pain. I can't do this, please just let me die. Why me? What did I do that was so horrible? I swear I'll never do it again, but please, please help me.

No one replied to Nita, though. No one came in the door to the little room. No one heard her sob as agonising spasms ripped through her.

The worst thing was she didn't even understand why it was happening. She hadn't understood what had happened since she'd been taken in from the market place and put on the godforsaken container.

Momentarily, she wondered what had happened to Elvie. The kid had been nice to her; she'd made sure Nita had water and food when no one else had cared, the other women all too caught up in their own misery and fear to even contemplate helping each other.

Nita hoped Elvie had escaped from wherever they had taken her.

An image appeared in her mind, Elvie leaning over her as she slept, rubbing her face and telling her that everything was going to be OK.

But it wasn't real.

The only thing that was real was the small cage she was in, the agonising cramps she felt, and the fear of what was yet to come. Curling into a tight ball, she hugged her knees to her chest and wept. Great hacking sobs that shook her to her very soul.

How am I going to get out of this?

5th November, 1925 hours – Desperado's Mexican restaurant, Sunderland

Connor sat at the corner table, his hand curled around the bottle of beer he'd been nursing for an hour now. He'd barely taken a sip.

He'd originally arranged to meet Ellie there for a meal. It would have been their third date, but his heart wasn't in it. He'd rang her and cancelled the minute he got off work, and in a spurt of spontaneity, he'd decided to go on his own. He wasn't in the mood for company.

Not tonight.

It had started when he had headed to his parent's house after work. His mum had been in her seat as usual, her face pinched as though concentrating on something really hard. She hadn't even acknowledged him when he'd sat down to speak with her, and after a few minutes, he'd wandered into the kitchen. His Uncle Fred had been sat talking to his dad, their heads huddled together as though discussing the world's greatest secrets.

When he'd entered, his dad had left the room to see his mother, and then it had started.

'So, lad, any interesting raids scheduled at work? Anything I need to know about?'

'Dunno, Fred, I work for the dive team, don't see much of the regular cops.'

Connor had watched as Fred's eyes narrowed and his mouth had grown hard.

'I take care of this family, Connor. I don't need to remind you how much it costs putting sweet Marie through her degree. When you count in the tuition fees, the cost of living and buying all those books. Did you know I bought her the latest mac book pro a couple of weeks back? Poor bairn was struggling along on a crappy old laptop that was having some speed issues.'

Connor had felt his temper start to simmer. That 'crappy old laptop' Fred had mentioned was only eighteen months old. Connor should know: he'd paid for it. And it hadn't been the cheapest of the cheap either. Marie had been grateful, knew he'd paid for it even though his dad had said it was from all of them. But he didn't know anyone who would turn down a mac book.

He sighed into his beer, recalling the rest of the conversation.

'Dunno how you can keep working for the shit-arse place you work anyway to be honest. Bloody pigs are as dirty as they come. You'd be better off coming and working for me. I could use a good lad like you. But I know you wouldn't do it. Your heads stuck so far up in the clouds.' Then he'd leaned in, become threatening. 'People who fly so high have to watch the sun doesn't burn their feathers. I'd hate to see all this come crashing down around you, lad. Just think how awful it would be for Marie to have to leave uni if I couldn't pay her way, or for your dad and your mum to end up on the streets so close to their retirement. This mortgage is like a noose at times. Sometimes I wonder if I can afford to keep it up. Information helps of course. The last thing I need is the cops treading their big size nines all over my crops, if you get my meaning.'

And Connor had sat there, just taking it. Like he always did. Within seconds he'd been spilling his guts about a raid to a cannabis farm he'd heard about on the rumour mill. A big one by all accounts. As always he didn't say when it was happening, or at what address, but he gave his uncle the area of the raid and that was enough.

Until next time anyway.

His uncle had been becoming more persistent, asking for information more frequently, keen to use the information to improve his reputation.

When it was found out, Connor would be well and truly screwed over. And it would be found out. This sort of thing had a habit of coming out at inopportune times. There was no getting away from the fact that he was leaking information that made him a dirty cop. You could dress it up anyway you wanted, but it still amounted to the same thing. He'd end up getting kicked out of the force, his name in disgrace. And that was the best case scenario. At worst it would mean criminal charges.

Connor sighed again. He had no idea what to do.

Glancing up as a shadow appeared at his table, he realised Marlo was standing in front of him. 'Hey. What're you doing here?' he asked.

'Ordering Mexican food. You gunna nurse that beer all night or come and sit with us?'

'Actually, I've already eaten,' he lied, guilt nibbling at him even as he said the words. 'I was just gunna finish this then head off home. My girlfriend got called back to work. She was on call,' he embellished, feeling the need to explain.

'OK, no problems, just thought I'd ask. See you tomorrow.' Marlo turned and made her way back to her friend who was waiting at one of the window tables.

Wish I could tell her. Maybe she could help.

But he knew he wouldn't tell her. Instead, he left some money on the table to cover the drink, and left.

Chapter Eleven

6th November, 1450 hours – Unit 12b, Sunderland Enterprise Park

Danny knew he was in trouble. No one got taken to the business unit unless it was bad. The search for the girl hadn't even finished when he'd been shoved into the back of a white van and whisked away. It was like they knew he had helped her escape. So far he'd pleaded and begged his innocence, but he knew they didn't believe him. They thought he'd slept with her, after all.

And that's your own doing. Why couldn't I be more like Gaz and just crack on with the job at hand? Why did I feel like I had to help her?

Berating himself didn't help though. It hadn't stopped him being tied to a concrete post last night, and it hadn't stopped them leaving him there all day today. Chains bound his hands and wrapped around his chest, and he had a rag in his mouth that pulled so tight across his cheeks that the top of his face actually felt numb. He'd wet himself at some point during the night, unable to hold it in any more, and the initial relief of the release now churned in his stomach as the smell of the stale urine crept into his nose to taunt him.

Why the fuck did I help her? I should just tell them she's in the car and be done with it. She won't have moved: she was too scared. It'll be a miracle if they haven't found her already.

Suddenly the unit door opened, and Rocko stepped inside with Gaz. Both of them looked serious, their faces drawn in determination. *Oh God. They haven't found her. They're gunna kill me. Fuck. I don't do pain. Please, just release this gag and I'll talk I swear. Please don't hurt me.*

He tried to speak through the gag, tell them that he would help them find her if she wasn't in the car, but it came out as a muffled, strangled grunt.

He saw Gaz shake his head, look at him with evident disdain. Pleading, he shook his head and grunted again.

I'll tell you, I swear to God I'll tell you anything you want to know. Please, just let me take this rag out of my mouth and I promise you'll know as much as I do.

Rocko advanced first, a knuckle duster glinting in the dull light of the unit. It had been a talking point a couple of years before when he'd leased the unit for a pittance. A serial killer had been loose in Sunderland and had used the unit to kill someone, which had decreased the rental as no one wanted it. It had been empty for ages before Rocko had happened on it. Danny still remembered the grin on the man's face as he'd told them of the new business place.

Usually it was used for conducting meetings, the kind that needed to be conducted away from prying eyes. But it easily doubled for the dirty jobs too.

Danny winced as the knuckle duster glanced the side of his jaw, his whole face erupting into stabbing pain that travelled around his head to the back of his neck. Trying desperately to make them understand, he shook his head.

Jesus Christ, please listen to me. I'll tell you. Fuck, this hurts.

The second blow was harder, the third even harder still. Danny no longer knew where his jaw began and ended as his face just felt like an explosion of pain. The taste of metal hit his mouth and he felt blood start to trickle to the back of his throat from a tooth that had dislodged.

Please God, no. This hurts so fucking bad, I can't do this.

Searing pain suddenly spread across one side of his ribs, rapidly followed by pain on the other side, as Rocko hit him as if he was a punch bag, one blow following the next rapidly. Danny couldn't breathe; he couldn't even inhale before the next punch hit and he saw stars as he struggled to draw in oxygen.

You fucking fuckers, stop! Please stop. You bastarding fucking twats. I said I'll tell you where she is.

The blows stopped, and Danny gasped in a breath. His lungs felt like they'd shrunk to the size of a child's. Pain pulsed around his body and it was impossible to know where it began and ended. His head dropped forward. *I can't take much more of this.*

Gaz stepped forward now, and when Danny saw the knife in his hand he started screaming, struggling against the chains. But Gaz didn't use it. Instead he placed it along the side of Danny's neck, and leaned in to his ear.

'You know what's worse than the pain you must be feeling? The thought of the rats that are going to come and feast on your flesh. They love the taste of blood, can smell it from miles away. The back door is ajar, and they'll come as soon as it gets dark. Sniffing you out, scrabbling in the dark. You won't even see them until they're right upon you. We'll be back tomorrow; maybe you'll be dead, maybe you won't. Either way it'll teach you. You shouldn't have slept with the little bitch. She was reserved, now she's gone and the money Rocko would have got has to come from somewhere. Don't expect to be paid for the last month's work.'

Twisting the knife sharply, he cut the side of Danny's neck, not deep but enough to make blood drip down towards his chest. He repeated the motion on his arms and legs, before smiling at Danny.

'You disgust me. If you'd had a bigger set of balls we'd all be OK. See you tomorrow, stud.'

The slam of the door reverberated and Danny sagged in his chains.

Jesus Christ, they're sick. All of them. Why the fuck didn't I walk away. We could have gone to Scotland, or Ireland. Anywhere that was far away from here. I don't deserve this.

But the niggling voice in his head disagreed. He could have gone to the police at any point along the way and reported what was happening. Gaz was right, he had no balls. Desolation and despair swamped him as he let the chains take his weight.

I deserve to die. That girl doesn't. Even if they give me the chance, I can't tell them. They'll find her and kill her. She's a kid.

Maybe if someone had helped me when I was her age, I wouldn't be here, trussed up like the Christmas fucking turkey.

Stars still swam around his vision, and he realised his jaw crunched when he moved causing yet another cascade of pain. This time, he didn't try to fight though; he had nothing left to fight with. Closing his eyes, he sank into the welcomed darkness that beckoned him.

6th November, 2115 hours - Dive Team HQ, South Shields

Elvie slowly stood from her hiding place under the stairwell. She'd somehow managed to fall asleep and had slept for almost twenty hours, her body taking some much needed time to repair. But now it reminded her that she was hungry, thirsty and needed to find the toilets again. She had ventured out the night before but was terrified she would get caught so had urinated, had a drink from the bathroom sink then hidden again.

She cocked her head to one side, straining to listen.

The building remained silent.

She cautiously made her way up the stairs and through the door at the top. It led straight into some kind of seating area. There were tables and chairs and a fridge hummed away to itself in the corner. The need to pee was stronger than the need to forage though, and she made her way round the room and through the door at the end.

After finding the toilet, she made her way back to the room with the tables. It had smelt like stale food, remnants of last microwave meals and grease loitering in the air. She crept to the fridge and pulled the door. It squeaked as it opened and she froze, listening for anything that would indicate someone else was there to hear.

But she heard nothing.

Opening the fridge door further, the scent of deep fried chicken entered her nose, and her mouth instantly salivated. She didn't even care what it was, it smelled like heaven. Reaching her hand into the round red and white

K.A. Richardson

box, she pulled out a piece of chicken and sank her teeth into it with a groan. It was a little greasy, but it was good, and exactly what she needed. She took the box out of the fridge, along with a can of cola and a handful of items from the top shelf which housed all manner of chocolate bars, sweets and drinks cans, and she took her haul back down to her hidey hole at the bottom of the stairs.

It was quite a large area, and held tarps, old dive tanks, and various other bits and bobs. It had hidden her well when she slept, and she felt safe there.

Pulling a tarp round her shoulder to take the chill off, she sat and methodically ate her way through several pieces of chicken, only stopping when her stomach was so full that she felt sick. She popped open the can, and took a slurp, giggling slightly as she burped loudly.

The tarp was her safety blanket. The spot under the stairs was warm and there was no one there who could hurt her. It wasn't long before she had dropped off again into a deep sleep.

7th November, 0210 hours - Unit 12b, Sunderland Enterprise Park

Danny suddenly jerked awake, completely unaware of his surroundings. Then the pain from his jaw filtered back into his mind, he felt the chains digging into his arms and fear coursed through him again as he remembered where he was.

Fuck, I'm in the unit.

His arms and legs felt numb, he had no idea what time it was but it was still dark outside, at least all he could see was black at the rear of the unit where the back door was ajar.

His senses kicked into overdrive as he heard scurrying sounds around his feet, and he about wet himself as he realised they were rats. He hated rats. Always had. And now they were right around him.

Grunting he kicked outwards, feeling his toe connect with a small body that let out a squeak. He shuddered so

96

violently that the chains rattled loudly, breaking the silence in the room.

He tried praying: *Please God, let me live. I swear I'll be better, I'll get out of this business and focus on raising my daughter.*

But there was no great bolt of lightning freeing him from the restraints, no rumble of thunder as some magical being leapt down to earth to help him. There was nothing except the sound of tiny claws on a concrete floor as the rats came closer to him.

Really he supposed he'd been lucky, he felt like he'd been there for days but the rats hadn't attacked him. Maybe they would just leave him alone. He felt a surge of adrenaline; no way would he just let it all happen. He jerked from side to side, trying to loosen the chains and get free, but they held fast. There was no way he was getting out of there without help.

He felt his head drop to his chest in defeat, and realised that he was freezing cold. It had been a chilly November so far as it was: the temperature dipping below freezing point every night so far. And tonight was no different. It was already past the point where he would shiver. He knew if he could see his fingers they would be blue.

Danny remembered reading somewhere that hypothermia was a good way to die. He recalled something about a person just falling asleep and not waking up. It sounded good to him. Better than being eaten alive by rats at any rate. He didn't know if it was true, but he knew he was tired of holding on and fighting.

The last spurt of adrenaline died off, and all Danny wanted to do was close his eyes.

So he did.

His eyes closed, and he slowly drifted off.

He didn't feel the rats congregate around his feet, he didn't feel their tiny sharp claws as they climbed up his trousers and jacket towards his face, and he didn't feel any pain as one dug its teeth into the soft flesh of his bottom lip.

Where he was, nothing could hurt him.

Chapter Twelve

7th November, 0600 hours – Ryhope, Sunderland
He unlocked the door to the room and entered. It wasn't normal for him to visit at this time of day: he usually liked the quiet of the night to do his work. He would just check on her and initiate stage one of her learning process before leaving.

It was even darker in the small room than it was outside. He snapped on the light.

He watched as the girl uncurled herself in the cage, and looked up at him with big brown eyes. She looked like she had a cold; snot had dried around her nose and on her top lip. He could see her pupils were dilated and the vomit in the cage indicated she'd brought up the sandwiches he'd left for her. He felt momentary anger. *What a waste. My mother would have tanned my hide if I'd eaten then been sick afterwards.*

But this girl wasn't him. And he sure as hell wasn't his mother.

He turned on the video camera in the corner, double-checking the view hadn't changed, then made his way to the cage.

'Subject seven, day three. Subject is displaying symptoms consistent with a cold, but I believe this is due to withdrawal of the heroin that was in her system. I am unaware of how long she was at the address in Sunderland so don't know when she had her last fix. Today, I will provide her with some bruising. I expect her to be resistant.'

He unlocked the cage door and waited for Nita to clamber out. He knew she would think she had a chance of escape. They all did. He'd have to teach her escape wasn't an option.

Grabbing her arm as she exited the cage, he gripped hard and forced her into the chair, methodically securing her hands and feet. After the incident last time, he wouldn't be so careless as to forget to do that.

Knowing it would come without warning to the girl, he slapped her hard. The crack echoed round the room, and she cried out, tears springing to her eyes as redness flooded her cheek. She started mumbling again in her native tongue.

He changed tactic and gently ran his hand down the side of her cheek, placating her with his touch, or trying to anyway. She pulled her head away from him in fear, and he slapped her again. Before she could react to the pain, he punched her with an uppercut that sounded like it made her teeth rattle in her head, and followed it with another punch, this time to the girl's stomach. Her breath left her body with a whoosh, and she made a sound similar to that of a donkey as she gasped for breath. Her eyes were bulging now, fear creating the instinctive response. Pulling back slightly, he boxed her ears, knowing that when he stopped they would ache and swell.

Glancing at the clock, he registered the time. That was it for now, he had things to do and he couldn't delay here. He unhooked the straps and pulled her roughly from the chair, frowning as he saw tears streak down her cheeks.

'No. You must learn to cope with the pain. It's the only way you can survive. I'm teaching you this so that you may live, little one. It's the only way.'

He punched her in the stomach, causing her to double over, and giving him the perfect angle from which to shove her inside the cage. The door to the cage slammed with a screech – metal on metal.

And for the first time that morning he smiled.

He had a good feeling about this one. She would learn, he was sure of it.

Turning the camera off, he pushed his messy hair into a semblance of tidiness, and left.

7th November, 1835 hours – Sunderland City Police HQ

Ali rubbed his hands over his eyes, and not for the first time that week, he wondered what the hell he was doing. In the last week, he'd had two bodies in the water. Something that in his whole career had probably only happened a handful of times. Which was good: the less the better as far as he was concerned.

Every time he was near the water, he felt his gut tighten and the nausea appeared from nowhere. It had always been the same.

Except it hasn't. I used to love the water. I loved the feel of it on my skin, and the weight of the tank on my back. I loved the bobbing of the RIB as we went out over the Forth, and the good feeling from recovering something that only the dive team could do. I would still love it too. If it hadn't happened –

He pushed his chair back suddenly and stood. He wasn't going down that route, not here and definitely not now. It was just the two deaths that were bringing his memories to the forefront, he knew that. He just had to keep fighting and leave them in the box where they were in his mind.

Packed away in the recesses where the bad stuff was sent, never to see the light of day.

Damn, I need a break. Why didn't I just tell Alex 'no' when he asked me to cover his damn shift today?

His mind wandered back to the recovery of the body two days before. Deena, one of the CSIs had arrived seconds after the RIB had been launched. They'd stood together and gasped as the hull of the RIB had made a beeline for Marlo's head.

He'd been ready to ditch his shoes and jump in, he knew he had. He'd been too busy to ponder on his almost-action until now, and he didn't know why his subconscious chose this moment to pop the memory back in front of him.

He could still swim – wasn't afraid of pools – but he hadn't been near a river since *it* had happened. It was so long ago but it was as fresh in his mind as if it had happened yesterday, even if he never opened the box to let it out. He knew if he did, he'd be able to smell the salty breeze from the water, his body would feel the gentle lull of the boat on the waves, he'd be able to smell the jasmine in her hair... Pulling himself from the edge of the steep cliff of remembrance was harder today than usual. Unresolved issues had a habit of coming back at inopportune times, and this was definitely one of those times.

Suddenly realising he was standing beside his desk, in the middle of a crowded office, was enough to pull him back this time, back from the place he didn't want to go. Taking a deep breath, he steadied himself and headed to the kitchen. *Coffee, that's what I need right now.*

'Liar!' his mind taunted. *'What you need is her not to be dead.'*

Guilt threatened to open the catch to the box, and he strode purposefully to the kitchen. Changing his mind last minute, he decided to work the rest of the shift on call from his flat. He had things to do, but there was nothing urgent and nothing had happened as yet. He could be at a scene in a flash, and at least at the flat he could use the running machine that his brother had left with him. Ali had inherited the flat from Alex when he moved in with his wife, Cass. Cass's cottage was smaller, without the room for the makeshift gym Alex had used at home. So he'd left it in the flat and just came round when it suited, though that had been much less often since the baby had arrived.

Picturing his niece in his mind, Ali realised it had been too long since he had visited the cottage. When they got back from seeing the family, he'd make more of an effort. His niece was coming up on a year old. He had to go round more often or he'd miss the important stuff.

Filling his mind with thoughts of his niece helped his mind push the bad stuff back. He told Charlie he was going home for a bit, and she nodded at him in acknowledgement before turning back to her computer. He knew she'd call if anything major happened, as would the control room.

8th November, 0540 hours, Dive Team HQ, South Shields

Elvie stretched with a yawn. It was toasty under the tarp, but she'd been there for over two days now and had barely moved. After everyone had gone last night, she'd raided the fridge again, bringing some snacks down to her 'den'. She'd even found a shower room and, once she'd figured out how to turn it on, had washed her hair and herself. Her dress was still smelly, though: she hadn't managed to find any clothing to wear while she washed it.

Pulling herself out from under the tarp, she shivered as a blast of cold air hit her. Peeking out through the window of the rear door, she saw the shimmer of frost on the windscreen of the vehicles in the back yard. It was icy cold: she wasn't used to weather like this. If she was going to leave the confines of the building she'd been staying in, she would need warmer clothing.

Frowning, she realised that a big part of her didn't want to leave. She knew she should: the chance of getting caught if she stayed was high; she was in a police station, after all. But it felt safe. If she left she didn't know where she would go, or if anyone would help her.

Climbing up the stairs to the break room, she pulled some more chocolate bars from the fridge, folding the bottom of her dress up a little to hold them.

She'd found the kettle and figured out how to turn it on to heat water, and had found the staff coffee and tea. She'd tried both, the coffee making her nose curl with its bitterness. But she liked the tea. Belatedly realising she had to put the chocolate bars down to make a hot drink, she dumped them unceremoniously on the table.

No one was here, anyway.

She hummed to herself as she made her drink, an old song Noni had sung to her when she was little. It was in her native tongue and it made her feel safe, '*sleep now, youngest one, your mother is far away, and she can't come for you.*'

Picking up the chocolate bars, she turned and made her way back to the stairs.

Maybe I won't leave. Maybe I'll just stay here instead. I like it here.

She pushed open the door at the top with her hip, then froze as she heard the bottom door open and footsteps start coming up.

Oh my God. There's someone coming!

She felt her heart pounding in her chest as panic threatened to keep her frozen to the spot. If she stayed though, she knew she'd get caught. Turning quickly, she pushed open the door to the female toilets and entered. She went into a cubicle, silently put the chocolate bars and the hot cup down on the top of the loo, and sat on the seat.

Terrified, she couldn't stop shaking. *If they find me they'll send me back to that house, I can't go back there. They'll kill me. Please don't find me!*

She jumped as the top door of the stairs closed with a crash; it was spring loaded and if it wasn't caught then it shut itself, loudly. She imagined she could hear footsteps outside in the corridor that led to the break room, and she would have sworn she heard them stop outside the toilets.

Holding her breath, she waited for the bathroom door to open.

But it didn't.

She heard another door open and close somewhere further past the rest room, and deciding that now was the time, she moved from her position. Gathering up her snacks and drink, she snuck out of the bathroom, tiptoed back to the stair door and opened it. She tried not to breathe in case someone was lying in wait for her, and cocked her head to one side, listening for any sound that the person was nearby.

Only silence greeted her though, so she went through the door, using her hip to close it softly so that the only sound it made was a click. She wanted to run down the stairs, and hide under her tarp and never come back out. But she couldn't. If she ran she'd spill her tea and someone would realise. So she silently went down the stairs, navigated around the piles of equipment and found the place she'd been calling home. Pulling the tarp over her head, she sat and finally exhaled.

That was close. I need to be more careful. She wrapped her now cold hands around the warm mug of sweet tea and took a couple of sips.

Noni had loved her tea, preferring it freshly brewed from a pot rather than the bagged form that was more popular. And because Noni had enjoyed it so much, Elvie had been brought up on it. It had been a tradition of sorts, Noni having a cup ready for Elvie before bedtime, and Elvie getting up and having a pot ready when her gran had got up in the morning.

Thinking about her gran made her sad. It had been so hard. People telling her what to do and how to act during the funeral. Her great aunt had taken care of the arrangements, but they'd never been close. The only person that mattered to Noni was Elvie, and Noni's sister had always been jealous of their close bond. The second the funeral was over, her aunt had left Elvie in the house on her own, saying she'd come and sort out Noni's things in a couple of days. But she hadn't come back.

Elvie didn't know why. She didn't know how the men had known to take her either. All she knew was that she wished she was back there, with Noni still looking after her.

She was pulled from her thoughts by the sound of the outer door opening again, and more footsteps heading up the stairs. Snuggling down into the tarp, she silently finished her tea and fell into an uneasy sleep.

Chapter Thirteen

8th November, 1010 hours – Unit 12b, Sunderland Enterprise Park

Danny didn't want to wake up. He felt consciousness try and pull at him, and fought it every step of the way. But finally his eyes cracked open a slit.

Sunlight shimmered through the crack in the rear door and for a moment he forgot where he was, staring as the light danced with the dust particles in bright rays.

Slowly though, the pain invaded his mind. He pulled his bottom lip inwards, it had felt dry and cracked, but as his tongue flicked over it he realised that something wasn't right. It was the metallic taste and the feel that it was all rough and cut up. He felt like every limb was burning, and suddenly he remembered the rats.

Tears sprang to his eyes as he imagined them crawling all over him, biting at his flesh and eating his lip. *Oh Christ, fucking hell. I'm still alive. How am I still alive? There must have been hundreds of them.*

He shuddered in disgust; all he could see in his mind was dirty great rats with huge teeth baring down on him.

And then the door behind him opened.

Rocko and Gaz entered the unit, Gaz immediately coming round to face Danny.

'He's still alive. The rats have done a good job of munching at his face like. Looks like something out of the Walking Dead. Gross, look at his lip. It's hanging off.'

Gaz slapped him hard across the face, and Danny groaned as his cheek started burning. He felt his lip split and blood started to drip down his chin.

'What we gunna do with him, boss? Leave him for the rats or finish him off?'

'What a fucking pain in the arse. Why'd you have to mess up, Danny? I had big plans for you.' Rocko's voice penetrated the fog of agony, he sounded disappointed, pissed off even. But Danny no longer cared. *Just end it you fucking twat, finish it. Please, God, just let me die. I can't take any more.*

'Do you know what I do to people who screw me, Danny? And their families? I'm not going to leave you here for the rats, they get fed enough shite. You're gunna die knowing that because of you, your little girl is gunna grow up without her daddy, your girlfriend is going to find your body and be traumatised for life, always looking over her shoulder wondering if she's gunna be next. And eventually, when they finally feel safe, I'm gunna come for both of them. They'll see me and realise in that moment that their lives will be over. And I'll make sure they both understand that it's all your fault. That if you had kept your dick in your pants and not fucked one of my girls, not helped her escape, and not been caught yourself, that their lives would have carried on as normal. And both of them will hate you for what you've done, in those last few minutes they will curse the piece of shit you are and wish to God that they'd never met you.'

Anger burned in Danny's stomach. *No! Please no, not my family. I didn't shag the girl, I swear I didn't! Please don't hurt my family.*

His silent screams echoed round his mind, but he knew Rocko couldn't hear them. He shook his head from side to side, grunting, trying to beg to tell them not to do that, to tell them the truth about the girl and what had happened.

But it was no use.

He felt the blade cut across his neck, the silky smooth feel of steel on skin almost deceptive in its intent. Blood gurgled in his throat, and he saw a red streak fly past him onto the rear door and ceiling. His last thought as he drifted off was of his daughter, and how she would grow up not knowing him, not knowing that he had died trying to do the right thing.

'You really gunna do that to his family, boss?' asked Gaz, once Danny's eyes had glazed over and his chest had ceased to rise. 'I can take care of that for you. I'll make them both wish they'd never met this useless sack of shit.' He kicked at Danny's leg before turning to face Rocko, his eyes sparkling. 'I could bring them here, boss. Make her watch while I bleed the little one dry. I could fuck her, all over. Then kill her too. I don't mind, boss.' Gaz was almost salivating at the thought.

'No.' Rocko's voice was sharp. 'What he did isn't their problem. It'll be enough that they live without him and that he died thinking they would suffer.'

'What shall we do with the body?'

'Untie him, wrap him in plastic. We'll dump him after dark. Then you can come back and clean this place with a gallon of bleach.'

8th *November, 1905 hours – Buchanan Residence, Sunderland*

'God damn stupid lift, always on the blink when I have shopping to carry,' mumbled Marlo, balancing the large box on her arms while the carrier bags dangling from her hands cut off the circulation in her fingertips. 'Always bloody happens when I've got shopping. I'll be emailing the maintenance man about this.'

Griping didn't make her feel better, but she did reach the top in what seemed like record time. She manoeuvred herself around the door to the corridor and tried to pull the handle down with her little finger.

The door suddenly sprang towards her, hitting the fingers that held the bottom of the box and causing her to instinctively release her hold on the box. Marlo cried out, partly in pain as her fingers suddenly realised there was blood flow, and partly to warn whomever was about to barrel through the door that she was there.

Tins clanked down the stairs as she moved back to allow the other person through. 'Jesus, you could've bloody looked,' she snapped, not bothering to look up. She didn't know her neighbours anyway, but no one went barrelling through a stairwell door without at least considering someone might be coming the other way. It was just plain rude.

Placing her carrier bags on the floor, she bent over and tried to retrieve a tin of tomatoes that was rolling towards the top of the stairs.

'Anyone ever tell you, you have a habit of bumping into people?' said Ali with a smile, bending to help her pick up the items that were now strewn over the landing.

'Just living up to my name I guess,' she grumbled back, remembering him calling her a jerk the last time they had collided.

Even his confusion didn't stall her, and she looked him in the eye. 'Next time you wanna call someone a jerk, at least have the decency to do it to their face.'

Ali's confusion was blatant, 'Jerk? I didn't call you a jerk.'

Marlo threw her hands up and shrugged in exasperation, 'And he can't even own up to it. At least have the decency to admit when you're at fault.'

'Marlo, I didn't call you a jerk.'

She felt her temper start to rise. 'I heard you,' she said. 'You knocked me over and asked me to carry that bloody box to your office, and as I was leaving you called me a jerk!'

She saw the moment Ali realised what she was on about, his expression changing from confusion to acceptance. But she froze as he surprised her by taking her hand, 'I didn't call you a jerk, Marlo. I was referring to myself. You carried my box and said something that I took the wrong way. I was calling myself a jerk for dismissing you like it was your fault.'

Marlo raised her eyebrows, questioning him even as her pulse quickened under his touch. He hadn't released her hand, and it felt warm where his lay on top.

Whoa there girlie, don't even go there.

Ali sighed, 'We were talking about the murder case a few months back. You said it wasn't my fault that the guy had escaped, and I snapped at you. I was the jerk, Marlo, not you.'

Marlo pulled her hand back, considering his explanation. It did ring a bell. Her tone softened, 'It really wasn't your fault you know.'

'I know, it feels like it, though. You're a cop, you know what it's like. A man died. Maybe if I'd done something different, he'd have lived.'

'Not at your hands, Ali. You're not responsible for a prisoner once they enter the prison system. There wasn't anything you could have done differently to change the outcome. Brown wanted to escape and he did what he needed to do to facilitate that. The prison service staff messed up, every Tom Dick and Harry knows you don't leave a high-risk prisoner like that with one staff member to look after him. The other guard shouldn't have left. But Brown will get caught again, and when he does the prison service will throw away the key.'

'I know you're right, but still. I'm sorry for being a jerk, and I'm sorry for knocking your shopping down the stairs. I'll go grab what's down here,' he said, leaving her sitting on the floor and picking the items off the steps and bottom landing. His cheeks coloured slightly as he handed her a box of Tampax that had gone astray, but it was nothing compared to how hers felt. Burning wasn't the word! *Of all the things he could've picked up, it had to be these? It couldn't have been a tin of bloody beans?*

'What are you doing lurking in the stairwell anyway?' she asked, suddenly wondering how he came to be there.

'I live here. Fourth floor.'

'Howay, pull the other one, it's got bells on it. I live on the fourth floor. Surely we'd have seen each other?'

'Seriously, I'm in flat E. Inherited it when Alex moved in with Cass last year.

'No way. Flat E? You're the Luke Bryan fan?'

'I play it too loud then,' said Ali with a rueful grin.

'Never too much volume for Luke Bryan. I have all his music. Love him. Wouldn't have pegged you for a country fan, like?'

'Always have been. Dad brought us up on the likes of Don Williams and Kenny Rodgers. He always said it was music that spoke to the soul.'

Marlo grinned at him as he handed her a bag full of tins. 'Would you mind returning the favour and carrying them to my apartment for me? Could do without having to chase them all down the corridor.'

'Sure,' he smiled back.

Wow, when he smiles his face changes completely. It's like he's a different person.

She unlocked her front door and pushed the door open with her hip, holding it open to allow Ali past. 'Thanks, Ali. You wanna stay for a coffee?' It was an impulsive question and she felt her cheeks flush with colour. She didn't do that, ask men to her apartment for coffee. It was almost unheard of.

But she got a reprieve as Ali replied, 'I'd love to but actually I have plans. I'm just on my way out. Rain check?'

'No problem,' said Marlo, 'thanks for the hand with my shopping.'

'Least I could do seeing as how I knocked it all out of your hands. See you later.'

Marlo closed the door thoughtfully. In that few minutes she'd learned more about him than she suspected most people learnt in a long time. Ali always came across as a good inspector, but he could also be standoffish, distancing himself from his colleagues. Or so she'd heard anyway. Shaking her head, she decided it was none of her business. She never listened to the rumour mill anyway, she made her own judgements. And her judgement about Ali was that he was a good man. Turning back to the kitchen, she turned the CD player on and smiled as Luke Bryan's voice came from the speakers.

Chapter Fourteen

8th November, 2205 hours – Ryhope, Sunderland

He sighed as he unlocked the door to the room. It had been a helluva day and the last thing he wanted to do was check on the girl. He wanted to go to bed.

He was tired right through to the core of his bones, the kind of exhaustion you got from being mentally and physically challenged all day. He felt the beginnings of a migraine niggle at the side of his head.

Maybe I should just leave her today; she'll still be here tomorrow. But he shook his head, if he didn't do the breaks today then his schedule would be all to pot. He already felt behind because he was more than a day late doing the breakages.

Why do I do this? I could just stop, let the girl go and not get any more.

But he knew he wouldn't: how would he get his teachings across if not to these girls who were so in need of guidance.

He felt his nose wrinkle as he entered; she'd soiled herself. He couldn't expect anything else really, he supposed. He had been thoughtful, though, and given this one a bucket: better a vessel to hold the waste than finding it all over the floor again. Such a simple idea really, he didn't know why he hadn't thought of it before. Still, it smelt ripe.

His memory faded back to a time when he was a child. He'd been given a dog off his mum, an old dog not a puppy like he'd asked for. It had grey all round it's muzzle, and she'd said he could name it himself. It only took hours to realise that the dog had a chronic wind problem, the smell so bad that he'd found himself pinching his nose and trying not to breath. He'd quickly decided on the name Stinky, and once named, the dog and he were inseparable. At least until Stinky disappeared. He frowned as he remembered his brother had been the last to see the dog. He'd denied hurting Stinky but he'd always wondered. It wouldn't surprise him. His brother had always been a nasty piece of work.

His mood changed and he found himself grinning as he closed the door behind him. He'd thought of the perfect name for the girl.

Pulling her from the cage, he said, 'Come on now, Stinky. It's time to play.'

8th November, 2210 hours – Ryhope, Sunderland

Nita was finally starting to feel more human. The shaking had stopped, the gnawing hunger was easing and despite the fear she had for the man, it was less than she'd felt in the house. In there she wouldn't have managed to survive much longer, she knew that.

She hated that her body had craved the drug so much though, despised the fact that she'd felt like she needed it, and worse would have done anything to get it.

This man might keep her locked in a cage, but surely it was preferable to needing brown liquid, and accepting the things the men had done to her in that house. Nita shuddered: it didn't even bear thinking about. All she could do now was try and get away, find out where she was, and then see what she could do about her situation.

Hoping it would work in her favour, she flashed a quick smile at the man as he opened the cage door and extended his hand to help her out.

She glanced round the room he held her in.

The wall behind the chair held tools mounted on hooks, and a work bench that was dusty but clear of debris. It wasn't a large room; the cage, the bench and the chair in the middle pretty much filling it, though there was a gap to the right of the doorway. *Something was there when I arrived... something plastic? Where's it gone?*

The man applied the straps of the chair to her wrists and ankles, then went into the corner and turned on the video camera. *Why does he video me? I don't get what he does with it. I don't know why I'm here. If I could understand him, maybe he would let me go.*

She heard him say the words softly to her, she didn't know what they meant but they were the same words he spoke every time he came into the room. She felt his hand touch her cheek gently, then withdraw.

The explosion of pain she felt as his fist hit her nose was unexpected and sharp, and even as blood dripped down the back of her throat she gasped. This caused her to gag, and she coughed loudly, blood exiting her mouth at speed and landing on the man's trousers.

Through the red haze, she heard him curse and looked up to see his anger. She pulled her hand back as he roughly bent her thumb until it cracked. Nita screamed. *Why is he doing this? Please stop. It hurts.*

Blood poured from her nose, she felt its warmth on her lips and her chest as she struggled to breath. Her thumb was pulsing with pain, she didn't even know if she could move it, but she didn't want to.

She hadn't even realised he'd unhooked her hand until she felt him pull her arm taut. Her mouth dropped into a wide 'O' as she saw him raise his other hand in the air, the hand that held a large mallet.

Blood gargled in her throat as she tried to scream, and attempted to pull her arm from his grasp. But he held fast and the mallet connected with a crack. She knew instantly the bones had shattered, feeling them crunch beneath his fingers as he reapplied the restraints, as if she was going to pull away with the agony coursing up her arm. Nita couldn't stop the tears falling down her face, she could barely breath through the blood in her throat, and felt it thicken as her body tried it's best to stop the blood flowing by clotting and congealing. *Why was he doing this? What kind of freak did this?*

As he put his hand back on her cheek, she pulled her head away, shaking her head vehemently from side to side. *Please let me go, please, just let me go. I won't tell anyone, I swear.* She felt herself whimper, her breath quickening as her body went into a panic. Within seconds she was hyperventilating, unable to stop the reaction as she struggled to draw breath. Black stars appeared in her vision as her panic grew, and suddenly, it all went black.

8th *November, 2230 hours – Ryhope, Sunderland*

He hadn't expected that; the blood flying from her mouth and covering his grey trousers with red spots. He knew they would wash out but still, it wasn't pleasant. Maybe he should invest in some clothes just for use out here. That way he wouldn't have to worry that someone would see.

Working methodically, he cleaned up the blood from the floor, putting the cloth in the bin under the work bench. He wiped down the chair and replaced the mallet on its hook on the wall.

Finally he opened the cage and placed a salad bowl, a sandwich, water and a section of a strip of paracetamol inside.

And now he sighed deeply. He knew he would sleep tonight. There was rarely a night he didn't sleep, but he didn't particularly want to. He had a sudden urge to go to a bar and get shit-faced. It had been a long time since he'd been so drunk he'd managed to force himself to forget everything. The last time had been about three years previously, and he'd been so drunk he couldn't even remember where he lived. He'd sat in the taxi and giggled to himself as the meter had ran onwards, the taxi driver charging for every minute he couldn't remember. Eventually the woman he'd picked up in the bar had told the taxi driver her address, and had let him go with her. He'd woken up the next morning in a strange bed, with a strange woman lying beside him and no recollection of how he'd even gotten there.

Maybe getting drunk was a bad idea. He had so little control over his life; he definitely didn't need to lose the control he had over himself now as well.

He rubbed a hand across his face, feeling the initial stage of the migraine progress into what was going to become a whopper. Locking the door behind him, he acknowledged it was time for his medication. It was sleep he needed, not alcohol. Decision made, he headed home.

Chapter Fifteen

9th November, 0820 hours – alleyway, Sunderland City Centre

Ali pulled the car over alongside the two marked vehicles that were already in the alleyway. He and Charlie clambered out, signed in with the loggist stood beside the police tape that worked as a cordon, and made their way over to the body.

'Wow, looks like he's had a number done on him. How'd his lip end up like that?' Ali asked the pathologist, Nigel Evans, who had just arrived at the scene. He'd seen the gaping wound across the male's neck, of course, but there was just something off about his lip. It was hanging, looked like it had been ripped.

'Give me a few minutes to look over him. Don't want to jump to any assumptions.'

Ali nodded and made his way over to the uniformed sergeant. 'Harry, how's things? What have we got here then?'

'Body dump I reckon, gov. His throat's been cut, but no way he bled out here. ID in his pocket says he's Daniel Burton, lives over Southwick way. I've got someone heading to the home address now, unless you wanna do the notification?'

'No thanks, I'll let your guy handle that. I'll see what happens next then head over later. He married, do we know?'

'Not married, no, but he lives with his girlfriend and their baby. PNC shows warnings for drugs, but that was a few years back.'

'No problem, we'll be looking into every angle. Wonder who he pissed off? His face is a mess.'

'Rats,' muttered Harry under his breath.

'Rats? What do you mean?'

'Some of the wounds look like gnaw marks. Attended a death years ago. Rat breeder had had a stroke in the shed where he kept the horrid little things. He was still alive and they'd just eaten him. He was found a few days later. When I got there a huge white one crawled out of a hole in his gut. Was disgusting, gov. He'd cared for them since they were babies, always handled them and made sure they were friendly. Then they turned on him in his moment of need. He haemorrhaged and bled out from the wounds .'

Ali felt his lip curl, 'Rats? That's gross. You really think that's what happened to him?'

'Honestly don't know, gov. Looks that way to me. Guess we'll find out in the PM.'

Ali nodded thoughtfully. He hoped it would end up being later this afternoon and not tomorrow. He was finally on his rest days and he had every intention of hiding away, possibly even going home to see his mum. Alex was due back today so there was no reason for him not to go. He'd even been invited for dinner at Cass and Alex's cottage that evening.

Making his way back over to the body, he waited for Nigel to finish looking around.

'I've got a slot this afternoon for a PM as long as the mortuary technician can get prepped in time. It'll be 2 p.m. at Sunderland Royal.' Nigel's voice was efficient and to the point as he addressed Alex.

'Initial thoughts, Nigel?'

'Looks to me like he's been gnawed on by something, possibly rodents of some kind. He has some bruising and lacerations consistent with being beaten, but I'd hazard a guess he bled out from the neck wound. We'll know more after the PM.'

Ali turned and made his way back over to Charlie who was stood talking to Deena, one of the CSIs.

'Hey, Deena. Anything to tell me?'

'No, not really. I've seized the plastic sheeting he was dumped in. Chemical lab might get some prints off the plastic itself. Couldn't really touch the body 'til Nigel had been so nothing there yet, but Kev, Johnny and Faith are doing the PM later. You gunna be there?'

'Aye I'll try and make it over. Just while I've got you, anything come back yet from the wee lassie we found over Washington? There wasn't much to work with I know. We haven't even managed to come up with an ID as yet.'

'No. To be honest the samples I recovered at the scene were all general debris stuff, I doubt very much it'll come to anything. More than likely it was just from people walking along the river.'

'Bummer. I've copied you in on the email regarding the strategy meeting, haven't I?'

'Honestly couldn't tell you, Ali. Haven't had time to scratch my backside today let alone read any emails. This is my second job already, I had a list of about ten to head out with when this came in. I've got staff drafted in from the Volume Crime Team dealing with a spate of theft from vehicles over Silksworth; some little scrote's been on an allotment rampage in Houghton that Kevin's gone out to, and Cass is on her way here after being summoned in the early hours and dealing with a rape case.'

'Christ, talk about one of those days. It's not 'til next week anyway, so no rush.'

Deena nodded and headed back to the CSI van that was parked out on the main street. Glancing around the area, he noted that the alley was to the back of an Aldi store. Limited chance he was sure, but it was possible they had CCTV. He made a mental note to have that checked into also.

There was CCTV all over the city centre, though to be fair, quite often at any given time probably at least half of them were off-line. The council just didn't have the funds to adequately maintain every camera and street light in the city. So they let them lapse and kept up on the ones that covered the main trouble spots.

He knew there were already a number of officers involved in the house to house enquiries. But it was doubtful that anyone would come forward. The area wasn't known for its high-class, law-abiding citizens. Still you never grew an oak tree without planting a few acorns: he'd just have to wait and see what the enquiries came up with.

Ali already had a gut feeling though, the rats, the beating, the cut neck – it all pointed to Daniel Burton being involved in something or other, possibly even linked to the drug offences Harry had mentioned. Organised crime? He didn't know anything for sure.

Opening the car door, he pulled a fresh Policy Book from the glove box and started writing. His notes at this stage could be vital, the book recorded the errant thoughts he might forget or misplace later, and he quickly made a bullet point 'to do' list.

It was gunna be another long day.

9th November, 1425 hours – Connor's parent's house, Sunderland

Connor pushed open the front door with a groan. He could already hear the screaming from the street: his mother was on one, again. He heard his dad bellow from the kitchen, and then the sound of glass breaking. He found himself running towards the kitchen door with dread.

As he entered, he saw his mother with a knife in her hand, her arm raised as she ran at his father. *What the fuck?*

'Mum! Stop it, what the hell are you doing?'

Running forward he grabbed hold of his mother's arm as she motioned towards his dad's face, which was as white as a sheet, his eyes bulging outwards, the vein in his right temple pulsing rapidly with his heartbeat.

'Dad, get in the other room. Mum, stop fighting against me! What the hell do you think you are doing?'

His voice sounded harsh even to his ears. All his police training flew out of the window. This was his mum, dammit. He'd never thought he'd see the day when his own mother would go for his dad with a knife. *Thank God I'm here. If I hadn't been I don't know what would have happened.*

He felt his mum struggle against his grip, reminding him that she still had hold of the knife. 'Let it go, Mum. Drop it, now.' He tried his best to keep his voice calm, but he was panicking. If he hadn't turned up when he did, his mum would have buried the knife deep into his dad's back.

Finally he heard a clunk as his mum dropped the knife on the floor.

'There's my boy,' she said with a smile, her mind suddenly popping back into the present from wherever it had been. 'Would you like a sandwich?'

Connor shook his head. How could she do that? Jump from being a violent psychopath one minute to being his mum? He didn't get it. It didn't matter how much research he did on Alzheimer's, how much he understood the basics. He'd never be able to grasp the severity of her changes.

Gentler now, he guided her into the living room, and positioned her in the seat by the window. Once she was settled he turned back towards his father.

'Dad —'

'Don't say it, Son. She's not going in a home. "In sickness and in health" I said, "for better or worse". It's my job to look after her now she's ill.'

'But Dad, she would have —'

'No, Son, she'd have stopped herself. She wouldn't hurt me, despite everything, somewhere deep inside I know she loves me. She threw the glass out of frustration. It was just bad luck that it hit the sink and not the pile of clothes waiting to be washed on the side.'

'Dad, she had a knife. If I hadn't grabbed her arm, she'd have stabbed you with it.' Connor felt his voice rise with exasperation. How could his dad not see what would have happened?

'You're wrong,' said his old man, shaking his head firmly. 'Your mother would not cause me any pain, not deliberately. She's calmed down now. It's all fine.'

'And what about next time? What about me not being here if she gets her hand on a knife then? Stop burying your head in the sand, Dad. You can't cope with this anymore. She needs to go into a home.'

'I said NO!' his father roared, before getting to his feet and storming from the living room.

Connor put his head in his hands. What the hell was he supposed to do when his dad was in complete denial and couldn't see what was happening, let alone do anything to help himself, or Connor's mum. Marie was due back at the weekend; she'd have a heart attack when she saw how bad things had become. It was getting to the point where Connor might have to move back home to help his dad, or go over his head and report his mum himself. His dad's pig-headed stubbornness was going to end up getting him hurt, Connor was sure of it.

'Always did have a temper, your father.' His mother started up. 'But I always told him, if he ever hurt you kids then he'd be out of that door faster than you could say "daft mick". You never saw, you were too young, and make-up did a wonderful job.'

Connor sat back and digested his mother's flippant comments. He'd never seen any evidence that his father had hurt his mother. Was this just the Alzheimer's talking? Or could it have been a relationship she'd had prior to meeting his dad? Shaking his head, he knew he'd never find out the truth. His mum would ramble on and then end up on a tangent, and his dad would storm off if he was confronted. But it had him worried. Maybe he needed to talk to his dad about it, see whether there was any truth to the allegation.

It had been such a flippant comment, so brief and just in passing. For a moment, he wondered whether he'd even heard it at all. Maybe his Uncle Fred would know better, and he would be less likely to kick off. Though Connor hated approaching him for anything. His dad's brother had a tendency to side with his father, believing in the values of family taking care of family. His dad was adopted and

Connor found the strength of Fred's feelings a little strange. He believed blood was thicker than water. Resolving to ring his uncle later, he left the house. He shouted goodbye to his dad – but got no reply – and locked the door behind him. Wherever his old man was, he was wrapped up in his own thoughts, and Connor would be damned if he'd make it easy for his mum just to walk out.

9th November, 2045 hours – Cass and Alex's Cottage

Ali pulled his car through the wooded driveway and parked next to Alex's white Audi. He sighed loudly. After the day he'd had all he wanted to do was go home, bury his head under the duvet and never come back out.

The post mortem in the afternoon had been relatively fast. Nigel had quickly ascertained that the cause of death was the laceration to Daniel's neck. He had confirmed that the male had indeed been a feast for animals of the rodent variety: he'd actually found two sharp teeth inside one of the man's wounds. Ali shivered as he thought about how terrifying it must have been for Daniel Burton – if he'd been conscious. *I really hope he wasn't though. I'm gunna have nightmares about this poor bloke.*

Giving himself a mental shake, Ali got out of the car. He was here to spend time with his family, not dwell on the happenings at work. It was getting to him though, that was the trouble. The dead eyes of the people he dealt with day in and day out had started invading his dreams, causing him to wake with a jolt virtually every night. It all reminded him of things that were better left in the back of his mind where they belonged. The water deaths had been especially hard: his memories fought to escape every time he thought about the cases.

He wasn't the kind of person who made connections easily and he held back on friendships offered, but his family meant the world to him. Not that it had always been that way, when he was younger he'd had a huge number of friends. But since *it* had happened he'd regressed, started doubting himself more, and backing away from the people that he used to call friends.

Tonight though, he wanted to forget. He wanted to forget he was a cop and just enjoy some time with the family.

He took in the sight of the cottage as he walked towards the front door. He could completely understand why Cass and Alex loved it so much. It was a fairy-tale come true. The porch light was on – it was left on permanently now – but he remembered being there when he'd been looking after Cass after she'd wound up with a killer stalking her a few years back and the light had never worked because Cass always felt so safe in the cottage. The light made him both happy and sad.

Not pausing to knock, he opened the door and entered. The smell of garlic and herbs hit him instantly: obviously some kind of pasta for tea. It smelt divine. He hung his coat on the rack near the door and turned just as Ollie, Cass's huge dog launched his oversized paws in the direction of Ali's shoulders. He held his weight and let the dog greet him, sloppy kisses covering his cheek and chin, before pushing the gentle giant off him.

'Unc' Awi,' squealed an excited voice from the top of the staircase, her small hands rattling the stair gate impatiently, knowing that he would go and lift her over. And dutifully he did just that, sweeping his niece into his arms and giving her a huge kiss.

'Hey, sqwudge. How's my favourite niece?'

He carried her downstairs and into the kitchen.

'Look who I found at the top of the stairs, a burglar!'

Alex and Cass both turned with a grin.

'A burglar,' said Alex, 'my goodness. We all know what happens to burglars in this house, don't we?'

He advanced towards Ali and baby Isobel squirmed in his arms.

'No tickle, no tickle,' she giggled hysterically before Alex even reached them. He tickled his daughter making her belly-laugh loudly, before grabbing her from Ali's arms and walking towards the door. 'You, little miss, should be in your big girl bed until morning time. I'll read you another story then you need to go to peeps, OK?'

The kitchen door closed behind them, and Cass grinned at Ali. 'You look tired, you OK?'

Ali took the mug of coffee offered. He hadn't even noticed her making it. He nodded. 'Yeah I'm OK, just knackered, I think. Was due on rest days tomorrow but we had a murder in this morning. Some kid involved in drugs somehow, we think, but nothing conclusive as yet. Been a long week.'

'Haven't you got any leave due? Your mum was saying it's been months since you've been home. She was almost set to come down here and frog march you back up there for some R and R.'

'Yeah, have plenty due but you know what staffing's like at the minute. If you're not off sick, you aren't getting off. Already had my rest days cancelled due to this bloody murder. Am hoping I'll be able to take them next week at some point. I'll head up to see her if I get them authorised.'

'She just misses you, Ali. She misses Alex too. She was saying she wants to come down and see Izzy in the next couple of weeks. Mary's brood are on about coming too. It'll be like a madhouse!'

'They're all wanting to stay here? Where on earth will you put them all?'

'Dunno to be honest, but we'll manage. We've had some quotes about getting the extension done at the back so hopefully that'll be going ahead shortly, though it won't help this time. Be good to have the extra room though. Especially when –'

She paused, her face blushing slightly.

Ali immediately realised what she'd been about to say: he should have noticed immediately. A contented glow was emanating from her like sunshine itself.

'Congratulations. I'm going to be an uncle again.' He got to his feet and pulled Cass into a warm hug. 'That's fantastic.'

'We just found out this morning, haven't told anyone else yet.'

Alex came back in, and Ali broke apart from Cass with a grin. 'Congrats, bro.'

He punched Alex on the arm with a smile.

This was what he needed, this feeling of belonging and warmth. If he could move in here and forget all his demons he would. He felt a little acid rise from his stomach as he realised that it would never be the case. Swallowing hard, he focussed on enjoying the evening and tried to ignore the lead feeling in the base of his stomach.

Chapter Sixteen

10ᵗʰ November, 0810 hours – Dive Team HQ, South Shields

Marlo was late. She was never late, but today she hadn't a hope in hell's chance of making it in on time. 'Sorry, Sharpie, had a nightmare of a morning. Some tosser keyed down the side of my car and slashed one of my tyres. I've put the spare on but then, when I was at the nick making the report, a pisshead decided that I was a taxi and nothing I said was going to convince her otherwise. One of the traffic lads ended up taking her home. And it doesn't bloody stop there! On my way up the A19, happy as you like, and some knobber decides to undercut me almost causing me to hit a lorry, then speeds off as if nothing happened; and another bloke using his mobile phone was so far up my arse he could practically see my teeth! God I need coffee. And Valium.'

Sharpie nodded with a grin. 'Must be the day for it today, kiddo. Had a similar thing on my way in, though without the keying and tyre. At least you didn't have to wait for the RAC or AA, you'd have been there forever. Don't worry about it. Mac and Doc are late anyway. Mac's on office duties only, but he's coming back in for a few hours today. Doc went to pick him up as he's not cleared to drive yet. Connor's down in the kitchen making a brew so the kettle will have just boiled. Go and make yourself a cuppa.' Taking a final long slurp of his own, he handed her his mug and added, 'and make me another while you're at it.'

Marlo headed down the corridor and decided that her bladder suddenly couldn't wait until after coffee. She reached the bathroom door and froze as she heard what she thought was a sneeze at the bottom of the stairs. Suspicious, she quietly made her way down and paused, her head cocked to one side as she listened intently.

Silence reined, and she pulled open the door, sticking her head outside and glancing around the rear yard. There was no one there.

Must be my imagination, could've sworn that sneeze was real. All the crap this morning must have me on edge. Definitely in need of caffeine!

She made her way back upstairs and within minutes was seated back in the briefing room. Taking a moment, she glanced around. Mac and Doc were both sat together, and Mac looked pale but his eyes were sharp. Doc looked relieved. Marlo knew it had been hard seeing his friend collapse like that. Connor looked exhausted, his eyes were bloodshot and he had dark circles shadowing his cheeks.

Edging a little closer to him, she quietly said, 'You OK? You look like hell.'

'Gee thanks, Marlo. Had no idea how shit I looked this morning.' His sarcasm was evident but before she could respond, he sighed and added, 'Parent issues. Been up all night trying to keep my mum calm. She has early onset Alzheimer's and last night was a bad one.'

'Sorry, hon. Do you look after her on your own?'

'No. Dad looks after her, but sometimes… well sometimes he just can't cope. So I help out. She should be in a home, somewhere that can give her the care she needs, but Dad's stubborn. He won't even entertain the idea. He's old-school where his marriage vows are concerned.'

'Nightmare. Is there anything I can do?'

'Take the lead if we get a job? I could so do with not diving today.'

Marlo nodded, and was soon interrupted by Sharpie as he said, 'Right folks, we have a job.'

Both she and Connor sighed as he told them the details.

10ᵗʰ November, 0810 hours – stairwell, Dive Team HQ, South Shields

Elvie froze after a sudden sneeze escaped from her without warning. Her heart started to thud in her chest as she heard footsteps coming down the stairs.

Someone heard! They're going to find me!

She held her breath as the footsteps approached, hearing her heart beat pounding inside her ears. She was convinced whoever was coming down the stairs would find her, and then what? She'd be in big trouble, that's what.

Her eyes widened as the woman came into view. Elvie was well hidden by the tarp. The woman would have to actually come looking, but it didn't stop the fear. She felt bile rise up into her throat from her tummy. All that junk food was doing nothing for her constitution.

She saw the woman cock her head to one side, listening intently, and almost gasped as the woman opened the door that led out to the yard.

For a moment, Elvie contemplated running. Just pushing past the woman and heading out of the door as fast as her legs would carry her, but she couldn't. Deep down she knew if she ran she'd get caught. Then the police would do whatever police did in this country. She had no reason to believe that would be anything good. In her country, they would take her to the station, and she would be treated with disdain, if not violence. They operated under the pretence that they were law enforcement, but the reality, especially in the outlying small villages, was that any enforcement was on their terms. Sure, there were a few good ones, but they didn't come with a flashing sign on their heads saying 'I'm a good guy'.

So she stayed where she was.

She heard the woman mutter under her breath, and then the woman's boots thudded as she made her way back up the stairs towards the break room.

That was close. I need to find somewhere else to hide. Maybe I should just leave, go and find Nita and we can find somewhere together.

'*Yeah right,*' her conscience argued back, '*As if there's anywhere to hide for two girls who don't have any money or know the country. You wouldn't know where to start.*'

But I can't stay here forever.

'*No one's saying stay forever. But you go out there and there'll never be anyone to help you. Stay here and figure it out.*'

Elvie felt a giggle rise and quickly put her hands over her mouth, stifling it. What the hell was she doing? Arguing with herself? The nervous laughter dissipated.

What on Earth was she going to do?

10th November, 1420 hours – Sunderland City Police HQ

Ali juggled the three files with a cup of steaming coffee as he made his way to the meeting room on the floor above his office. He wasn't happy. The team had their own meeting room next door to the office – it was used for all the forensic strategy meetings, the daily briefings and so on. But the superintendent had booked it solid for the next month. Ali didn't even know what for, but it all seemed very hush-hush and it didn't sit well.

He bent slightly, using the elbow he held the files in to open the handle to the meeting room door, and then used his hip to push it open. His coffee sloshed precariously close to the edge of the cup, but somehow stayed inside.

He glanced around as he made his way to the top of the table, at which point his files dislodged slightly and went to fall. He put his cup down first, spilling half his coffee on the desk and swore as he used his free hand to grab at the tumbling files.

Acting sergeant Charlie Quinn pulled a wad of tissue from her bag and mopped up the coffee, flashing him a grin.

'One of those days, boss?' she asked.

'Every day's one of those days at the minute. Right, let's get started. Where are we at with the Burton murder?'

He turned his gaze towards Tony Cartwright first. He was in charge of the POLSA search team that had been on duty the day Burton had been found.

'Just a load of trash, boss. No knife or other bladed implement in the area. Evidence seized is just the generic stuff we'd expect to find in an alley: cans, crisp packets and the like. We did find a couple of syringes which may tie into the drugs link. They're in freezer storage so we can use them if need be. We did a search at his home too. Came up with 20k hidden under one of the floorboards. All unmarked, non-sequential bills of different denominations. His lass looked as shocked as we did, though she's already asking for it. She seems to think he's been squirreling money away for her and the bairn. There was a black notebook found also, but it reads like gobbledegook. It's possibly some kind of code, but I don't know a thing about that stuff.'

Ali nodded, and looked at Charlie expectantly.

'We've done the house-to-house. Surprisingly no one saw or heard anything. Checked the Aldi store for CCTV but it's been hit by vandals wanting to nick from the store without being watched. The engineer's apparently scheduled to repair it next week – which doesn't help us.

'I've spoken with his girlfriend… Tracy I think her name is off the top of my head. She seems to think it's down to his old life. Apparently Burton was into some not so sweet and light things. She didn't know what exactly but said that his old bosses had had her kidnapped when she was pregnant with the bairn, which is now a few months old. It was never reported to police, but Danny apparently got it sorted, and is now out of the life. We all know it's not that easy though.'

'What was he into?'

'She doesn't know. She suspected it might be drugs but never found any evidence and he kept her right out of it. Said he just called it "business". She did say he hated it, though. The kidnapping was the last straw, apparently. To her knowledge he had finished with it all and was working at a garage in Southwick. The garage have never heard of him and confirm he's never been an employee there. We've checked the associates on the intel systems, one listed as...' Charlie paused as she checked her notes. '... Gary Dobson, though the intel's a few years old now. The last address listed must be an old one, as the current tenants have no idea who Dobson is. We have a warrant out for a fail to appear from a couple of years ago, but it's a reasonable assumption that Dobson is in the wind.

'Danny's younger brother, Kyle, is also listed. I'm attending his home address later today. The notebook Tony mentioned is being looked at by HQ at the minute, but they may well send off to a cryptographer to decipher if they can't work it out up there.'

Kevin waited until Ali glanced his way before speaking.

'Not a lot from the scene as it stands. PM showed the laceration to his neck to be cause of death. He bled out, though not in the alley. The body was dumped there. The initial crime scene is still to be established. We did swab the skin on his face. Burton had been beaten so there's a chance of mixed profile DNA. Might give us a lead. Submissions have already authorised it to be sent off. We did find trace amounts of sawdust on his clothing which might be identifiable if we can locate something to compare it to. His mobile phone's been sent over to Jacob Tulley in the digital forensics lab. He's putting a rush on it, though you know how slow a rush is over there. Never seen such a busy department.

'His nails were scraped at the PM but Nigel doesn't think there's anything there as he had no evidence of defensive wounds. I'd hazard a guess he knew his attacker, but he might equally just have been surprised. His clothing is in the property store. I've tasked Johnny to do fibre tapes, and check for trace today. You never know, our killer might've left us a hair or two.'

'Great, thanks guys.'

Kevin stood to leave, knowing it was the end of his part in the meeting. And Ali opened the second file.

10th November, 2040 hours – Ryhope, Sunderland

He couldn't do it. For the first time, he felt something akin to regret. He just wanted this all to be over. His control was slipping and there wasn't a thing he could do about it. Panic threatened to overwhelm him. Not panic that the bodies would be found, the chances of that happening would be a miracle. He'd put them somewhere that no one would ever find them.

It wasn't even the girl in the cage. He'd gone in the night before and fed her, given her some pain killers, and documented the session. She was stronger than the rest, he could tell. She would last the longest, which meant months of her learning. He knew she would be the one to understand, too, to comprehend that he was just teaching her to be able to cope with the pain. It wasn't his intent to be cruel, but they *needed* to learn.

No one should have to go through what he was feeling. It was so raw and strong at times that he thought his heart might actually split in two. Today was one of those days.

He was standing outside the room, his head leaning on the door frame, and was ashamed to admit that he was crying. Not massive great heaving sobs, but the silent tears that trickled down your cheek when you didn't even realise they were there. The soul-destroying kind of sadness that hid so deep inside it was rarely released. It felt like it would never stop, had been building in momentum for weeks. A thousand dead souls screaming at him and telling him that all the shit in the world was his fault.

Maybe it is. Maybe I should just kill myself and be done with it.

At this errant thought, his expression stilled. He somehow managed to push the sadness and tears back inside the box from whence they came, and a slow burn of shame appeared instead. He was too much of a coward to kill himself.

He swiped at the remnants of the salty rivers on his cheeks, set his expression, and went inside.

Chapter Seventeen

10th November, 2050 hours – Dive Team HQ, South Shields

Marlo stepped out of the shower in the functional ladies' room and wrapped her towel around her. She'd been in the shower for twenty minutes and could still smell the sickly sweet stench of 'dead guy'.

The job they'd been called to that morning had turned out to be a long one. The RIB had to navigate through reeds and water lilies to get to a small island in the middle of a river. How the body had even been spotted she didn't know, but it had been there for a while and was ripe.

It had been a man, at least she thought he was a man. Most of his head was missing – the blast from the shot gun at his feet had turned his brain to mush and shattered the bones in his face and skull. She knew that both the pathologist, and Deena who had attended the scene, would agree it was a suicide. The note tucked in his pocket had been the clincher.

As the team had manoeuvred the body, the flesh had released its hold on the muscles due to the build-up of gases. The skin had split, covering both Marlo and Deena in stinking body fluids. Among those fluids were the decaying lipids that stick to your hair and clothes, and even lodged in your pores. Marlo had only ever had it happen once before. And that hadn't been this bad.

Even now as she stood drying her hair, she caught a waft of the stench and almost gagged. Sharpie and Connor had had the grace not to laugh, but she could see they were glad it hadn't been them. They'd all gone home an hour before, but there was no way she was leaving the nick smelling like she'd crawled backwards through a rubbish dump filled with toxic waste and dead fish.

Sighing, she unwrapped the towel, and stepped back under the shower head, setting the temperature to a notch below scalding. Her dry suit had been bagged for the incinerator: there was no getting back from the filthiness and biohazard dead guy juices presented. It seeped through the white crime scene suits, soaked into the top of her boots, and the cuffs above her gloves. It was standard procedure in cases like this that all clothing and shoes be burnt and new kit issued. She sighed again. *Damn, that means breaking in a new pair of boots.*

Squirting a huge blob of shower gel onto the scrubber, she started rubbing it hard over her skin again. This was her fourth shower: maybe this one would get rid of the stench.

Suddenly, the door to the bathroom opened, and she stilled, listening.

'Hello?' she called out, turning the shower off and pulling her towel from the hook on the back of the door. She heard footsteps retreating, soft footsteps, not like those from police issue boots. *What the fuck?*

Marlo was the only female diver: no one else would be in the nick at that time of night. Pulling open the cubicle door, she stepped into the bathroom and grabbed her mobile phone from the sink. Quickly dialling, she waited for the control room to answer.

'This is 5402 Buchanan from the dive team. I'm at HQ in South Shields. Everyone has gone home, and I think there's an intruder in the building. I'm going to do a walk-through but don't have my radio on me. I'll leave this line open.'

She pulled on her sweat pants and t-shirt, and softly padded out of the bathroom and into the canteen area. It was almost in darkness, the street lights from the car park outside the only glow. Listening intently, she heard nothing. But she was certain someone had opened the bathroom door. *Or did they? I am tired. Maybe I just thought they did?* Doubt trickled in and suddenly she felt like an idiot for immediately ringing comms.

'What you doing sneaking about?' came Sharpie's voice from behind her. Marlo jumped about twenty feet in the air and turned, punched him on the arm and then put her hand to her chest. 'You bloody idiot! Are you trying to give me a heart attack?'

Sharpie backed away, his hands held out in front of him. Unable to stop himself, he started laughing loudly, tears springing to his eyes as he held his sides. 'Priceless...' he gasped, 'your face was a picture. Jesus, I wish I'd recorded that! Would've got me £250 on You've Been Framed, that bad boy.'

'Jackass. Did you come in the bathroom too, just to get me all on edge? I thought you'd left with the guys?'

'I did, forgot my mobile though, and then started working on a report. Besides, you know I don't like the idea of a female being left in the nick on her own. Didn't come in the bathroom, though.'

'Yeah, you don't like that idea, yet you're willing to scare said female half to death,' grumbled Marlo. *I must have imagined the door opening. How weird. What a dufus.* Deciding she would get her own back at a later date, she turned back towards the bathroom. 'I'll be ready to go in a sec. Let me grab my bag.'

10ᵗʰ November, 2100 hours – Dive Team HQ, South Shields

Elvie had almost died when she had walked in the bathroom and heard the woman in the shower. She'd pegged it into the canteen and hidden beneath a pile of jackets and the like, certain that her luck was out and that she'd be caught now.

She'd jumped herself when the man had come into the room and spoken to the woman. She really needed to learn to check people had gone before coming out from under the stairs. When he'd started laughing though, for a moment Elvie had wondered if maybe these police weren't the same as back home. Maybe she could ask them for help and not be punished. *I just don't know what to do. I need some help. I miss you, Noni. You'd know what to do.*

She stayed hidden beneath the coats until she heard the cars leave, then slowly emerged. The pile consisted of jackets, waterproofs and kit. Most stations had one similar somewhere. Since the dive team's headquarters didn't have locker rooms, it accumulated in a corner of the recreation room.

Elvie felt a stab of guilt as she pulled open the fridge. No matter how much she tried to sugar-coat it, stealing was wrong. But she had to eat.

She opened the top of a Tupperware box that had been left on the shelf and sniffed suspiciously. It was a rice dish, with lumps of chicken and vegetables. Grabbing a fork from the draining board, she tucked in, her mouth watering as she tasted the tang of chilli. When she was done, she flicked through the magazines left on the table. One thing she could say about being holed up with no one to talk to was that it gave her time to read. And her reading skills were improving rapidly. She was even starting to understand some of the slang terms used. She made a conscious effort to listen whenever she heard conversation, then when everyone had gone home, she'd been practising her words.

She wanted to be able to leave the station, venture out and find help, but to do that she knew she had to be able to speak. Noni had taught her, but she wanted to be better, and reading helped her learn. Besides, there wasn't a whole lot else that she could do cooped up in the police station.

10th November, 2105 hours – Ryhope, Sunderland

Nita was confused. The whole situation was just surreal. One minute the man who came in was hurting her, then the next he was stroking her face, talking softly and feeding her painkillers.

In the time she'd been there, he'd gotten her off the drugs she never even wanted to be on, broken bones, beaten her and then dressed her wounds to alleviate her discomfort. She had no idea what he wanted, or why he was keeping her there. And she was losing track of time: the lack of natural light made the days indistinguishable from the nights.

The last few times he'd visited, he'd taken to staring at her, his gaze what she could only describe as compassionate. It was unnerving. She'd tried talking to him, but he never understood. He seemed pleased when she didn't show the pain she felt, so she'd started not crying out when he hit her, not whimpering and crying despite the fact the fear kept her chest so tight she thought it might burst at times.

Right now the room was pitch black, even the portable heater wasn't giving off any light that she could see. She couldn't hear a thing either, except the ticking of the clock on the wall above the workbench. Not that she could see it: she remembered its position from the times the lights had been on. She hated the clock: it ticked so loud that sometimes she found herself twitching in time with it. Given half the chance, she'd rip the horrid thing off the wall and smash it to smithereens.

Nita had taken to trying to sleep whenever he wasn't there, but it was uncomfortable. Even now she could feel the metal bars of the cage digging into her skin, causing bruises on bruises. She couldn't stretch out fully, couldn't even stretch her legs out if she sat up. Her neck ached permanently from being bent at an angle, and many of the grooves to her skin off the cage had started getting sore and weepy.

She was lucky if he was in the room for a couple of hours over the day, and she felt like she was slowly going insane. She had full conversations with herself, dreaming about when she would escape, then arguing with herself and saying that it would never happen and that he would kill her in this little dark room.

Truthfully, she didn't know what to think. She knew he had had plenty of opportunity to kill her if that was what he wanted, and she had no idea why he kept her alive.

Turning slightly, Nita repositioned herself on the other side, and fumbled in the dark for the water bottle she knew was somewhere near the cage door. Taking hold of it in the crook of her bad hand she used the other to subconsciously rub at the welts on the leg that had been against the base of the cage.

There's only me, no one knows I'm here. No one will ever find me. If I'm going to get out of here, I need to do something.

She fought as tears of desperation threatened to fall again. The tears did no good, they couldn't help her.

Angrily, she swiped at the salty rivers on her cheeks. No more. Whatever happened, this situation was down to her to resolve. If she didn't help herself she would die. It was that simple.

Next time he comes in, I'll be friendly; I'll make him understand that I won't tell anyone. I'll look for an opportunity to escape. Maybe when he puts me in the chair I might be able to distract him.

Resolve made, she took a sip of the water then curled herself into a tight ball to preserve what warmth she had. Slowly, she dropped off into an uneasy sleep, her fingers tapping on her leg with the ticking of the clock.

11th November, 1910 hours - Connor's parent's residence, Sunderland

Connor screeched to a halt outside his parent's house and ran inside. He'd had an absolute nightmare of a day. He'd ended up being nominated lead diver with Marlo and had spent the better part of three hours in the freezing cold north sea, alternating being in the water with a little time on the boat to warm up. *God damn training exercises.* Just once he'd like to have a day where training consisted of sitting inside, with a cup of coffee and his feet up.

He sighed as he reached the front door, his body shivering slightly. Even now, a couple of hours since they'd gone back inside the nick, he was bitterly cold. He had been looking forward to a nice, hot bath and a couple of beers, and had just got in his car when his phone had rang.

His mother screaming down the phone had chilled him more than the temperature of the sea water could, and he'd broken every speed limit getting to the house.

Hearing his mum scream again from inside, he pushed the door open and practically ran inside.

Racing into the living room, he found his dad towering over his mum, his fist raised. His mum already blood streaming from her nose and a bruise forming on her cheek. She had an arm raised, trying to protect herself as her husband brought his fist towards her again.

'Dad!' screamed Connor, pushing himself between his parents. 'Stop it!' He felt his face burn as the blow meant for his mum glanced off the side of his chin.

Immediately his dad looked distraught and devastated as the red haze lifted and he realised what he'd done. He took in the pain-filled incomprehension on his wife's bruised face, and he started to sob, falling to his knees and putting his hands over his face. 'I'm sorry, I'm sorry. What have I done?'

Connor was torn.

What the hell was he supposed to do? His dad loved his mum, he knew he did, but that couldn't excuse this behaviour. He could have killed her. Connor knew how hard it was when his mum wasn't lucid: heck, he had the fading bruises and scabbed scratches to prove it. But his dad was supposed to look after her and protect her; not lose it and beat the crap out of her.

He sighed deeply as he pulled out his mobile phone. He knew what he needed to do.

'Wouldn't do that if I were you, lad. I'll take care of this mess.' Fred's voice came from the doorway to the hall. 'You ring this in and your dad will be arrested for domestic assault. Your mum will be shipped off to some God-forsaken home where she'll wither away in a pool of her own piss.'

'He hit her, Fred. I can't just do nothing. I've got an obligation to report –'

'You have an obligation to your family,' said Fred, grabbing Connor's arm and pulling him into the hallway, and shutting the living room door with a soft click. 'You're not doing this, Son. He might get off, he might not – but you're not getting my brother arrested. Your mother will stay here at home where she belongs. You owe her at least the comfort of her own home, not a council run shit-hole.'

Connor was ready to argue his point, but Fred continued, 'Look, I'm here every day as it is. I'll come more often, make sure your dad has some time to himself so this doesn't unravel again. You know he loves Sheila. Taking her away will break him. God knows she doesn't make it easy, but he loves her. Don't you want your mum to be looked after?'

Connor nodded slowly. 'Yes, but not at the expense of everyone else. It's time she was in a home, Fred. It's not up to you to look after her, and I work too much to be here more than I am now. It's safer for her, and better for Dad that she goes in one – and the sooner the better.'

'He's my brother dammit, we take care of our own.'

'Adopted brother,' Connor corrected, getting frustrated.

'Besides, imagine how bad it would look if you reported it. Your mum always could spin a yarn. What if she mentioned to one of the social workers, or one of your cop friends that her precious son gives his uncle information on raids and the like. I can't imagine being exposed as a rat would go down all that well at work, Son.'

'You bastard,' spat Connor, clenching his fists.

'Like father like son,' said Fred, his eyes cold as he flashed a glance down to Connor's hands. 'You wouldn't know a set of balls if they jumped up and bit you on the arse, you jumped-up little shit. And you definitely don't have the cojones needed to take me on. I've enough dirt on you to have you put away for three life-times, and don't think I wouldn't squeal to high heaven if you don't do what I say. You... Will... Not... Tell... A... Soul.' He punctuated each word by jabbing a finger into Connor's chest, his face so close that Connor could smell the stale stench of cigarettes and whiskey.

'I'll deal with it. You can go.' Fred dismissed him with a nod towards the front door.

'You can't just kick me out of my parent's home.' Connor tried to sound certain, but he knew it was already a foregone conclusion. He would be leaving any second. Fred was right, there was no way he could report this. It would mean his job.

'I believe I just did.' Fred turned his back on Connor and entered the living room, closing the door firmly behind him.

Connor stood still for a moment, his mind reeling from the exchange. He couldn't report it. He'd been guilty of passing so much information that there was no solution with work. If professional standards found out, they would bury him. But he wouldn't do it anymore, he wouldn't feed Fred any information. Family or not. But even as he thought it, he knew he was fooling himself. For one, what Fred wanted Fred got, and for two, everything they had as a family depended on Fred continuing to pay the bills.

For the hundredth time, Connor wondered how he had come to be on this path. How his dream job could've ended up turning into the nightmare from hell thanks to his actions, and how he had come to be this person he despised so much.

Life fucking sucks.

Chapter Eighteen

11th November, 2320 hours – Ryhope, Sunderland
He was angry.

The kind of anger that simmered beneath the surface, ready to blow with the ferocity of a volcano. It seemed to him that the older he got, the harder it became to contain the fury. One shitty day and he wanted to lash out to anyone and everyone, kill them where they stood just for looking at him.

He tried to rein it back in. Going in to see the girl when he was this mad would probably be a bad idea. Too much, and he could do irreparable damage to her, and he knew that would blur the lines, make this whole thing about him and not about the lessons he had to teach. There was a fine line between teaching someone to cope with pain, and inflicting torture.

Pushing open the door, he took in a breath and flicked the light switch.

Her eyes widened, blinking as the bright light made her pupils dilate.

For a moment, he realised he couldn't remember when he had last visited her, last brought her food. The last few days had blurred into one, no specific action clear to him. *I'm too old for this shit.* And maybe he was, but it wasn't something he could stop doing. He was destined to do this, karma had shown him the path he had to take and regardless of how angry he was, he had to follow it. Doing this would make everything right. It had to.

The girl's face was apprehensive, but also accepting and it threw him off balance. Normally it took weeks for them to get to that stage. How long had she even been here? It wasn't weeks though, he knew that. It was more like days. The acceptance was strange though. Had her life been so shit before that this was actually better?

He stood for a long while, just staring at her.

She was attractive, he supposed, though not to him. With everything he'd dealt with in recent years those kinds of stirrings were a thing of the past. And even when he'd had them back then his wife had always serviced them, before she'd gone anyway. And afterwards, well he'd just learned to ignore them. Or head to the brothel if he needed to. He might've liked this girl though, with her long, dark hair and brooding brown eyes. Even curled up in the cage, in need of a bath and a hair brush, she could still captivate.

Suddenly he wondered what she was called, where she had come from.

Knowing that information would be a bad idea. It would make it personal, and he couldn't afford to get emotionally attached. Not to her, not to anyone.

Emotion caused pain.

His anger dampened now, he unlocked the cage and held out his hand to her. He saw her wince, and knew her muscles were tired of being in the same position and would be sore.

Despite the pain, she paused. Then softly slipped her hand into his.

Again, he found himself surprised. He'd never had a girl so accepting of her fate. Usually they kicked and screamed until they realised that doing that meant more pain.

He put her in the chair, fastened the straps and stepped back.

Before he even realised what he was doing, he pointed to his chest.

'Jim,' it had been his father's name but she didn't need to know that. Repeating the motion, he said it again and then looked at her expectantly.

Understanding gleamed in her eyes and she replied. 'Nita.'

Nita. Pretty name, it suits her.

Then he realised what he'd done.

God damn idiot. What did you go and do that for? Now it's all going to go to hell in a hand basket.

Stepping back, he waited for the lightning bolt to strike him down, but there was nothing. Just the girl, still strapped in the chair in front of him.

'Sorry,' he said, reaching for the Stanley knife from his pocket.

Maybe I shouldn't do this; maybe she's already had enough pain. He realised he felt sorry for her. He knew the girls Rocko brought in had no life, wouldn't be missed by anyone. They already knew pain to a point. And he knew what went on in the houses, and had seen first-hand, how hard it was for them to come off the drugs. Maybe she had suffered enough.

Told you not to ask her name. Now it's personal, and you're soft.

Setting his mouth in a straight line, he tried to ignore the argument in his head. He slammed the Stanley knife back down on the bench, cursing loudly, making Nita jump fearfully.

He couldn't do it.

Unstrapping her wrists and feet, he pulled her roughly from the chair and pushed her back towards the cage.

The first he knew of her resistance, was the feel of her fingernails scratching across the side of his neck, ripping his flesh. She screamed like a wildcat, clawing at him again and kicking at him with her bare feet.

He'd let his guard down, and now he was paying for it.

He grabbed her hand and did the only thing he could to control her; he twisted it hard, the movement and the pain knocking Nita to her knees with a loud cry.

She whimpered as she looked up at him, apologising and pleading with her eyes, but it was too late. His eyes flashed with anger, and he couldn't stop himself if he tried. His fist slammed into her face, again and again, bringing blood forth and breaking teeth. His feet kicked her in the stomach and ribs, harder and harder until he was so exhausted he could barely lift his arms any more. She'd slipped into unconsciousness somewhere along the line, and didn't struggle as he pulled her limp body up and practically threw her back inside the metal box that had become her home.

Locking the padlock, he left the room, and realised he was devoid of any feeling now. There was no guilt, no anger, just a massive expanse of darkness.

12th November, 0940 hours – Dive Team HQ, South Shields

'For Christ's sake, I've had enough of this. My chicken and rice was taken the other day, and now someone's troughed my bloody sarnie!' Sharpie's voice echoed round the canteen as Marlo exchanged looks with Mac and Connor.

'You're not the only one. We've all had stuff taken, and the tuck shop's been coming up short. Do you think it's Bravo Team being dicks? It's ridiculous like. It's a police station not a flipping school playground.' Marlo's questions had the others nodding their heads in agreement.

She watched as Sharpie's gaze hardened. 'I have no idea, but I'm damn well gunna find out. I'll not have this childish behaviour. I'm going out to grab some breakfast and run a couple of errands. If anything comes in buzz me on my mobile.'

As he left, Connor asked, 'Do you think it is Bravo Team?'

'Dunno, but something's not right. Don't think I've ever seen Sharpie that pissed off. Am sure there's an old line that says never come between a man and his food!'

The team chuckled, then sobered, lost in their own thoughts, at least until Marlo's radio burst to life a few minutes later.

'5204 Buchannan. Go ahead LV.'

'Marlo, I've tried contacting Sergeant Sharp but can't raise him on his radio, can you have a look at an incoming job please? It's a bloke who was seen to go underwater near a buoy just off the coast of Seaham. Apparently the old boy has swam in the ocean three times a week for the last fifty years. Coastguard is asking if you can assist: they've got a ship in distress down Blackhall way so can't dispatch a full crew.'

'Yeah, no problem, LV. I'll try Sharpie on his mobile. What's the log number?'

'It's 132 of today. Thanks Marlo.'

Marlo sighed and pulled her mobile out from her pocket. 'So much for a leisurely morning for once,' she muttered as Connor and Mac made their way out of the break room and down to the equipment room.

12th November, 1235 hours –off the coast of Seaham, County Durham

Marlo pulled the mask in place over her face, and stood to allow Doc to check her connections. She felt the cool oxygen brush over her face and spoke to test the radio inside the mask.

'Testing, Buck to RIB, over.'

'Picking you up loud and clear, Buck. Dive safe, don't let Davy Jones catch you.' Sharpie's dive message was always the same no matter who was getting wet. It had become a kind of safety mantra for the team.

Connor was fully suited and ready to go next to her, though he'd been in a foul mood all morning, snappy and frowning constantly. She'd try and catch him after shift and ask if everything was OK.

One thing she was sure of though, was that the weather wasn't helping his mood any. The wind was bitterly cold, biting into any exposed flesh with its icy tendrils. Dark clouds floated ominously above the RIB and the smell of rain overwhelmed the normal scent of salt. The North Sea was always chilly to swim in. The temperature warmed slightly in summer but it was cold enough from September onwards to give even the hardiest folk cause to consider before dipping their toes in.

Obviously the bloke that had gone swimming was made of tough stuff.

Marlo made sure the Kevlar gloves were snug over her hands, then sat down on the edge of the RIB. Letting her body fall backwards, she landed in the water with barely a splash.

Sharpie had already assessed the tidal flow and given her an initial search grid of approximately twenty metres around the area of the buoy where the male had last been seen. It sounded like a small area, but twenty metres on a day like this would take some time. Virtually all searches conducted by the dive team were done in near-zero visibility, and today's was no different. UK diving was definitely not the same as diving abroad where the waters were crystal clear. Marlo couldn't even see her hand in front of her face.

She kicked her feet, pushing herself forward as she blindly felt around for anything that resembled a human body. She monitored her direction, swimming in a circular pattern, and did her best to ignore the piercing cold seeping through to the bones of her fingers. The drysuit kept her body temperature at a decent level, but the Kevlar gloves were awful and provided no protection at all.

'They really need to invent fur-lined Kevlar,' she muttered.

'That's next on my patent list,' responded Sharpie. 'How's it going down there?'

'Crap visibility and freezing temperatures, my favourite kind of diving,' said Marlo. 'Has the sonar picked anything up?'

'Couple of forms but nothing big enough as yet. You've been down twenty minutes, you ready to switch?'

'I'm good for a bit yet, I can still feel my knuckles.'

Her light heartedness was acknowledged and her mask fell silent again.

It was the life of a diver: you either didn't mind the quiet, claustrophobic nature of being underwater and stayed in the job for years, or you hated it and didn't dive. There wasn't really an in-between. Over the years, people had commented that it couldn't be all that bad underwater, that the UK had clean water ways didn't it? Marlo just responded that it was like swimming through 'poop soup', dark, dingy, and often smelly when you were above the surface line. Despite this though, all of Alpha Team bar Connor, and the members of Bravo team had been in the job for years. Spaces were scarce on the team and didn't come up often. Most wannabe police divers resorted to other roles in the hope that one day their dreams would be realised.

She groaned a little as her hand started going into cramp. It was time for a break.

'Coming topside,' she said before kicking powerfully towards the surface.

12th November, 2135 hours – Marlo's flat, Sunderland

Marlo rubbed the towel through her hair and pulled it through the bobble into a loose, messy ponytail. Her bones finally had warmth seeping into them and she'd stopped shivering under the scalding heat of the bath she'd just clambered out of.

The silent screams in her head were exceptionally loud tonight, and she frowned as she placed the bottle of red on the side to rest. She suddenly felt incredibly lonely.

She'd never told a soul about the things that haunted her, not even Deena who knew her better than anyone. She'd like to say it was being brought up in care that prevented her saying anything: a lack of skill with boundaries and relationships, but it wasn't. She was ashamed, it was that simple. *If I hadn't – nope, not going there.* She pushed the screams aside, and made an impulsive decision.

Loneliness fuelled by red wine was an accident waiting to happen, so she grabbed the bottle of wine, and made her way towards Ali's front door. It was only once she arrived that her common sense kicked in. *What the hell am I doing? I'm not the girl who knocks on a guy's door in the middle of the night.*

'*But you're lonely and he did say rain-check,*' argued her mind mercilessly.

Yeah rain-check on coffee, not wine. This is a bad idea.

She turned to leave, and jumped as she realised Ali was standing behind her, obviously assessing her reasons for being there.

'I was, erm... just...' Marlo fell silent, her panic now so deep she could barely follow her thought train, let alone string the sentence she didn't even know how to say together.

'Bringing me a bottle of wine? Great, after the day I've had I could use a glass or two. I've just ordered a huge pizza, way too much for me so you're welcome to stay and join me if you like?' Ali grinned as her stomach grumbled in response. 'Guess that's a yes then, come on through.'

Her cheeks pink, she followed him through the door and into the flat. Glancing around, curiosity got the better of her, and she wandered to the huge mantelpiece in the middle of the lounge. The décor itself was simplistic, neutral colours that were neither here nor there, but there were photos all over. They adorned the top of the mantle, and were mounted on hooks around the room. It made it very homely, and she couldn't help but look at them. Most had the same dimple in the chin as Ali, and she realised they were all family.

'Are all these people your brothers and sisters?' The minute she spoke, she realised how incredulous she sounded, and looked at him, ready to apologise. She didn't need to though, Ali's face was steeped in pride, he loved his family and hadn't even noticed.

He moved closer, and then reached round her to point.

'That's my mum and dad; Dad's been dead a long time now but that's one of my favourite photos. This one is all of us kids when I was like twelve. It's in age order so you've got Alex, me, Mark and Annie are twins, then there's Joseph, then James and Max, and finally our little Mary who's the youngest. This one's my siblings with their respective partners, and this smiling lot on the walls are my nieces and nephews.'

'Big family,' said Marlo, turning her face towards him and smiling.

'Yeah, they're fab. How about you? Brothers and sisters?'

'No, well, kind of, but not really,' realising she sounded confusing she clarified, 'I grew up in care. I guess the other kids in the homes classed as brothers and sisters but not in the real sense. I grew up alone.'

'Sorry to hear that,' pausing not knowing what else to say, Ali pointed at a large picture of a blond toddler, grinning a toothy smile. 'This is Izzy. You know my brother Alex, he's a DCI? Currently working out of Newcastle?'

'He's married to Cass right? The crime scene manager?'

'Yeah, Izzy's their daughter.'

Forgetting where she was for a moment, Marlo leaned back into Ali's chest. He froze instantly, and she scrunched her eyes together tightly. *Way to go Marlo, just do shit that's totally inappropriate as usual.*

Ali didn't say anything though, and he hadn't moved away. She felt his fingers brush her arm and her heart thudded in response, then suddenly, the door buzzer sounded.

'Saved by the bell,' joked Ali lightly, stepping back and making his way over.

Retrieving the pizza, he took it into the kitchen and took the rubber cork she'd replaced in her flat, off the wine, pouring them both a large glass. He struck a match and lit the large church candle on the coffee table.

Marlo stared at the flame for a moment, the hairs on the back of her neck standing to attention. Her senses were on overdrive as the silent screams threatened her composure. She leant forward and quickly blew it out.

Ali looked surprised. 'Not into candles?'

'No,' she said quietly, staring at the smoke curling up from the wick for a second. 'They're just dangerous. Always worry they'll spark or something. Sorry.'

'No need to apologise, I get it. Here,' he said, handing her a slice of pizza.

The food was hot, and the wine was smooth – too smooth as one glass turned to three. Marlo didn't even notice he'd popped the cork on another bottle. She felt more comfortable now, the alcohol easing whatever discomfort there might've been. She sat on the sofa next to Ali, her legs tucked up under her bum.

'Thanks, Ali. I needed this.'

'Tough day?'

'Yeah. Hours spent diving off the coast of Seaham and we didn't even find the old boy that went under. We're heading back out tomorrow, expanding the search area.'

'Sorry, love. Was he a swimmer?'

'Yeah apparently so. He supposedly swam the same stretch three times a week and has done for fifty years according to the log.'

'Tough as old boots then. There a chance he might've swam further away and made it out?'

'Not really. Coastguard reported a bad rip tide out that way; he probably got caught in it and didn't have the strength to pull free.'

Marlo's head dropped onto Ali's shoulder and the last sentence was muffled against his shirt. She fell silent and her breathing deepened a little.

12th November, 2250 hours – Ali's flat, Sunderland

Well I'll be! She's asleep. Ali let his thoughts run free. They'd had a moment when they were stood by the pictures.

He knew it. He'd wanted to turn her around, crush her to him and kiss her hard. His whole body had screamed at him to do it the second she'd leaned back into him. That wasn't good. He didn't know if he could do it again, hell it had been so long he didn't even know if anything still worked as it should. He'd not been with anyone since Tina. He frowned as he tried to remember her face, and all he could see was Marlo. *Weird.*

Not wanting to wake her, Ali carefully pulled his legs up onto the couch and shuffled down so his head rested on the sofa arm. Marlo mumbled in her sleep then snuggled into the crook of his arm.

This was dangerous territory, it felt comfortable. He figured he'd just lie there for a couple of minutes, maybe watch the end of the movie they'd started, then try and manoeuvre from under her. But before he knew it, his eyes closed, his mind cleared and he fell into a deep sleep.

13th November, 0640 hours – Ali's flat, Sunderland

Marlo stretched as consciousness pulled her forth. She didn't want to get up, she was comfy and warm and… on top of someone!

Jumping up rapidly, she blinked several times, eventually understanding she had fallen asleep on Ali. The movement had woken him, the harsh pressure of her hands on his chest as she'd risen waking him suddenly too.

'What the hell?' he jerked, sitting up.

'Sorry, I didn't realise where I was and then… oh crap. Sorry, Ali. I didn't mean to fall asleep on you. You must think I'm a right idiot.'

'Don't be daft, I meant to wake you, but I must've fallen asleep too.'

'Oh God, the wine,' muttered Marlo, her head banging to remind her of the multiple glasses she'd consumed.

'We fell asleep is all, don't worry about it. I should've woken you, but you looked so comfortable and cute, I just didn't have the heart,' Ali smiled at her.

Cute? Cute? I haven't been called that since, well, ever! But, she supposed, she'd never fallen asleep on a guy either. It seemed to be a night of firsts.

Glancing at the clock on the mantelpiece, she struggled to focus and when she saw the time, she paled. 'Shit, I'm going to be late. I've got to run!'

Without giving Ali a chance to reply, she grabbed her sandals off the floor, and rushed out of the door and back to her own flat.

Taking a second once inside, she rested her head on the doorframe for a moment. What the heck was the matter with her? How brazen she must seem to walk into his flat with a bottle of wine and fall asleep on him. This will be round the nick in no time. *Idiot!*

Berating herself wouldn't help though, and besides she really was late. She dropped a quick text to Sharpie apologising for her tardiness, pulled her uniform on and left the flat. After locking the door, she noticed Ali stood in the corridor waiting for her, also dressed for the day. He held out a travel mug that was steaming and smelled suspiciously like freshly brewed coffee.

'Strong and black, you won't have time to grab any. You need milk?'

Marlo shook her head, surprised at his thoughtfulness. 'Strong and black is perfect. You didn't have to do this, thanks, Ali. And again, I'm sorry about last night.'

'I'm not,' replied Ali, handing her the cup and heading for the stairs without another word.

Eh? Not what?

Dropping like a lead weight she understood: he wasn't sorry. *Well what does that mean?* Groaning she took a quick sip of coffee, he was a bloke. She'd fallen asleep on him all damsel-in-distress like; of course he didn't mind. *That had to be what he meant. Right?*

Not having time to over analyse, she followed his lead and headed for the stairs.

Chapter Nineteen

13th November, 0720 hours - Dive Team HQ, South Shields

Marlo rushed into the briefing room and sat down silently.

'Second time in a week, Marlo,' scolded Sharpie. His tone was light but Marlo knew if she was late again she'd be in bother.

'Know we're supposed to be rest days today but that's no excuse. Anyway, busy day ahead. Back out to the coast to continue the search for the missing swimmer, though he hasn't shown up at home so it's very likely now that we are looking to recover a body. Doc, you're lead diver today, Mac and Marlo on pumps. Connor, you're second diver. Any questions?'

The team shook their heads and left the room.

'Pumps, I hate pumps,' grumbled Marlo as she turned to leave. Her head was still thudding dully, and she knew she'd have to take some paracetamol before heading out.

'Marlo, hold up a sec,' said Sharpie.

Feeling her heart sink, she figured she was in for a bollocking.

'Everything OK?' asked Sharpie, 'It's not like you to be late, or to grumble on like that. Normally you take it all in your stride.'

'Yeah, am fine. My stupid alarm didn't go off. Phone's been playing up for weeks, am about due my upgrade so I'll pop down when we're off and look at getting a new one. Sorry.' She wasn't lying; her phone had been playing up. Just not today.

'It's fine: as long as you're OK. You know you can always talk to me if anything's up.'

'I know, Sharpie, thanks.'

'Go on then, go suit up, I'll be down in a bit.'

Marlo made her way down to the wet room and paused as she heard the rest of the team talking inside.

'... she's never late, Fiver says she was out getting laid.' Mac's voice resonated around the corridor.

'Nah, she's gay isn't she? That's what I heard when I started?' said Connor.

'Gay? Buck? I don't think so. I'm totally happy with my missus, but if I was ten years younger and single I'd tap that.' Doc sounded almost wistful as he put in his two-penn'orth. Deciding to do a little ribbing of her own, Marlo pushed the door open and put her hands on her hips, her best pissed off expression on her face. They all had the good grace to look embarrassed.

'Not gay, didn't get laid, and, Doc? You'd need to be a lot more than ten years younger and single to tap this,' she grinned and did a quick spin, 'besides, you guys are like family. You don't *tap* family.'

'Never a truer word spoken,' said Mac, coming over and flinging his arm around her shoulder.

'So,' he whispered conspiratorially, 'why were you late?'

'Ladies' time,' she whispered back knowing full well which buttons to push, 'had to make sure my Tampax was in securely. Those little buggers are finicky.'

Mac went a little green around the gills. 'Errr,' he said, dropping his arm from her shoulder and stepping back. For someone who swam in the murky depths of the North East waterways, Mac was incredibly squeamish. Leaving her side, he pushed open the door to the yard. 'I'll go sort the RIB.'

'Right, are we set?' came Sharpie's voice from the doorway.

The journey back to the launch point at Seaham Harbour was quiet; the mood in the 4x4 unusually sombre. Sharpie had eventually turned the radio on to cover the silence. The last song cut out mid-sentence as he pulled the key from the ignition.

'Quick as we can, the sooner we find him, the sooner we get our rest days.'

The wind ripped at them as the RIB sped to the buoy and slowed to a stop. No sooner had they slowed, the heavens opened and icy rain started falling down. Doc and Connor worked quickly, prepping to dive while Marlo hooked up the lines and checked the pressure.

It was going to be another long day.

13th November, 1005 hours - Ryhope, Sunderland

Nita groaned as her mind pulled her from unconsciousness. She'd barely even stirred since he'd thrown her inside the cage, but now her body reminded her of what had happened.

As she struggled to open her eyes, pain burst to life in places she didn't even know she had. Her chest crunched and hurt with every breath in. She cried out as she tried to sit, and gave it up as a bad job when she accidentally put weight on her injured wrist. It hurt so much that she felt physically sick, and without being able to stop it, she turned her head and feebly threw up on the floor of the cage.

One eye opened a slit; at least she thought it did. The room was still dark, and for a moment she panicked, thinking that he had hurt her so badly that she'd gone blind. Slowly though, she saw the soft glow of the heater tucked into the corner by the door.

Gingerly, she manoeuvred herself around and cautiously pulled herself into a sitting position. Her stomach felt swollen and sore, and hot pain rippled through it with the movement, causing her to gasp. She fought the dizziness that threatened her consciousness, and gently touched her face.

Her left eye was swollen shut, and she felt dried blood all over her nose and cheeks. Her whole body felt like a mass of agony, so much so that she couldn't distinguish which part felt worse.

Her tongue felt dry and cracked, and she felt around for a bottle of water.

As her fingers closed around it, she realised there wasn't a lot left, but it would quench her thirst. Taking a sip, she winced as sharp needles of pain roared through her lips.

As she replaced the lid on the water, her head spun. She felt like she was on a merry-go-round in the dark, and the bottle slipped from her grasp as her head lolled to her chest once more, the pain easing into nothingness as she passed out.

13th November, 1410 hours - off the coast of Seaham, County Durham

'OK guys, pack it up for now. We'll break for half an hour or so, warm up and what not. Start her up, Mac,' said Sharpie. He ran his hand through his hair and looked weary. 'When we come back out me and Marlo will dive.'

They pulled the RIB up on the shore, and Mac caught the 4x4 keys as Sharpie threw them over.

'Chips and coffee, please, mate,' he said with a grin.

Mac took the rest of the orders, and knowing Marlo would come with him, headed for the car.

'Not chips then,' he said to her as he turned the key.

'God no, you know I can't bear those greasy horrible potato sticks from the sea front.' Marlo grimaced at the thought. She knew the others thought it odd, but she couldn't abide chip shop chips. 'I'd kill for a cuppa and a pee, though. You going to the chippie near the amusements? There's a cafe round the corner: I'll pop and get something from there.'

When they got back to the shore, Connor, Doc and Sharpie clambered in the back, unwrapped their chips and dived in.

Marlo breathed in deeply, for all she hated the taste, the smell of chip shop chips couldn't be beaten. Unwrapping her ham salad sandwich, she waited for the ribbing to start. Never one to miss a trick, Sharpie chimed in, 'Rabbit food? Thought your suit looked a little snug on the hips. Put on a few pounds have you?'

'Cheeky git,' said Marlo, knowing he was joking. She was one of the lucky ones, her body weight rarely altered from the lean, physically fit shape she'd had for years. She knew other women hated her for it; it wasn't even like she tried to keep it steady. She loved her wine, ate takeout a couple of nights a week and if she wanted chocolate she had it. She acknowledged it was probably why she seemed to get on better with blokes: there was less competition and more comfort. Granted they ribbed her about being afraid of blood, but that was par for the course. Hell, she could fart in front of these guys if the need took her and it would just be accepted as matter of course. Not that she did that. She smiled to herself, that sort of stuff was best kept for when she was diving.

Taking a sip of the coffee she nearly gagged. 'Blurgh, trailer coffee. Still, it's hot and wet.'

'Chips... good ...' mumbled Doc with his mouthful.

'Take it easy, you don't want to cramp up.'

'Aye OK, *Mum*,' he replied. Knowing she was right though, he ate a few more then wrapped the rest back up.

'Couple of minutes wander about and we'll get back to it,' said Sharpie, pushing open the rear door.

14th November, 0910 hours - Dive Team HQ, South Shields

Elvie paused at the base of the stairs, listening intently. She'd heard the team leave a few minutes ago, not the team with the girl on – she wasn't sure where they were – but the team of all men had left in a mass of raucous laughter, one of them obviously sharing something funny. There didn't seem to be anyone upstairs and the whole building had fallen silent. She couldn't wait any longer though, she was desperate for the toilet.

She padded up the stairs to the bathroom at the top and dipped inside swiftly. She'd gotten into the routine of knowing when the teams were on duty, and she tried to time venturing from her hiding place around the hours they weren't there.

Yesterday she'd even wedged open the door to the rear yard, and had found a heavy coat that almost drowned her slight form. Venturing outside, she'd been surprised at how cold it had been. Did it get even colder in this country? She didn't know, but either way it had been nice getting outside and breathing in the fresh sea air. The village she came from was near the coast, a good bus-ride from the main city of Manila. She missed the smell of the ocean, and the people. She'd never felt as lonely as she did in this country. Her grandmother sprung into her mind as she washed her face. She'd have moved heaven and earth to get Elvie back. She'd have died stopping those men from taking her. For the first time since her Noni had died, Elvie was glad she wasn't alive to witness where she was now, was glad she hadn't had to put up with the pain of losing her. She was surprised to find that the easy tears that had sprung to her eyes every time she thought of her grandmother, this time stayed at bay.

She jumped in the shower, rinsing herself down and dressing in some of the clothes she'd found the night before. The combat trousers hung off her, but she tied some string around the waist as a kind of make-shift belt, and they stayed resting on her hips. The t-shirt she donned had the old dive team logo on, not that she would know that. The insignia had changed a few years ago when the three forces had amalgamated. The old, out-of-date stock was left lying around because no-one had quite got around to returning it to stores for destruction. The whole building was very untidy, with bits of kit and equipment lying in the rooms that were not used on a regular basis. The building had originally held some admin staff, as well as three dive teams and had facilitated training courses for a lot of the police divers from around the country. The job cuts in the force had left the whole building being used by the two dive teams alone.

Finishing in the bathroom, she peeked into the canteen area to ensure no-one was there, and entered, making a beeline for the fridge.

One shelf was full of food, boxes containing sandwiches, yogurt, and other goodies, and one box that held something that looked like roast chicken with all the traditional English trimmings. Making her choice of chicken, she grabbed a couple of chocolate bars and some pop and headed back to the make-shift den under the stairs.

The guilt she'd initially felt at stealing had abated; at the end of the day she had to eat and had no other means than those at her disposal to do so. One day she'd find a way to replace all she'd taken, but for now she'd eat whatever was left.

As she finished the cold chicken and vegetables, she realised she felt restless. She didn't want to go to sleep, or sit here thinking all day. It felt like forever since she'd spoken to another person. The last person had been Danny. She wondered again what had happened to him, why he hadn't come to get her like he'd said he would. And Nita, what had happened to her? Nothing good, Elvie knew, not judging from how out of it she'd been in that horrid building on Wear Street. But was she even still alive?

Leaving the empty plastic tub that had held the dinner on the ground near the pile of coats and tarps she slept under, she grabbed the jacket and threw it over her shoulders, wedged the door open and went outside.

The people who worked there had taken one of the larger rubber-bottomed boats. She knew they had two more under the shelter in the yard. Wandering to the edge at the back, she looked out onto the sea. It was dark and menacing, nothing like the sea near her home. Thick black clouds raced over her head, and she shivered, pulling the edges of the coat tighter to her middle. The yard was only open at the side that backed onto the sea. Large pointy fencing surrounded the other sides and the only access to the yard was either through the building or through a mechanical gate that didn't open unless something went over the sensor embedded into the concrete. Even if she decided to leave by it, she knew she'd never get back in.

Burning off some of her energy, she raced from one end of the yard to the other. It felt good to exert herself, she could feel her heart start to pound and her breath turned shallow and fast. Finally spent, she made her way back inside.

14th November, 1620 hours – Sunderland City Police HQ

'... anything else to add?' asked Ali, glancing around the table at his team. Seeing the repeated head shaking, he nodded and closed his folder and stood, effectively dismissing them. Mumbled speech ensued as they left the room.

He hated these meetings. A known paedophile had been released from prison and had been seen near one of the local schools. The meeting had held police, social services and the man's probation officer. 'Dirty Darren' was well known around the nick, and the neighbourhood. Ali had thought the last offence would have kept him locked up for much longer than the twelve months he'd served. Not long enough by any means: rehabilitation wasn't an option for Darren, either. He got off on looking at images of young boys, and there was no way twelve months behind bars would change that. But until they had something definitive to get him on, they'd just have to watch and wait.

Leaving the room, he almost collided with the superintendent.

'Sorry, ma'am, I wasn't watching where I was going.'

'My office, McKay,' replied his boss, motioning with her hand for Ali to pass.

Bloody great, here we go. He couldn't help but think about the last meeting where he'd been told there might not be enough funds to keep paying him.

'I've had a look at the financial situation. At the moment it looks like we are OK to keep you on as a secondment – at least that's how it looks at present. You're a good cop, McKay, and I think the force benefits from you being here so I'd rather not send you back up to Scotland. You hadn't put plans in place to head back up, I trust?'

Ali felt lighter than a feather at that point, and shook his head. 'No, ma'am. I'm happy to stay here as long as you need me.'

'Good to know. This may be a little pre-emptive, but why don't you fill in your transfer papers. Cooper and Mathers are taking their thirties this year. It'd be helpful not to have to advertise externally. It's no guarantee of acceptance of course, but I'd be happy to endorse your transfer and give you some coaching on the application if you need it.'

Ali sat back in his seat, shocked. Less than a fortnight ago he'd been told they mightn't be able to pay him and now they were telling him to transfer in on a permanent basis. He wondered if there was a hidden agenda he was unaware of, but nodded at the woman sat in front of him.

'That would be great, ma'am, thank you.' He left the super's office, and smiled to himself. Whatever the hidden agenda was, he didn't care.

Even before the secondment had come up, he hadn't been happy. Everything in Edinburgh reminded him of Tina. He couldn't even walk down Princes Street without something slapping him in the face, forcing him to remember what he'd lost. He felt the ache in his chest, but today it seemed a little less severe. He let himself remember her wavy hair and sparkling hazel eyes, and the wide smile she'd given whenever she'd been with him. They'd been so happy. It wasn't fair. Even now he'd have given everything to have gone instead of her.

Panic threatened to rise from his belly as he remembered the large expanse of dark water, and he found it difficult to push the memories back. He knew he'd have to face them one day, be able to think about what happened without running away. But he couldn't imagine how he'd ever be ready to do it.

Spending the night with Marlo though, had left him... What? Hopeful maybe? At peace? He didn't think it was the latter, not yet. But he felt kind of like there was now a potential for it, where before remembering had always swamped him. He'd never been able to picture himself being able to move on.

Now though, he just didn't know.

It felt good though, to allow the grief close to the surface without thinking it would consume him. Maybe there was hope for him yet.

He sat at his desk and pulled the top file from the pile to his right.

He'd find Marlo later; maybe try and talk through some of the awkwardness from the day before.

14th November, 1810 hours - Ryhope, Sunderland

He unlocked the door and entered the room, apprehensive as to what he'd find. He felt bad for beating the girl so severely. He barely remembered anything except blind rage. Part of him expected to find her dead. It had scared him, if he was honest. He'd never in his life lost control so horrifically.

He flicked the light switch, illuminating the room in bright, artificial light.

As he saw the girl, he gasped loudly.

Cuts and bruises covered her face and arms. He could only imagine what the rest of her looked like. She was slumped against the side of the cage, her head lolling onto her chest.

What have I done? The poor girl. She didn't deserve this. I didn't mean for it to happen, not this way.

He opened the cage door and pulled her out as gently as he could.

I should take her to hospital, I could tell them I found her like this. But he shook his head, they'd get an interpreter and she would tell them the truth about the monster who had kept her in a cage and beaten her.

Stepping back, he knew what he had to do. He'd done it before.

It was different this time though: normally he didn't care. If they died during his teachings then they weren't strong enough to cope with pain. It was never about him killing them. They had to learn to cope and if they didn't, then they died. But he was connected to this one somehow, it made him sad to think he would have to end it.

Out of habit, he turned the video camera on and started speaking: 'Subject seven, day ten. I lost my temper with the girl yesterday, beat her too much. It wasn't her fault. I lost control. She gave me her name, Nita. She's hurt badly, barely even stirred as I took her from the cage. I couldn't stop.' His voice broke on the words, and tears filled his eyes. 'I need to make sure she doesn't tell anyone. This is the last time. I'm not taking any more girls. I can't do this again.'

He took a breath and stared at her, knowing he would never forget her face, and always remember how hard she fought to live. It was definitely time to stop, he was tired, so exhausted with his whole life that it felt like it physically hurt him.

Sighing, he clamped his hands around her throat and squeezed hard, ignoring the feeling of desolation that flooded through him.

He heard her try and catch her breath, felt her feeble struggle beneath his hands.

She was too spent, though, to struggle hard, and he felt the moment she gave up fighting. But still he held on tight, sad tears trickling down his face and onto her cheek.

What's happened to me? When did I get to the point that I could kill without mercy, just to protect myself.

He only stopped squeezing when he could no longer feel the flutter of her heart against his fingers. And he wiped his hands across his face, clearing the tears.

He had no right to cry. This girl had needed teaching, but he'd moved from that and made it personal. That was his fault.

Leaving her in the chair, he left the room and locked up.

The red light on the video camera blinked, still recording.

Chapter Twenty

14th November, 1940 hours - Dive Team HQ, South Shields

Marlo was exhausted, the kind of tired so deep her bones ached. She'd spent three hours in the water, alternating times with Sharpie, but despite several blips showing on the sonar, they were no closer to finding the old man who'd gone under.

Mitchell, the DI handling the investigation, had stood them down when they returned to station. It wasn't viable to conduct further dives. The likely scenario was that he had gotten into difficulty and drowned. His body would probably wash up somewhere along the coast thanks to the tidal movement.

It felt bad, not finding the body. Marlo knew the family wouldn't get any closure until he was found.

Not every case got to her, in fact most didn't. She had become good at compartmentalising, the same as anyone who saw and dealt with what she did on a daily basis. But this one had. She hadn't wanted to negotiate the drive home while full of emotion. She made an excuse about having paperwork to do and stayed behind after everyone left, reassuring Sharpie that she was fine so he would go too. Then she'd had taken a long shower and cried. Deep, wracking sobs for the old man she couldn't find.

She could imagine how he'd felt, taking the same swimming route he took three times a week only to be caught out by a rip tide. She could feel him struggle against the pull, using his strength trying to get out but only ending up further in. And she could imagine the very second when he gave up, the second he became too tired to fight any more. She wondered whether he'd whispered goodbye to his family as Davy Jones pulled him deeper into the locker.

K.A. Richardson

Feeling tear prick at her eyes again, she realised she was more tired than she'd initially thought. It wasn't often she got emotional like this. It was time to go home.

By the time she came out of the bathroom, she'd calmed down.

So when she came face to face with a young girl in an extinct piece of uniform, she'd frozen in shock.

The girl looked to be about sixteen years old; slender framed with dark hair surrounding her petite face. She looked terrified.

'Easy, love,' said Marlo softly, holding her hands out in front of her, trying to make herself as non-threatening as she could.

It didn't work though; the girl spun on her heels and practically flew down the stairs.

Marlo followed, and heard the door at the bottom slam into the external wall to the building seconds later.

She put her hand out to stop it closing and winced as the force reverberated through her elbow and shoulder. As she entered the yard she saw the girl, who was frantically looking around for a way out. Her eyes were wide with terror and she was obviously desperate.

14th November, 1945 hours – Dive Team HQ, South Shields

Elvie had nearly had a heart attack when she'd almost walked into the female diver. Even now her heart pounded deep in her chest, every scenario of what could happen next running through her mind, and none of it was good. Even if the cops here weren't like they were at home, she'd end up shipped off to some little room where the paint was peeling and be forced to answer questions.

She looked around, already feeling dread in the pit of her stomach. There was no way out. She was trapped.

The woman would kill her, she was sure of it. Well, almost sure. A voice niggled at the back of her mind. *Maybe she'll help you, maybe she's as nice as she seems when you've been watching.* But she knew in her heart she couldn't take the risk.

So she did the only thing she could do, she turned and leapt as far as she could into the pitch black sea at the bottom of the wall.

14th *November, 1945 hours – Dive Team HQ, South Shields*

'Shit!' exclaimed Marlo as she heard the girl land with a loud splash. She raced to the edge of the wall, but she couldn't see the girl. She knew the wall was solid, built to hold the water back, not allow it under like some ocean walls. There was nowhere the girl could have gone.

Thankful for the torch aspect of her mobile phone, she shone it back and forth over the water, looking for the girl or any sign indicating where she could be. Finally she saw a small burst of bubbles spill over the surface, and putting her mobile phone down, she pulled in a deep breath and jumped into the water.

The icy cold water was like a slap to the face, and she instinctively wanted to breathe in, but she didn't; instead she swam powerful strokes to the rough area she'd seen the bubbles, bent double and pushed herself beneath the surface. Kicking her feet to propel herself forward, she blindly felt around for anything that felt solid. She felt something fabric, with weight behind it, so she pulled with all her might, resurfacing only centimetres from where she'd gone under.

The girl's body was motionless, and Marlo swore softly. Turning the girl onto her back, Marlo put her cheek up to the mouth of the girl, feeling for breath.

There was nothing, not even a whisper of breath.

Treading water to support the girl's weight as well as her own, she firmly pinched the girl's nose and filled her lungs with air from her own. She repeated the process, willing the girl to wake.

Suddenly the girl jerked beneath her, and started coughing, sea water splashing up onto Marlo's face. 'Easy, love, you're OK.' She soothed, twisting slightly so the girl could cough up the briny water.

Placing her arm across the girl's chest and under her arms, Marlo swam them both to the edge of the wall. The ladder was illuminated slightly by the lights in the yard, but she held no illusion. Getting herself up the ladder would be challenging enough, the cold starting to set in now as her adrenaline abated, and she wondered how she'd manage to get the girl up too.

'Listen, can you hear me? I know you're cold, and I promise we'll get warmed up as soon as we get back into the building. But first, I need your help, OK?'

The girl just mumbled in response.

'Hey, girly, look at me. Open those pretty brown eyes and look. I need you to help me, or we will both die in this freezing cold sea, do you understand?'

Understanding flashed across the girl's face, and suddenly her fight came back. Whatever Marlo had planned in relation to carrying the girl up the ladder went out of the window as the kid reached past her, grabbed the lowest rung and pulled herself forward. Reaching as though her very life depended on it, she stretched again and dragged herself further.

The second her feet hit the lowest rung, Marlo reached up and grabbed a rung too. Spurring her on, Marlo muttered encouragement until both of them finally hoisted themselves over onto the concrete of the yard. The danger now was that both had spent their energy. The girl had already collapsed with her eyes closed, Marlo was close to doing the same.

But she pushed herself, knowing they had to get inside the building. She got to her feet, and grunting, she hoisted the girl over her shoulder in a fireman's lift. Her legs wobbled under the excess weight, but she managed to maintain her balance and made her way into the building.

Her swipe card was still dangling from her neck so they could gain access.

She could feel the warmth as soon as she entered, but she knew it wasn't enough.

Her body screamed with each movement but she slowly navigated up the stairs to the top and rushed through the canteen and into the men's bathroom. The men had shared showers, not individual cubicles, which meant she could get some instant heat into both of them simultaneously. Hitting three of the showers, she waited a moment until the water began to steam, then gently lowered the girl directly underneath one of the hot sprays. Holding her up, she managed to get herself under the next one along too.

The girl gasped, struggled a little, then realised the water was warm. She sagged back into Marlo's chest, sighing as the water cascaded over them both.

'Shhh, it's OK, I've got you,' whispered Marlo against her hair, her fingers rubbing the girl's arm in a soft circular motion.

Both now conscious, the adrenaline ebbed to nothing and they started shivering, not just small ones either, huge judders that shook teeth and made the body believe it was in the middle of an earthquake.

'Stay here,' said Marlo, getting to her feet and leaving the girl under the shower. Her legs were still wobbly but she made her way to the kit room and retrieved a couple of packaged space blankets. Pulling at the plastic wrapping with her teeth as she made her way back to the bathroom, she told the girl to come out from under the water.

Knowing the girl would follow her lead, Marlo pulled her clothes off down to underwear and wrapped a blanket around her. As hoped, the girl followed suit.

Marlo led her back into the canteen and made them both a cup of hot, sweet tea.

The whole thing felt a bit surreal, like it had happened to someone else and Marlo had just happened to have been watching. Her shoulders ached as she moved: she was going to be stiff tomorrow. The body had funny ways of dealing with trauma, but she could manage that when it happened. For now, she handed the girl a steaming cuppa, and sat down beside her.

'So what was that about then?' asked Marlo, glancing over the mug she held with both hands.

'I think you will hurt me. Police hurt me where I come from,' whispered the girl, tears filling her eyes.

Marlo felt her expressions soften. 'Where do you come from?'

The girl started crying, not able to answer for the sobs heaving through her shoulders. Marlo shuffled closer, put her arms round the girl and pulled her to her chest.

'Shhh, it's OK, everything's going to be fine. Sh.'

The heat from the extra body, and the fact they had both warmed up caused both of them to become sleepy. One after the other, they both fell fast asleep.

Chapter Twenty-One

14th November, 2320 hours – Ryhope, Sunderland
He pushed open the door and entered the room. It was time to get rid of Nita, clean up and figure out what he had to do next.

She was exactly where he'd left her. Her skin had turned grey and parts of it had darkened where her blood had settled. Her expression was peaceful. At least he'd been able to give her that. It was a small mercy, though. The guilt for hurting Nita was threatening to overwhelm him. He'd been thinking about it all day, how his hands had squeezed the life from her as though she didn't deserve to live.

Maybe it would have felt different if he hadn't known her name. She was the first one he'd asked. When it had come to killing the others it had been like second nature. Routine almost: it had been a task that had needed to be done. It was almost as though his mind had detached from his body, only now returning. The fuzziness and control he'd felt was ebbing. And he felt sorrow. Sorrow for the lost lives and for what was to come. Like taking the bodies to his favourite location. His wife had loved it there. They'd gone every few weeks before she'd gone, and done it for years and years. They would get up in the morning, and she'd fill a flask, make sandwiches, and away they'd trot. He missed those times.

Raw pain flooded through him. *Why her? It just wasn't fair.* He would have preferred it to have been him. She'd always been so full of life, bursting at the seams and always happy. Then she wasn't any more.

Shaking his head, he knew he couldn't dwell in the past.

He caught a sob as he dragged Nita from the chair and onto a large expanse of plastic, the same kind of plastic used to cover seedlings on farms and in allotments. He'd picked it up years ago, and had kept it, firmly believing that one day he'd need it. One day had arrived with the death of number one.

His head started to pound dully as he wrapped the plastic around her and secured her with tight knots. Hoisting the body onto his shoulders, he took her to the car and placed her in the boot. Two large cinder blocks were already inside, and he tied them to the bag with the strong rope he'd purposefully left loose for that task.

He drove in complete silence. The only noise was the sound of his tyres gliding over tarmac, then eventually over a stony track that led to what had been his favourite place. It was always deserted at this time of night. He still came here to think, even when he didn't have to leave one of the girls. It was peaceful, serene. He could hear the wind rustling the trees he knew surrounded the path, the occasional hoot of an owl, and the water lapping against the reservoir wall.

The path led to the wall by the tower. It was only because he left his headlights on that he could see where he was going. Nita was heavier now he had the cinder blocks tied on too, and he struggled lifting her high enough to pitch her over the fence. Something felt different tonight: it didn't seem like the sanctuary it usually did.

He pushed her over, listened for the splash then retreated to the car. Something was definitely out of place this evening. Not wanting to be caught, he pulled the car in a circle around the car park and drove off.

14th November, 0135 hours – Dive Team HQ, South Shields

Marlo fought to stay asleep, but her body had other ideas. Her neck ached and slowly she registered two things: she was sitting up and she was way too warm. She remembered having a dream, jumping in the sea to save someone, and being so cold afterwards.

Suddenly she remembered it wasn't a dream, and her eyes flew open.

The girl was laid on the floor in front of her, sound asleep. She looked so innocent and peaceful that Marlo was loathe to wake her, but she had questions that needed answering.

Gently, she shook the girl's shoulders.

'Hi,' she greeted, smiling at the girl who stared back with distrustful eyes. 'I'm Marlo, what's your name?'

The girl just stared back, huge brown pools of fear and fear.

'Do you speak English?' asked Marlo, keeping her tone neutral.

Again the girl didn't speak, but Marlo was certain she understood.

'Let me help you, love. I know you've been staying here, taking food from the fridge and hiding, but without knowing what you're hiding from, I can't help you. If I can't get any information from you, I'll need to contact an interpreter, maybe even immigration. But I suspect you know exactly what I'm saying, don't you?'

Elvie had a decision to make. She couldn't run, the woman wouldn't let her. If she didn't speak she'd be deported back to the Philippines where she had nothing and no-one and would potentially get taken again by the same men. Her fear grew as she contemplated her options. She couldn't go through all that again. She knew that if they found her they would kill her. There would be no selling her to the highest bidder, nobody trying to touch her. There would be just death. She was terrified and her lips were trembling, but she made the decision.

'Elvie,' she whispered. 'Please no send me back. Men will take me again. Bad men. They hurt me.'

'What men?' said Marlo.

'Bad men,' repeated the girl gravely, 'they take me from house, bring me here. Many other girls die but I live. I help Nita from truck. Then they take her, do things to her. They take me to big house. Try to make me marry man. But Danny help me get away.'

'How old are you?'

Elvie looked confused.

'Age? How many years?'

'Fifteen,' replied Elvie, understanding. 'Danny nice man. He help me. I need to find Nita, help her. She in bad place.'

The girl's words were now running into each other, she was babbling, trying to pass information that made little sense to Marlo. She had goose bumps from hearing what had already happened to the girl. Who was Danny? And Nita? She was out of her depth. Marlo knew she needed help. She would have called Sharpie but he had kids and they would all be tucked up at this late hour. *Ali,* a little voice niggled in her mind.

'Elvie, I will help you. I'll not let anything bad happen, but you need to trust me. Can you do that?' Her words belied her own uncertainty. The girl had a long hard road ahead of her, navigating immigration and possibly even a criminal investigation. Would she be better off?

'I trust Marlo,' said Elvie.

'I'll get us some clothes, then we need to go see a friend of mine, OK?'

Despite the fear in her eyes, Elvie nodded.

15th November, 0215 hours - Ali's flat, Sunderland

Ali groaned loudly then cursed even louder. Who the hell was knocking at this stupid time in the morning. He pulled on a pair of shorts, and headed for the door.

It had been late when he'd got to bed anyway. He'd found himself listening for movement in Marlo's flat so he had an excuse to knock. Which was ridiculous, he knew, but he'd still done it.

Flinging open the door, his face quickly softened from thunderous to much less annoyed when he saw Marlo stood

178

with a young girl beside her. The girl looked ready to bolt, and he instinctively knew it was partially in response to his demeanour when he'd yanked open the door. He stood aside to allow them access, one eyebrow rising up in question as Marlo caught his eye.

'Sorry to wake you, Ali. This is Elvie. I think you need to hear what she has to say.'

To be fair, the girl had already piqued his interest. He didn't see Marlo as the type to pick up waifs and strays, so there must be some connection there. He could feel the cogs turn rapidly as Elvie bombarded him with information. It didn't take him long to realise she had been illegally trafficked into the country. He should be taking notes, preparing to hand information over to the NCA, National Crime Agency, who dealt with human trafficking, as well as contacting the likes of immigration and his own supervision. But instead he found himself enthralled. From what she said, it was a miracle the girl was still alive, let alone sat in his living room. And he didn't want to rush things. Besides, he knew what would happen when he informed immigration. She'd be detained in one of the immigration buildings, pending an asylum investigation. The details of the case would be handed off to someone other than him, and he would likely never even find out the outcome. And Elvie deserved more than that.

Deciding he had time to take the official route, he looked the girl up and down. She looked exhausted, her skin paling as she struggled to stay awake. Getting up, he pulled the throw from the chair behind him, and covered her shoulders, telling her to go to sleep.

Motioning with his head at Marlo to follow him, he headed to the kitchen.

'Is she OK?' he asked, concerned.

'She took a dip in the sea trying to get away from me, had to give her mouth to mouth. She's fine, coughed up all the water, but she's had a lot to deal with. I think it's probably just stress and exhaustion to be honest. Do you think I should take her to hospital?'

'No,' Ali shook his head, 'that'd just open up a whole can of worms. I'm sure you're right; she'll be exhausted with everything she's put up with.'

'She's been hiding in the dive HQ building. Stealing food and the like. She's been there at least the last few days.'

'Few days?' said Ali incredulously, 'How on earth does someone hide in a police station for a few days? When that gets documented no doubt the shit will hit the fan.'

'For sure,' agreed Marlo. 'Listen, I'm sorry I woke you to deal with this. I'd have called my sergeant but he has kids and I figured he'd be flaked. Besides, he's a stickler and probably would have just woken the super for advice. Just figured you'd probably know what to do for the best. Can't believe this sort of stuff happens on our doorstep. I'm a bloody cop, and I'd never thought for one second that human trafficking would be happening here.'

'Know what you mean. It's some scary shit. All we do and see, you'd think we'd be better equipped to stop this stuff happening, or at least be more accustomed to it all.'

'What're you gunna do?'

'Honestly? I should ring this in now, get immigration up to speed and get her interviewed. But that stuff can wait. She's already stressed to hell. I think she could use a day to get her head straight before she has to start answering the questions that will be asked, don't you? I'm happy to take the fall if there's any blowback. Though, I'm sure we can get around the red tape with a bit of explaining. She's welcome to stay here until I have to make the report. Right now, how about we put the world to rights with a cup of tea?'

Marlo shook her head with a smile. 'I'd best not to be honest, I'm supposed to be on rest days but I know Bravo Team was called to assist with a search down near Barnard Castle late yesterday afternoon. They'll be tied up with it for a couple of days, and you can pretty much guarantee we'll get called in to deal if something comes in.'

'Yeah, you're right. I'm on earlies too, swapped shifts with Alex again. One day I'll call in these chips – reckon he owes me a fortnight so far.'

'Must be nice having a brother on the force too?'

'Yeah. Dad was killed in the line of duty. It was the only thing me and Alex ever wanted to do. We virtually passed our training at the same time with the same grade. Mum worries of course, but she knows we do it for the love of the job.'

'Sorry about your dad.'

'Ancient history, but thanks. Was pretty tough growing up without him like, but mum was amazing. I truly don't know how she managed to do it. We all take care of her now, though.'

'Must be nice,' Marlo's voice had turned wistful without her realising, but Ali had picked up on it.

'What happened to your parents?'

Marlo paused, her usual lie of a 'car accident' turning her tongue sour. Deciding on the truth, she answered. 'Never knew my dad, he's not listed on the birth certificate so I wouldn't even know where to start looking. And Mum was a junkie. She overdosed. I must've been about four I think. I don't really remember. The care home told me as I got older that I'd been lucky. She'd died with me in the house, surrounded by needles and filth apparently. I was too old to be wanted by the people looking to adopt, and the number of foster carers was as scarce back then as it is now. I grew up in a communal home.'

'What was that like?' asked Ali.

'Awful,' she said with a grim smile. 'This was back when kids fell through the cracks with social services, not like now where they try and dot every i and cross every t. I slept in a small room with four other girls. The beds were bare even in winter. There was damp on the walls and the bathroom was disgusting. We had to bath in the same water once a week. Mrs Reay had a water metre so didn't want to waste good money. She fed us enough so questions didn't get asked, and clothed us in second hand clothes. Needless to say, it wasn't very nice.'

'Jesus, I thought places like that only existed in musicals like *Annie*. How'd you end up turning out so right with all that crap to deal with?' He had the grace to look embarrassed at his slip.

'I had a good teacher at school, Mrs Black. It was the stupidest thing, she saw something in me I didn't even know was there and she encouraged me. She paid for school trips so I didn't miss out. Gave me extra tuition so I could stay at school longer. Without her guidance, God knows what would have happened.'

Marlo paused. Mrs Black would have turned in her grave if she'd known about the screams Marlo heard, and what had caused them. And what on earth had caused her to tell Ali the truth? She never spoke about her past.

'I presume you'd like to stay with Elvie? I'll grab you a blanket. The chair's a recliner. Or you can take the bed? But I think the bairn would be more comfortable if she woke up and saw you rather than me.'

'You don't mind? The chair is great, thanks, Ali.'

Marlo had turned to face him, and for a moment she thought he was going to kiss her. She felt heat surge through her body, and knew instantly that if he did, then she'd have kissed him back. But the spark in his eyes faded and he pulled back, stepping past her into the lounge. Had she imagined it?

She wondered what she'd done wrong as he handed her the blanket and retreated to the safety of his bedroom, a dark frown across his face.

Chapter Twenty-Two

15th November, 0830 hours - Sunderland City Police HQ

Ali had made it to work on time which was surprising, seeing how he'd practically had a domestic with Marlo before coming in.

He had planned to bring the girl into the station with him to start hashing the whole situation out. That was the right thing to do.

But Marlo had begged him to let Elvie spend a rest day before the ordeal to come. 'Elvie will stay inside your flat and she won't leave,' she'd promised.

Ali had argued – even though he knew it was pointless. Marlo had stood her ground and eventually – just to keep the peace – he'd acquiesced, giving Marlo his spare key.

He was more than aware he had come close to kissing her last night, and knew fine well she had picked up on his intention. The fact that he'd pulled back had caused her to be snippy that morning, and he understood why. He'd sent out the right signals, then backed away like an idiot. He knew that was the right word. Half the nick would have been over the moon to be in a position to kiss Marlo, if only to challenge the reason they called her Buck. He'd heard the banter, knew many had tried to take on Marlo but failed saying 'the bucking bronco strikes again', indicating she'd bucked them off before they'd even gotten close. He understood her reluctance though: hell, he was hardly one to talk.

He'd felt a yearning to feel her lips on his, and then, just as he was about to act, Tina had popped into his head and he couldn't do it. He knew it was irrational, stupid even. She'd been gone for years now, but it had felt like she had been watching over his shoulder.

Shaking his head, he pushed thoughts of her from his mind. Deciding he really needed to deal with the issue of

Elvie, he stood and put one arm through his jacket. Feeling around for the second arm, he jumped as the phone rang.

Jacket still only half-on, he answered, 'DI McKay.'

'Hey, boss, it's Inspector Whatmore in the control room. Just wanted to make you aware of a job just coming in. It's a serious assault: caller reporting that two masked men have just forced entry into her house and hit her husband over the head with a bat. He's alive; we've got ambulance travelling.'

'OK, no problem, acting sergeant Charlie Quinn will deal.'

'Great, thanks. I'll pop her down as allocated. It's log 103 of today.'

Pulling his arm out of his coat, he sat down with a sigh. He'd deal with Elvie later. Right now he had other things to do.

15th November, 1010 hours - Connor's parent's house, Sunderland

It all seemed quiet as Connor made his way up the path to the front door. It was a rarity, to not hear any noise for once. He actually felt dread at the thought of what was to come when he walked inside. His sister was due home at the weekend for a visit. She'd delayed coming the weekend before as she had an assignment to hand in. It had been a few months since she'd been back. He'd told her snippets on the phone but he hadn't wanted to burden her initially, then as time passed it just became more difficult to talk about. Besides, she still had exams and course-work and he wanted her to be able to do it without having to worry.

On entering the kitchen, he was surprised to find his mum bustling about while his dad sat drinking a cup of coffee. It looked like any normal family environment –

anyone else's, anyway.

'What's going on?'

'Me and your mum are going out for the day. We're going to the seaside.' His dad sounded pleased as punch, and his mum turned and smiled.

A moment of lucidity in a life of turmoil.

'You sure that's a good idea, Dad?' he asked quietly, sitting down at the table.

'Can't hurt, Son. Your mum seems OK today. And she rarely leaves the house now: it'll be good for her to get out and about.'

'But what if –'

'No buts, you're not a goat,' said his mum, brushing a kiss on his forehead. Just for a minute, he let himself enjoy it. It was how she used to kiss him when he was a boy, her lips as light as butterfly wings. It reminded him of how happy they'd been when he was growing up. They were always out and about, making quick picnics whenever the mood took them. Even if it rained, they would go to the airport to watch the planes.

It had been almost four years now since his mum's diagnosis, and he could count on one hand the number of times she'd kissed his head like this.

But, as suddenly as it had started, her mood changed. She stepped back and he saw confusion on her face. He didn't have time to react as her hand slapped him hard across the face, and she started screaming.

His dad sat there, shrugged his shoulders as if saying 'you can deal with this one' and took another drink of his coffee.

His mum had just calmed down and he had her seated in her chair by the window when the front door opened and Fred strode inside. He hated that, his uncle just walking in unannounced as if he had the God given right to do so.

'Fred,' he greeted coolly.

'Just off, are you? Never could stick around when the going got tough, you. You're a disgrace. Your mother should have drowned you at birth.'

'Well she didn't so you're shit out of luck on that point. Go fuck yourself, Fred.' Connor felt his blood start to boil. A confrontation was well over due. He was sick to the back teeth of being blackmailed and pushed around by his uncle, and today, for the first time, it showed.

'You wanna watch who you're talking to, lad. I've shivved people for less. You think you're so hard, the big tough cop. You're nothing but a bloody water rat. That last intel you passed me was a crock of shit, too. Doing it on purpose, are you? 'Cos if that's the case, I might as well kill you. You've never been of any real use anyway.'

'So shiv me then, you bastard,' spat Connor, 'cos I've had it leaking intel to you about raids, and having you sneer in my face. You don't know jack about me. I'm better than this.'

'You think? I doubt it like. Gunna go in and fess up are you? Tell the big boss that you've been slipping your uncle confidential information about raids and the like?'

As Connor hung his head, Fred grabbed him by the throat and slammed him against the wall. His shoulder blade hit the metal edge of the mounted mirror.

'Just try it, you little shit, I swear to God, you come after me and I'll show you a side you'll wish you'd never unleashed. Not only will I make sure I drain every single penny from your beloved parents and pack their bloody boxes meself, I'll bring that lovely little Marie home and teach her what it's like to earn her keep. She'll learn just what her education cost me in the most heinous of ways. And all you'll be able to do is sit and watch.'

'Get off me, you fucking prick,' said Connor, pulling free of his grasp. He raised his fist and swung it round, connecting with Fred's face. Fred stumbled, then turned in full rage. Grabbing Connor's shirt, he swung him round and threw him against the unit in the hallway. One of his mum's vases flew and shattered on the floor. Then Fred brought a knee up into Connor's stomach, causing the breath to expel from his lungs and making him gasp as he tried to draw in oxygen. His uncle was full of rage, and Connor couldn't avoid the fist that impacted with his nose. His eyes streamed as blood spurted forth and gurgled in his throat.

Connor heard a roar from the kitchen door, and saw his dad barrel through and tackle Fred. He was like an animal possessed, raining punches down on Fred's face, grunting and red cheeked.

Connor grabbed his dad and pulled him off, 'Dad, stop, it's OK. I'm OK, stop it!'

His dad sagged against him, 'He hit you. I'm sorry, Son. I'm sorry.'

'Son? He's not your son.' snapped Fred, pulling himself to his feet. 'Your shitty sperm couldn't even create a speck of life, you useless twat. It was damn lucky I was on hand to help old Sheila out, wasn't it, or you'd never have had those bloody spawn you call yours.'

His dad paled, and whispered, 'No. You swore you'd never tell. You bastard. Get out of my house.'

'*Your* house? I think you'll find the mortgage is in my name. I'll have my solicitor pen out your eviction notice. Or even better I'll just send round some of the boys. Let them give you a helping hand. I'm done with this shit. You're a bunch of ungrateful fucking arseholes. Good luck on the streets. And as for you, *Son*, I'll be looking out for you.'

Fred then turned and left, slamming the door so hard it shook the house.

Connor was in shock. *What the hell just happened? Not my dad?*

Silent tears fell down his dad's face. 'I'm sorry, Son,' he repeated, his voice shaking.

'What did he mean, Dad? He said you weren't my dad. Is that true? Is Fred my dad?'

His dad fell silent, his head shaking from side to side, his eyes filled with sorrow.

'Dad,' pushed Connor, turning him round and looking at him. He looked so sad, so full of pain that Connor knew instantly what Fred had said was true. Instinctively, he stepped back. 'Jesus. That prick is my father? Why would you and Mum do that, Dad? Why would you turn to him?'

'He used to be different,' defended his dad feebly, 'before …'

'Before what? Before he got into the whore and drug business? Before we were born? Jesus, why the hell would you keep something like that from us. Marie's going to be devastated. Fuck.' Connor paused, hurt filling him completely. *How the fuck am I meant to deal with this?* He knew he couldn't, not now. 'I can't be here right now, Dad. I need to go.'

As he walked down the path, he wondered what else in his life would turn to shit. Everything he knew to be true was falling apart. Christ, his mother had shagged his uncle. More than once. And his dad knew. Did life get any more fucked up than that?

Chapter Twenty-Three

15th November, 1620 hours – Ali's flat, Sunderland
Ali precariously balanced the shopping bags in one arm whilst trying to unlock the door to his flat. He didn't know if Marlo was still inside with Elvie, but he figured the two eggs and spring onion that were in the fridge wouldn't feed one of them let alone three, so he'd stopped at the supermarket on the way back.

Pushing open the door, he heard laughter from inside. Laughter that sounded awfully familiar.

Stepping over the threshold, he peeked round into the living room, and was surprised to see his mum sitting on the couch, chatting to Elvie and Marlo.

'Ma?' he asked, stepping through. He was confused. Had he invited her down then forgotten? Or was she staying with Cass and Alex, and his brother had failed to mention it?

'Alistair,' she greeted warmly, pulling herself to her feet and coming to him. She wrapped her arms round him and squeezed tightly, 'Surprise! I thought I'd pop down and see my sons. Is that shopping? That's good because what ye had in was pitiful. How do ye expect to feed a woman and bairn if you dinnae keep food in the fridge? We had chips for lunch, from that place round the corner. Quite nice, it was. Not a patch on Clyde's Chippy near us but still good.'

He followed his mother into the kitchen and stood silently as she started unpacking the bags. After a few seconds, he decided he couldn't hold back.

'What're you doing here, Ma? I wasn't expecting you.'

'I know that, Son. That's the whole point of a surprise, ye know. I just missed ye, is all. It's been months since ye've been up, and Alex mentioned ye might be having a tough time of it at the minute with work and what not. It's nae bother if me being here's an issue: I can go and stay in a hotel.'

189

'No. I didn't mean that, Ma. I was just curious. I've missed you too. Every time I plan to come up, something happens and it ends up not being possible. I'm sorry, Ma.'

'OK, I'll take the couch, though admittedly the flat seems a little crowded. I presume ye're aware there's a young lassie in there who needs yer help? She's had an awful time of it, the poor wee mite.'

'She told you about it?' Ali tried not to sound incredulous. Not only was he harbouring an illegal immigrant; now his mum knew about it too. He could picture the interview with professional standards now: *'No, I was not aware that she was illegally in the country, sir.'*

'Well your mother and colleague both were, so it stands to reason that you also knew, McKay, doesn't it?'

'Aye, she mentioned it in passing. The other lassie, Marlo is it? Nice girl that one. Head's well and truly screwed on. Dive team she tells me? Seems to think highly of ye.'

'Don't do this, Ma. That's none of your business,' Ali groaned.

'What?' asked his mother innocently. 'I don't know what ye mean. Cup of tea?'

Ali sighed and nodded, 'Want me to help?'

'Go get yourself in there and chat to your guests. Figure out how to help the wee one.'

Ali made his way through. 'Sorry, I didn't know Mum was coming down.'

'It's fine, she's lovely. We've been having a good chat. I came back in about 2 p.m. Had some errands to run, and Elvie wanted to stay inside. Hope that's OK?'

'Course it is. How you doing?' he asked, turning towards Elvie.

'I have to go back, yes?' Her voice was barely audible, her eyes turned downwards. He could see she was dreading his response.

'Not if I can help it, love. I'm going to see what we can do. We need to speak to immigration, but I need you to come to the station with me tomorrow and answer some questions. Is that OK?'

Elvie nodded; she didn't have any reason to trust him, but he could see that she did.

Turning back to Marlo, he added, 'So you didn't get called in, then?'

'Nope, but tomorrow's a whole new day. Supposed to be off tomorrow too, but we'll see. Angelo from Bravo team has text to say their search will extend into tomorrow too. They're looking for a teenager, believed to have been drunk, who somehow wandered into a storm drain near the viaduct in Bishop Auckland. So if anything comes in we'll get the call.'

'Well hopefully it'll be as QT as today seemed to have been.'

'You've jinxed it now,' said Marlo with a wry smile.

Just at that point, his mother came in carrying a tray of tea and a plate of biscuits she'd apparently found in the cupboard. Ali didn't have the heart to point out they were probably there from Alex's time in the flat. He never bought biscuits.

He took one dutifully though, and as he bit down he frowned slightly. What would tomorrow bring? How would he explain holding Elvie at his home for two nights before bringing her in. This was gunna blow back and bite him on the arse. He could feel it now.

15ᵗʰ *November, 1825 hours – Connor's parent's house, Sunderland*

Connor found himself sat in the car outside his parent's address again. It seemed to be the only thing he did, sitting there dreading going inside. It was worse today though: he'd struggled all day with what he'd found out the night before. He'd spent hours looking over photos of him as a child, innocent with blond hair and blue eyes. And he'd examined them for hints as to his lineage.

Deep down, he knew what Fred had said was true. There was no reason for him to lie. He'd said the words because he knew he would hurt Connor, that it would cut deeper than any knife could. All these years of trying to hold the family together and cope with his mum's illness and his dad's reluctance to accept any help: it was all for nothing.

His whole life was a big fat lie.

His home life was a lie. Work was a lie, too. They didn't know who he was, didn't know that he was the son of a major criminal, that he fed him information on drugs raids to help ease the guilt he felt at not being able to look after his own parents. Which in itself was beside the point now, since his dad wasn't actually his dad so there was no reason to feel guilt.

But he did. Guilt threatened to overwhelm him, it was heavy and he didn't know how he could continue to carry it.

Sighing again, he tried to remember the last time he had been genuinely happy, the last time he had smiled so wide he'd actually thought his face would split. It took a minute, but he eventually recalled.

He'd been about fifteen years old. The girl he'd liked at school had passed him a note secretly in class, asking him to meet her later. That she'd sent him a note had been the highlight of his day, and later, when they'd met up under the cover of darkness after he'd snuck out of the house, she had made his night. They'd gone walking by the river, just the two of them. Holding hands and bumping into each other in that accidental way people do when they like someone, where it's not really an accident but they pretend it is so they can make contact and apologise. And under the light of the moon, he'd had his first kiss.

That meant it had been almost thirteen years since he had been totally and utterly happy. He'd come close when he'd made the dive team down south. Having a working brain he'd aced the tests and exams, and he had the natural affinity for the water that most divers had. But then they'd found out about his uncle. It hadn't got to the investigation stage. He'd transferred back up north to get away from Fred and the people he used to call friends. They'd dropped the case as he was no longer classed as an associate. Then his uncle had followed him up north, and the cycle had started again.

Now it was all threatening to turn to shit again, and he couldn't help but wonder whether it was worth it.

After sitting there for almost an hour, he decided it was time to head inside, and head bowed low, the feeling of intense despair flooding every pore, he made his way up the path.

16th November, 0830 hours – Crankle Reservoir, south of Sunderland

'Brian, move the pipe over to the north west corner. Schematics show a dip up there,' hollered Paul Deacon, pointing Brian Fellows in the right direction.

The work on the reservoir had commenced the week before. The council had decided to increase the size of the reservoir to improve flood defences. The first stage involved draining it in sections.

Brian nodded and made his way along the track to the other end.

Once the pipe was under the water, the machine trundled and pumped it over the top of the makeshift dam erected by the crew. Paul had been right: there was a hell of a dip at this end of the reservoir. Barry didn't know if it had been man made, or whether it was just to do with nature. The walled path led along the edge past a small water tower. It was a regular spot for walkers; they'd go from one side of the water to the other and back again to the car park. When it was all done, there'd be car parks at both ends, with a toilet block, too. There were also plans to erect fishing piers for those interested in catching rainbow trout.

Tourism would help pay for the work, but today no one was around.

Barry sat back in his chair and listened to the repetitive thudding of the pump. It was days like this he loved his job. The sun was trying to shine, though the air still held the bitter chill of impending winter. Birds were singing in the trees – at least he thought they were, he couldn't really hear over the pump but he liked to think they were.

Jumping out of the cab, he lit a cigarette and leaned over the wall to watch the water ebb from the shore as it was transported elsewhere.

Even now, twenty years into the job, it surprised him what people left at the bottom of a lake. He'd found endless bicycles, water drums and old boots. Once he'd even found a car. That had caused a stir: they'd initially thought there might be a body inside, but the car had been empty. Obviously just someone's idea of an easy way to get rid of a car for an insurance job.

He squinted as something started coming into view. It looked quite big, whatever it was. As the water level dropped further, he could make out something that looked almost cylindrical, and murky white in colour.

The water decreased further still, and Barry felt his eyes almost pop out of his head as he saw, at the top of the shape, a girl's face. Her eyes open and opaque, her face covered in bruises. He felt himself stumble backwards in shock. Unable to stop himself, he threw up the man-sized breakfast he'd eaten an hour before into the grass.

'Jesus Christ,' he muttered, wiping his mouth then making a cross motion across his face and chest. Jumping into the cab of the pump, he pressed the emergency stop button. The pump fell silent, and he reached for the radio.

'Paul? You need to get your arse over to the north west corner pronto. There's something here you need to see. Fuck, I'm going to throw up again,' he said, before sticking his head out of the window and heaving down the side of the truck.

Minutes later, Paul pulled up alongside the truck and jumped out. Barry pointed at the wall, and Paul leant over, gagging as he saw the girl in the water.

Grabbing his radio, he barked orders into the mouthpiece, 'Stop all drainage. All staff head to the cabin and wait there.'

He waited for the other workers to acknowledge, then turned to Barry.

'Have you phoned the cops?'

Barry shook his head slowly. 'Nope, told you first, boss.'

'OK, get yourself over to the cabin. Take my truck and bring the cops when they get here. I'll ring them now.'

Tossing the keys at Barry, Paul pulled his mobile from his pocket and dialled 999.

16th November, 1040 hours – Crankle Reservoir, south of Sunderland

'Yet another one,' greeted Sharpie, shaking Ali's hand as he arrived in the small car park at the reservoir.

'Yeah, tell me about it. Like I didn't have enough to do today,' grumbled Ali. He'd taken Elvie into the nick with Marlo, then the report of the body had come in and they'd had to leave the kid with the front office staff. He'd phoned his mum to come and pick her up but he'd still have it all to deal with once he'd sorted this mess out.

'You had a look yet?' asked Marlo, suddenly appearing beside him.

He felt his heart flutter at the sight of her in the tight black and grey dry suit. It definitely didn't leave a whole lot to the imagination, and despite the circumstances, he found it hard to tear his gaze away.

'No, wanna go look together?' An innocent comment, but in his head it felt almost like he'd asked her out on a date. He actually felt nervous in case she said no, which she didn't obviously.

Get a grip, McKay. Jesus, what are you? Twelve?

195

He followed her to the wall and both of them glanced over. It was obviously a body, fresh judging by the lack of damage around the mouth and eyes. The plastic she was wrapped in was translucent white, and looked to have been tied with rope, cinder blocks attached to keep the body submerged.

This was definitely no accidental death.

'We'll launch from the shore,' said Sharpie from his left.

16th November, 1050 hours – Crankle Reservoir, south of Sunderland

Within minutes, Marlo was aboard the RIB with the rest of the team. She'd already been nominated lead diver with Doc as second. Connor pulled the RIB over to the general area, and stalled the engine. Knowing she wasn't likely to require the oxygen lines, she sat and dipped into the water with a small splash. As she swam closer, she heard Doc jump in after her. It would be quicker to recover this one as a team rather than trying to work alone.

Swimming closer to the body, the extent of the girl's injuries became more visible. Dark bruising surrounded her neck, both eyes were black, and her nose was misaligned. The swelling from the injuries hadn't gone down. The body had started to bloat slightly under the water, and it gave her face a distorted, mottled grey look.

The plastic had been wrapped and tied tightly with rope, the only gap around her face. Momentarily, Marlo wondered why the killer had done it – left her face exposed when he'd taken such care with the rest, but she knew it was something she might never find out.

One thing she did notice immediately though, was that this girl had similar features to the one they'd pulled out at Washington a couple of weeks before. Similar to that one, and similar to Elvie. Dread settled in her stomach. Could it all be linked?

'Where the blocks are, we'll have to cut the ropes and mark the ends so it's obvious what we've done and which the offender's done. Don't wanna confuse the lab.'

'Yeah,' agreed Doc, 'trouble is if we remove the blocks, the rest of the plastic might well undo.'

'I dunno,' said Marlo pulled closer to examine the ropes. It looks like the blocks were added after the plastic. I think they're on different ropes.'

'Well we can give it a go. Know the forensics team would prefer the plastic intact around the body as opposed to floating out there in the water. Might be something trapped inside they can use. I'll go grab the bag.'

Marlo pushed off slightly, intending to go around the body to the other side – working as opposites meant the job got done quicker.

She swore under her breath as the front of her leg impacted with something hard underwater. Pain pulsed and she felt beneath the surface to ensure her suit was still intact. It was.

'Doc, grab my mask. Wanna check something out,' she shouted over to the RIB.

Making his way back over, he handed her the mask. 'Something up?' he asked, his eyebrows raised.

'Dunno, just hit my leg on something. Just wanna have a check and see what's going on beneath the surface.'

Spitting into the mask, she rubbed her saliva around the clear screen, donned it and pulled herself beneath the surface, carefully in case whatever object had caught her leg was closer than she thought.

Feeling around in the dark of the water, it would have been easy for her to forget which way was up. Her breath was comfortable. She knew she could hold it for several minutes if needed.

Suddenly her hand closed round something that crackled together and felt suspiciously like the plastic surrounding the body on the surface. It was obviously slimy, and even her Kevlar struggled to maintain its grip. Using the plastic to guide her, she pulled herself along the length, and pulled back when the corner of something hard hit her in the arm. *Fuck, it's another one. There's more than one body down here.*

Popping her head back up, she quickly swam to the RIB.

Ripping off the mask she breathed a couple of deep breaths before speaking to Sharpie. 'There's another one. Underneath the one on the top, there's what feels like another plastic sheet with breeze blocks attached.'

'You sure? Fifteen years on the job and I've never had multiple bodies at a dump site. It couldn't have been the same body?'

'Nope, too deep. The one on top seems to have snagged on a ledge on the wall, that's why it's exposed. The other is offset to the left a little, and is at least a foot further down.'

'OK, hang back a sec with Doc. Let me speak to Ali.'

16th November, 1420 hours – Crankle Reservoir, south of Sunderland

Ali stood on the shore, shaking his head for the hundredth time that day. He'd spoken to his mum who'd taken Elvie home from the station. There was no way he would have been back in time to help her with immigration. He'd rescheduled on the proviso he would ensure she saw the immigration officer when he was present.

He pulled himself back into the now – more than one body did not bode well.

The body of the first girl had been brought to the shore minutes before, and both Kevin Lang, and Ben Cassidy were photographing and applying the plastic bags required over the victim's hands and feet. They were both absorbed in the task, and he knew that Deena and Johnny were already in the car park to deal with the next one. Cass was finishing at an assault in the town then heading their way too. The full examination of the body would take place in the mortuary under the watchful eye of the pathologist; and Nigel Evans had lucked out again as the on-call pathologist today. He was due to arrive in ten minutes.

Ali watched as Marlo, now connected to the oxygen line, dipped below the surface to help Doc in recovering the next one. The chief super had already phoned to say he was on his way to the location: two bodies meant someone had thought very carefully where to leave them. Ali had never seen anything like it, and he knew that if it hadn't been for the draining of the reservoir for flood defence work, then it was unlikely these two would ever have been found.

Sharpie had called him to say they would use the sonar to get the precise location of the second body prior to recovery. That was what he figured they were doing now. He hoped that one would be as smooth a recovery.

He'd seen Doc half lift, half push two breeze blocks onto the RIB from the first body before the body itself had been loaded, and that stroppy Connor lad had brought the body to shore. It stood to reason the next one would have similar anti-floatation methods in place.

He couldn't hear what was said, but he saw Sharpie talk into the RIB's radio, and the next second Marlo popped above the surface. Both she and Doc swam over to the RIB and leaned over the edge with their arms, removing their masks.

For a second he wondered what was being said, and moments later he didn't have to wonder, Sharpie had been informing the team that the sonar used had picked up five more shapes beneath the water. All immobile, all too big to be a fish, and all of them a similar size and shape.

Holy fucking shit! Five more bodies? They're taking the piss. That can't be right. The chief super will have a bloody aneurysm.

Instantly he headed over to his team to let them know.

Chapter Twenty-Four

16th November, 1745 hours – Crankle Reservoir, south of Sunderland

The dive team had been working stoically and methodically, recovering the next couple of bodies which were now lined up on the shore. Connor was pulling up the fourth and the shore was lined with cops and CSIs. To prevent contamination, each body had been allocated its own CSIs which had meant calling in pretty much everyone on duty force wide. Cass and Kevin, as well as the other supervisor, Jason Knowles, were huddled to one side trying to shelter slightly from the freezing wind that buffeted the scene relentlessly.

The outer cordon had been set up surrounding the car park and the mobile lounge had finally arrived, providing much-needed warmth and hot drinks to the staff on scene. Even Nigel had called in support in the form of another pathologist.

The whole scene had a sombre feel to it. The officers talked in hushed tones, quietly taking in the fact that someone had managed to murder and dump seven bodies under their very noses without it even being noticed. The backlash would be a nightmare when it finally came. He wondered momentarily why one had been dumped in Washington and the rest here, then shook his head. That was something he could look at later.

There wasn't a lot Ali could do until the bodies had been recovered and he knew more of the circumstances. The three on the shore appeared to be of similar race, all were young, and all had been strangled, judging from the marks still visible around their necks. Each one they pulled out was slightly more decayed than the last - the killer had obviously been active for some time and had taken time between each kill. Ali suspected when the PMs were complete it would indicate some form of sexual assault: it was highly unlikely the girls had been taken for anything but that.

Darkness had already set in, the water becoming black and creepy as the natural light had abated. Large floodlights had been erected around the inner cordon, illuminating the scene so that the investigation could go on. Ali knew the dive team would recover the rest of the bodies before stopping. They would then be taken to the mortuary and the post mortems arranged. Once the bodies were removed, he could leave the scene with the nightshift cops on the cordon for preservation. Glancing at his watch he sighed. It wasn't even 6 p.m. Nightshift were still four hours from starting, but he knew it would take that long before the other bodies were recovered, photographed and removed from the scene.

How is this even possible? It made him sad. All those wasted lives.

Walking over to Cass, Kevin and Jason, he said, 'Any chance these girls will be in the system you think?'

'Doubt it, gov. They all look foreign to me, possibly Polynesian or something. This one's gunna stay with me a while like, they're all babbies for God's sake. Not one of them looks over about sixteen.' Kevin shook his head as he spoke.

'They look very similar to Elvie,' said Marlo. Ali hadn't even noticed her approach. She then blushed as she realised what she'd said. 'Sorry, I didn't mean ...'

'It's OK. You're actually right. I wonder if she knows these girls.'

'Who's Elvie?' asked Cass, raising her eyebrows.

'A kid I know,' replied Ali evasively. *Jesus I'm gunna be in so much shit over this. I should've just brought her in the first day, let immigration deal with her.*

But a voice niggled in his head that she might actually know the girls now being fished out of the reservoir. She had said there were others on the container, it stood to reason that if Elvie had been trafficked in, then there could

201

have been other containers. The thought made him sick to his stomach. It had always seemed so far removed from Sunderland. He knew it happened a lot down south, that the likes of London and even Manchester had seedy underworlds rife with trafficking and sex. But this was way too close to home.

It's probably a good thing I hadn't handed Elvie off - she might end up being useful on this case.

He knew he would bring her to the station the next day and question her in an official capacity. He needed to know as much as possible about these girls.

Glancing up, he saw the RIB coming closer to the shore with body number four.

16th November, 2105 hours - Ryhope, Sunderland.

James Maynard made his way down to the shed at the bottom of the garden. It had always been his refuge, up until now. He'd had it installed when the kids had moved out, a few months before Sheila had been diagnosed with the Alzheimer's. He liked the quiet solitude it gave, and no one ever bothered him there.

His head hung low as he turned the key in the lock. The kids would have had a heart attack if they had known what was inside, what he did inside. He'd had about eighteen months' worth of girls in there now. Girls he'd thought he could help but it turned out all he'd done was hurt them, causing them the pain he'd been so desperate to escape himself.

He hadn't slept since taking Nita to the reservoir. He had dark circles under his eyes and every time he closed them, he saw her battered face, bleeding and crying. Pleading with him not to hurt her. He felt her feeble attempt to survive every time one of his hands touched his own skin.

Tears streamed down his face.

He was a monster.

The realisation had been slow in arriving, but when it did, it had hit him like a tonne of bricks. He'd hurt people, hell, he'd hurt and killed *children*.

There was no sugar coating, no attempt at denial. He'd been to see Fred who'd been only too happy to oblige, and then he'd tortured them and then murdered each and every one of them. Without intending to, he'd turned into the brother he so despised.

He closed the door behind him and sank to the ground in the darkness, his head dropping to his knees as he began to sob.

He'd never felt like such a failure. It was like everything that had happened since Sheila's diagnosis had been leading him to this point. He'd promised to love her in sickness and in health, and he'd been driven to the point where he had struck her. His own wife. He'd gone and done the very thing he'd always sworn he'd never do. And then Connor had gotten in the way and he'd hit him, too.

James knew there was no way he was coming back from it all. He had travelled through the range of emotions before finally arriving at acceptance.

Acceptance that he wasn't worthy to grace this earth any more. He didn't deserve to live. Everyone in his life would be better off without him. He needed to get everything organised first, then, well, then he'd see – there was no way he could go on as he had been. It was time to sort himself out.

16th November, 2225 hours – Crankle Reservoir, south of Sunderland

After a whole day of diving and pulling bodies out of the water, the dive team was finally calling it a night. Connor navigated the RIB back to the shore line, each member silent and lost in their own thoughts.

Who did this? Who beat up and killed girls like that.

Connor had no idea, but he hoped to God they'd find enough evidence to catch the guy. There was enough crap going on in the world without that kind of monstrosity. For the first time in his career, his stomach had turned somersaults at the sight of the victims. Not from their varying stages of decay, that was a given with bodies that had been under water; it was more to do with the age and how innocent they'd looked. Each one of them beaten to a bloody pulp, but their faces peaceful, as if they were happy with their lot.

He wished he was at peace.

Connor didn't even know how to describe what he was feeling. It was like an emotional overload. First finding out that his dad wasn't his dad, then finding out it was Fred – it had all just been too much. So when he'd reported to work that morning, his mind had decided to shut down and ignore it all.

Now though, as he guided the RIB up onto the gravel shore, it all came flooding back. *What good can possibly come out of this situation? Marie's gunna be devastated. Or maybe she won't, maybe she'll understand. Fuck knows how though. I don't care how desperate for kids Mum was, in Dad's shoes I'd never have allowed it. And why, for bastard fucking fucks sake, did it have to be* him.

Connor shook his head – he couldn't do this now. Right now, he needed to get his head back in the game. This shit could wait until later, much later preferably. Like after he'd downed at least half of the bottle of single malt he had stowed away in the flat.

Shitty fucking day.

'Shitty fucking life,' his mind argued back.

Agreeing with himself, he nodded.

'You OK?' Marlo's voice beside him startled him and he jerked the rudder slightly. Rectifying, he nodded, then realised she probably couldn't see him.

'Yeah, long day is all,' he said.

'The longest. Can't wait to sit in a hot bath full of bubbles. It's bloody freezing.'

Connor watched as she blew air from her mouth into her cupped hands. He was surprised to feel nothing. He'd always been a little in awe of Marlo. Her easy manner made her impossible to dislike, and at some point he'd realised he found her attractive. And his emotions became unsettled when she was around, until today.

Doesn't matter, anyway: she'd never go for an arsehole like you.

Ignoring Marlo, he turned and jumped out of the RIB, dragging it with Mac further up the shore, then made his way over towards the edge of the trees.

16th November, 2230 hours – Crankle Reservoir, south of Sunderland

Marlo stared after him, a little confused. He'd been a grumpy sod all day; any attempts at conversation had been met with cold, unfeeling, one-syllable answers. She wondered what it was that was bugging him, but knew she wouldn't press. If he wanted her to know, then he'd tell her in his own time.

She shivered as she walked over to the 4x4. She hadn't been lying, it was freezing. All the vehicles that had been there longer than a few hours had a sheen of frost that sparkled under the artificial lights like the dust of a hundred fairies. Despite being cold to the bone, she smiled. She'd always loved the idea that frost was left by fairies. Stupid, but it allowed belief in something magic, something other than the real stuff like pulling six bodies out of the reservoir.

The sonar hadn't shown any more in the immediate area, but it didn't mean there weren't more. Sharpie had already given orders that they would be out scanning the reservoir again tomorrow. The area itself would be retained with cops standing guard for at least a couple of weeks, regardless.

It should have been creepy. Someone had used the area for dumping bodies after they'd had God knew what done to them, yet the location still felt serene. The wind whistled

205

lightly through the trees causing the branches to stretch and whisper to each other softly. It was idyllic. It didn't feel like a crime scene.

Now you're just babbling on about nothing.

Giving herself a shake, she pulled open the door to the 4x4, activating the internal light, and methodically stripped out of her suit. The vest and shorts she wore beneath were thin and offered no protection against the chill of the breeze. Pulling the bottom of the dry suit over her legs, she stepped out with one leg then repeated the motion on the other side, wincing as it scraped down what felt suspiciously like a bruise. Remembering bashing her leg whilst she'd been in the water, she glanced down to assess the contusion. Only it wasn't just a bruise. Blood had smeared over the whole front of her shin, drying and congealing around a large scrape and cut.

She looked up with glazed eyes as Ali came up behind her and started speaking. But his words swam together, blurring into a mess of garbled nonsense.

'I'm bleeding,' she whispered, her face going pale.

16th November, 2233 hours – Crankle Reservoir, south of Sunderland

Ali couldn't say the specific moment he'd realised something was off. One minute she'd been stripping in front of him and he'd been babbling as he tried not to stare at her stepping out of the figure-hugging suit, and the next her eyes had rolled back in her head as she looked at him.

He barely had time to grab her as she fell toward him, but awkwardly he managed and lowered her to the ground. 'Is Nigel still here?' he yelled in the general direction of Sharpie.

Both Sharpie and Nigel Evans were at his side in seconds.

'What the hell's that on her leg?' asked Sharpie, bending to take a closer look. 'Bloody idiot, she didn't tell me she'd banged herself. She'll be fine. Anything recovered she can handle, no matter what the condition, but the first sniff of her own blood and she's out like a light.'

Nigel agreed, checking her pulse and feeling it beat strongly beneath his fingers. 'Easy, Marlo, you're going to be just fine.' She groaned, opening her eyes and staring up at the three worried men.

Realisation dawned, and she blushed bright red. 'Aw shit, not again.'

'The sight of your blood that bad, Buck?' joked Sharpie with a grin.

Ali felt the gravel dig into his knees as he knelt beside her, but held his arm out to help her sit when she reached for him. She blanched again as she caught sight of her leg, and swayed towards his chest.

'I think maybe you should stay lying down,' he said.

'I usually deal with dead people – less arguments that way – but what say we get this patched up so we don't have any more fainting issues?' Nigel's voice was good humoured.

Sharpie handed him the first aid kit and left Marlo with Ali and Nigel.

'I don't do blood,' mumbled Marlo, her cheeks still bright pink.

'Heard a rumour it's more your own blood you don't do,' said Ali with a grin. 'I don't do it either. Mine or otherwise. Once had a murder scene in Edinburgh where arterial spray had hit the rotating ceiling light. Needless to say I walked in and turned the light on. I was laughed at for months – passed out in front of all the uniforms and fell out of the front door.'

'Oh God, you didn't? That's awful!' Her sentiment was there but she couldn't stop the wide smile. 'Bet you were mortified!'

'All done,' said Nigel from beside her. 'Keep it clean and change the dressing every day. Now, get some clothes on young lady, before you catch your death of cold.'

As Nigel walked off, Ali held out his hand and pulled Marlo to her feet. 'Never thought I'd see the day I told you to get your kit *on,*' he said before adding, 'your skin's already turning a pretty shade of blue.' As the words left his mouth he struggled not to let his feelings show. *Yeah that's the perfect time to come onto someone. Idiot.*

Chapter Twenty-Five

17th November, 0005 hours – Marlo's apartment

Marlo was so tired she felt like she could sleep for a month. But she was due back at work at 8 a.m. so a month was definitely not on the cards. She rested her head against the outer frame of her front door, almost too tired to turn the key and step over the threshold.

Hearing a noise, she turned towards the stairwell.

'Hey,' said Ali with a weary smile. 'Don't think I've ever felt so bloody knackered.'

'You do look pretty shite, like, but then I'm pretty sure I do too, so who am I to judge?'

Ali smiled, not disagreeing. 'How about a hot chocolate before bed?'

'Hot chocolate sounds amazing. Have you got some pods for the machine? If not I've got some Oreo ones if you fancy a try?'

'Aye, why not,' replied Ali, following as Marlo unlocked the door and stepped inside her flat.

'Am just gunna go get changed – would you do the honours? The pods are right by the machine.'

'Sure.'

Ali made his way into the kitchen. The flat was designed exactly the same as his, though the décor differed. It was still neutral colours, but was more feminine with pictures of flowers and metal wall art mounted where he had photos.

Marlo was back in seconds, dressed more comfortably in jogging pants and a T-shirt. 'Sorry, I don't normally wear my uniform to come home in but to be honest I was ready to get out of there today.'

Ali handed her a cup, and made his way into the living room. 'Mum rang me a couple of hours ago, said she and Elvie were going to bed so it looks like I'm on the sofa when I get back in. The bairn isn't looking forward to tomorrow.'

'Crap, Elvie didn't even cross my mind. That's awful of me, isn't it? Is she OK? Wait – tomorrow? I thought she was seeing immigration today?'

'Not awful, but completely understandable after today. She was – but I was at the reservoir. I rescheduled. I don't want her going through that alone. She's fine, love. I must take her to the station tomorrow though, can't keep pretending it's all OK. I'll give her a statement towards her asylum, but it's overdue time to get this sorted out.'

'I know,' said Marlo, her voice sounding small. She was mortified when she felt tears well in her eyes.

'Hey, come on, love. It's OK, she'll be alright,' Ali was startled, she could tell by his face, and that just made the tears want to come even harder. *What the hell is the matter with me? I'm not this sobby, emotional mess. Get a grip!*

'Sorry,' she whispered, putting her cup down and wiping her eyes with her hands. 'Dunno what the hell this is all about.'

'We all need a good cry every now and then. Come here.'

Marlo felt herself stiffen as he pulled her into his arms. Her tears refused to listen to her logic, and fell for a few more seconds, her mouth nuzzled into his neck. His arms felt good wrapped round her like that. They were warm, and made her feel like nothing could touch her as long as she stayed there. Sniffing, she let him hold her for a minute. It had been a long time since anyone had done that, just been there at the right time and held her just because she needed it.

The air shifted, moving from comfort into something else. Suddenly his arms weren't just protective, they were muscular and made her skin tingle. Her mouth was so close to his neck that she could feel his pulse jump against her lips, and not thinking, she leaned further in and kissed him there. He froze, but didn't object, and not quite ready to stop, she kissed his neck again, this time flicking with her tongue as her lips closed. He tasted like sweet and salt at the same time, and she pulled back to look at him.

Her mind didn't have time to forge any arguments as Ali leaned forward and his lips met hers, hard. She groaned into his mouth, and he deepened the kiss, pulling himself around and over her in one motion. She almost didn't recognise herself as her hands pulled at his shirt frantically, eventually ripping the last couple of buttons off. Her neck arched towards him as he nipped at her neck and closed his hands over her breasts.

Marlo had no idea how she became naked and was glad she'd kept the box of condoms in the drawer on her coffee table. As he pushed into her she felt herself open and move to meet him with the same enthusiasm. She gasped as he sank deeper into her, and he captured her mouth with his again. Her nails scratched down his back as they met each other's rhythm, both getting harder and faster until her orgasm broke around him, causing him to follow suit.

His chest was crushing her breasts, every sense tingling as he lay on top of her, spent for the moment. And then, ultimate tenderness, as he shifted his weight, and kissed her, more leisurely this time. His fingers played along the length of her arm, and she turned, snuggling into his chest, silent as he kissed the top of her head.

Ali reached up with one hand and pulled the mink effect throw down from the back of the sofa and covered them both. Tomorrow would be soon enough to wonder what the hell had just happened; for now, they were warm, comfortable and absolutely exhausted.

Chapter Twenty-Six

17th November, 0240 hours – Connor's parent's address, Sunderland

James Maynard sat himself in the chair in the room. It was almost dead silent, the padding on the walls blocking out any sound from outside, not that there was much at this time of the morning. The ticking of the clock was irritating, though: he'd never realised how loud it was when that was the only noise you could hear. How the girls had put up with it he didn't know.

Because you never gave them an option, dickhead. They didn't get any choice in what happened to them.

It wasn't right, what he'd done. The more he thought about it, the more he understood that there would be no explaining it away. There was no magic 'forget' pill, nothing that would ever make these feelings of desolated worthlessness and guilt disappear. And why should there be? He'd done the most horrible things to those girls. Unspeakable things that belonged in late night crime shows and documentaries.

He'd thought he understood at first, figured by teaching them pain that they would go on to survive and be stronger. But he'd never actually let them go so they could even try to survive. He'd played God, decided when things weren't going so well. He alone had made them cry and weep with pain and anguish, had terrified them every time he'd entered this forsaken room. He'd even had the forethought and planning to soundproof the walls. And he'd decided when to clasp his hands round their throats, and squeeze every inch of life from them. Except for Nita – she had been the exception.

James knew he deserved everything he was going to get.

His whole life had turned to shit. It had happened so gradually he hadn't even seen it coming, hadn't noticed its approach. How could he fuck everything up so royally?

He didn't even deserve to be on this earth. He was utterly useless, a waste of space and time.

Fred had told him often enough, always rubbing it in as he'd slunk into the whore house to pick out his latest girl.

He should have stopped ages ago, not given Fred the satisfaction of seeing him return time after time. Shouldn't have let his own brother see just how low he'd become.

For some reason, Fred had always seen himself as better than him, had bigged it up even as a kid when his knobbly knees knocked together as he ran through the fields they'd called home. And James Maynard had always just put up with the bullying, never moaned when he *knew* that it was Fred who had killed Stinky, didn't grass him up when their dad had found weed in the bedroom they shared so had ended up getting the blame as the oldest, and had coped with Fred kicking and punching him out of utter meanness.

When he'd met Sheila he thought he'd found redemption. He barely spoke to Fred any more unless he'd turned up at the house unexpectedly. It hadn't been a hard decision to move to the North East.

And then they'd found they couldn't have kids. His worthless body refusing to give Sheila the sperm she needed. She'd been completely and utterly devastated. Fred had a couple of kids, not that he saw them, but James had been jealous. It started to cause problems in his marriage, him being so desolate that he believed Sheila needed to find someone else.

He'd all but pushed Sheila into Fred's arms, practically begging the pair to make the child his beloved wife so desperately wanted. And she'd been so happy when she'd fallen, and all the heartache had seemed worth it.

When Connor had been born, he thought he'd have felt a niggle of unease, a shred of envy that the boy wasn't his, but Sheila had made sure that where he might've had doubts, she was there to bolster him up. They'd recovered, slowly, and finally he'd started to feel like a man again.

Then Sheila had told him she was pregnant again.

He hadn't even realised that she'd still been shagging his brother, had thought that with Connor, they had everything they needed together.

He'd left then, for a long while. Did some things he was ashamed of. Fred had hooked him up with some of his girls, hell, he'd been classed as a regular for a while. He'd lost his way, smoking dope and ending up high every chance he got, and always with a girl on his arm. A girl he'd paid for with money he should've been spending on Connor. Then Sheila had called him from the hospital to tell him Marie had been born and, curious, he'd had to visit. The tiny little girl had grabbed his fingers with hers, and he'd been completely and utterly lost. He'd moved home the next night, stopped smoking and getting hammered, hadn't stopped the girls though. He'd still been somewhat regular at the brothel. Not that Sheila ever found out.

He'd begged Sheila then to stop seeing Fred, pleaded with her to be happy with two children so they could be a family, and she'd agreed.

They'd said they would never tell the kids, would bring them both up as though none of the shit from the past had any impact.

And it hadn't.

Until now.

Sobs suddenly broke free from his body. All that pain, years and years of bottling it all up and never letting it out, years of coping now with the way Sheila was, all flooded to the surface and escaped. It wasn't right. None of it was right.

He'd had enough.

All the girls he'd tried to teach to cope with pain, and it was all for jack shit. It meant nothing.

All he'd done was inflict pain on other people. It was all he'd done for his entire life. His son now couldn't even bear to look at him. He'd watched earlier when he'd been round the house. Watched as Connor had made Sheila a cup of coffee, then sat on the sofa, his agony resounding around the room in a silent echo.

And James had finally understood.

Pain was normal.

Everyone had it in their lives. It had been wrong to pretend otherwise. But most people didn't pick girls out from a line-up like cattle, beat the crap out of them with bare hands. Normal people didn't do that. He already knew he wasn't normal, had struggled hiding it from Sheila as he'd visited the seediest of places and done things with the girls that she would never have let him do in a million years. But he'd always at least thought he wasn't crazy. That he could cope with his own life.

But the deeper into her Alzheimer's Sheila had got, the worse his behaviour had become.

He sat in the chair and sobbed until there were no more tears. His body eventually stopped shaking and he felt physically exhausted.

Standing, he turned on the lamp on the workbench and pulled out the notebook and pen from his pocket. He wouldn't back out this time. He couldn't live with who he had become and he needed to make sure that Connor and Marie understood.

Putting the pen to the paper, he started writing.

> *Dear Connor and Marie,*
>
> *I know you won't understand any of this, but it's how it has to be. I had to do this, it was the only way. I've done such terrible things.*
>
> *When your mum was diagnosed with her Alzheimer's, I was stupid and thought it would take ages to take hold, and that we'd been together so long that she'd never, ever be able to*

forget me. But she did, and at times it felt, and still feels, like my heart was being pulled out from my chest.

I thought, that if I took in some girls in trouble, that I could help them understand pain so that it would be easier for them, easier than it had been for me and you both at any rate. I thought they'd learn to handle pain, and then I'd let them go and they would just get it, you know? I never meant to strangle them. I never meant to keep going back to Fred and getting more. There were seven in total. I only took them so they could learn.

But I couldn't teach them anything but pain and fear. I couldn't even let them go to see if they could survive. They'd seen me, you see, knew my face. They would have ruined our whole family. As it turns out, it wasn't them that ruined us, it was me.

I'm so sorry I hit you Connor, and I can't even describe how I feel about you both finding out that I'm not your dad. It was never meant to be like this. I loved you both so much from the second you were born. The nurse placed you in my arms and it didn't matter who had got your mum pregnant, it just didn't matter anymore. You were both the children of my heart, and I was there for every football game, every dance recital, every school play.

I know this is the coward's way out, and I know you'll both be upset. But it really is the only way - without me you will both continue with your lives; your mum will go in the home you both want and maybe even she'll be happier.

All I know is I fucked everything up. I wish... well, wishing doesn't do any good really, does it. I've said what I wanted to say. I hope it's neither of you who find me, and I'm so sorry for everything. Look after your mother, and each other. And always remember that none of this is your fault.

My love always,
Your Dad.

This was it - the sum total of his achievements was in this room. And it amounted to nothing.

Calm now, he reached for the rope he'd rigged above the door, and wrapped it round his neck. The note was on the work top, the pen placed neatly beside it.

Having the rope round his neck didn't feel like he'd thought it would.

He'd thought that when his oxygen was cut off he'd feel panic, put the weight back onto his legs to relieve the constriction at his throat – but he didn't.

As the rope tightened further around his neck, he felt his lungs struggle for oxygen, and he felt calmer than he had ever felt in his life.

And when the darkness finally claimed him, for the first time in his whole life, he felt completely at peace.

Chapter Twenty-Seven

17th November, 0305 hours – Ali's flat, Sunderland
Elvie watched as the minutes ticked over on the clock in the bedroom. Agnes, Ali's mum, was curled up next to her and was snoring softly. But Elvie couldn't sleep. She couldn't shake the feeling that everything was going to go wrong.

She knew she'd have to face immigration, and she was struggling with the part of her that wanted to stay here where the people had been so warm and welcoming, and the part that wanted to go back home where everything was familiar. She knew how to act at home, what to say and who to trust.

If they sent her home, her great aunt would be asked to care for her, and Elvie knew in her heart that that wouldn't happen. The old crone would just throw her out on the street and expect her to fend for herself. Noni had always told her not to trust her sister, and she'd never given any reason to be trusted, always envious of Noni and the life she'd chosen to lead. If she was chucked out on the street, Elvie didn't know how she would survive. She'd had dreams of going to college, one of the big ones in Manila, but if she was sent back it would never happen. She'd have to work to pay her own way.

If she stayed here and was granted asylum, she didn't really understand what would happen. Agnes had tried to explain that the UK don't send people back if there's a danger to their lives, or for various other reasons, but even she didn't know what would happen if Elvie stayed. And Elvie hadn't been able to ask Marlo or Ali as they'd both been out at work all day.

She smiled in the dark as she remembered visiting Cass and Alex with Agnes. Their child, Izzy, had stolen her heart. She'd sat quietly while Elvie had haltingly read a fairy tale. The child had sucked her dummy, content that someone was devoting their attention to her. Elvie had had experience babysitting for some of the women back home: it was expected with so many of the women having to work, so when Izzy had fallen asleep, she'd carefully lowered her into the crib. Elvie had stood for ages watching the child's eyelids flutter, envying her the innocent knowledge that her world was safe enough to keep her in deep slumber.

Elvie had found herself wondering what it would be like to have a little sister, someone who she could care for and look after. And then she'd realised that she couldn't even take care of herself right now. Everything was so uncertain and it had been for weeks. She didn't know if she was coming or going, didn't know what would happen from one day to the next. And it scared her.

Once again, she was unable to stop the silent tears as they fell from her eyes, defeating her feeble attempts to wipe them away with the back of her hand. For the hundredth time in recent weeks, she wished for someone to tell her it was all OK, longed for her Noni's comforting touch, and wondered what would happen tomorrow.

As the hands passed 4 a.m. she finally fell into an uneasy sleep.

17th November, 0435 hours – Marlo's apartment

Ali stirred as Marlo jerked in her sleep beside him. The couch was only normal width, and she was right in front of him so there was no avoiding the sharp jab of her elbow to his ribs. He gasped and raised himself up on one arm, wincing at the force with which she'd hit him.

'Marlo?' he asked, touching her arm with his hand.

She didn't respond, her body twitching as mumbled words escaped from her mouth.

'No, let me go. It wasn't my fault. Let me go!'

Her head moved suddenly, the top impacting with his jaw causing his teeth to crash together loudly. Cursing softly, he pulled as far back as the couch would allow.

'Marlo, wake up,' he said, more firmly this time, gently shaking her shoulder.

She thrashed again, mumbling incoherently. Whatever she was dreaming about, she was deep asleep. Ali remembered reading somewhere that you were supposed to ease someone out of a nightmare, not just wake them abruptly as it could do – well what it did he couldn't quite remember, but it did *something*.

'Come on now, love, it's time to wake up,' he said, rubbing her arm a notch above gentle with his hand. Feeling her gather momentum for another struggle, he had no choice but to pin her with his weight otherwise she'd end up head-butting or elbow-jabbing him again. 'Marlo, wake up dammit!' Ali noticed his voice getting louder – how the heck was he supposed to wake her? Slap her face like they used to in the old films? He couldn't do that.

Suddenly she stilled beneath him, and her eyes opened slowly, still full of remembered pain from her nightmare.

'Easy sweetheart, it's just me. You had me worried. You wouldn't wake up.' He slid from on top of her to beside, and she turned her head towards him.

'Sorry,' she said, her eyes downcast and filled with anguish.

'Wanna tell me about it?' he asked.

'I can't,' she whispered, glancing up at him.

'Sure you can, it's easy. Just open your mouth and let the words fall out. It'll do you good to open up.'

'Like you do, you mean?' she snapped, surprising him. 'Every time you're anywhere near the water, you freeze up, stare into space. Your skin goes pale like water's the worst thing on earth, but that's not it is it? It's not just the water. Whatever *it* is, is what you don't open up about.'

Her cheeks had flushed with red, and Ali realised she had snapped through self-preservation rather than as a direct dig against him. Besides, she was right. How could he get her to trust him when he didn't do the same? Breathing deeply, he opted for the direct approach.

'You're right. I don't open up easily. I find it so hard to talk about it that I just block it all out and try and forget.

But I never really forget, it's always hovering at the edge of my mind. I was on the dive team in Edinburgh. Everything was going great. I had the job I wanted, the girl I loved.

'I'd booked a RIB from a hire place, took her out on the Forth despite her not really liking water. Champagne, nibbles, and the diamond ring in my pocket. I was building up the courage when the rain came – and I'm not talking a squall – massive heavy streaks of rain that stabbed like needles.

'The engine stalled and I stood to try and get it to work again. I rocked the RIB, and I didn't hear the splash over the rain. When I got the engine running a couple of seconds later, Tina just wasn't in the RIB any more. I dove in, cried her name every time I came up for air, but – I couldn't find her. I couldn't save her. All my training and I couldn't –' Ali broke off, tears filling his eyes.

'I was pulled out by a fisherman half an hour later. I still hadn't found her. She washed up a few miles upstream a few days later. I never should have taken her out.'

Marlo looked stricken. 'Oh my God, I'm so sorry, Ali. I didn't know, I shouldn't have pushed. But it wasn't your fault. Tina chose to go out on the river with you. You couldn't have known what would happen. I'm really sorry.'

Ali took in a shaky breath – it had been so long since he'd let himself remember. It was almost like he was there again. He could smell the salt in the air, feel the sting of the rain, and he could see Tina in front of him, her brown hair blowing in the wind. Giving himself a mental shake, he said, 'It was a long time ago. Kinda felt good telling someone about her I guess. She's been inside so long. I won't push, Marlo. If you don't want to tell me it's OK.'

'It's not that I don't want to. It's just, I've never told anyone before. It's too horrible.'

She took a deep breath and followed his lead. 'You know about my mum, right? Well, being an uneducated, rough four year old wasn't something that was appealing to adopters. I was pushed from foster care to group home more times than I can remember when I was young. Anyway when I was ten, I was placed with a lady called Ann. She seemed OK, helped me with my homework and made sure I was fed. I'd been there three weeks when her boyfriend, Chris, came home from the oil rigs. It was my eleventh birthday, and for the first time I allowed myself to get a little excited, thought maybe I might get a present or a cake. Other kids got all that but I never had a birthday cake, not once.

'Chris creeped me out, he had greasy hair and breath that smelled like stale fags. I didn't want to go anywhere near him, but Ann pushed me onto his knee and told me to sit there while she went and made tea. At first it was OK, he just stroked my leg, but then his hand went under my dressing gown. I didn't know what to do. When Ann came back in, I thought he'd stop but he didn't. He touched me, and I started crying. I ran to the bathroom and threw up.'

Marlo paused, lost in her thoughts for a moment.

'I was so afraid he would come for me when I fell asleep that I forced myself to stay awake until I heard them go to bed. And I lit the candle – Chris said I wasn't allowed to put lights on so Ann had given me a candle in case I got scared. I crept downstairs, and I remember stopping on each stair to make sure they didn't wake up. I didn't want him to follow me, so I took the keys off the hall table.'

Marlo's voice dropped to a whisper.

'I crept out of the back door. I realised after I'd got outside that I'd left the candle in the kitchen. It was so dark outside, I was petrified of the dark anyway and I didn't know what to do. So I hid in the shed. I didn't even realise anything was wrong until I saw the orange glow in the kitchen, and smelt the smoke coming from inside. I tried to go inside, to shout for Ann, but the fire was too hot. And then I heard them screaming. They couldn't get out. I'd taken the front door keys and they couldn't get the door open. I could hear banging, like they were throwing something, and Ann was screaming and screaming. The firemen found me in the shed once the fire was out. Chris had told them that Ann must have left the candle on in the kitchen. He knew though. I think he thought I did it on purpose. They sent me back to the home the next day. I didn't get any more foster parents after that.'

Ali had been silent throughout, but his blood was boiling. How the hell did that sort of thing still go on? He could picture Marlo in his head, sweet and innocent and so happy to be getting presents and cake, only to have something so horrific happen. He had no doubt that if she hadn't run to the shed, Chris would have come into her room and hurt her even more.

'You know that wasn't your fault, Marlo, the candle was an accident. What kind of person doesn't let kids turn on lights when they're scared anyway? You did the only thing you could do: you ran away before something bad happened, worse than him touching you and that's bad enough. Why didn't you tell?'

"Cos I was an idiot,' said Marlo, her eyes glistening. 'He told me if I ever told that he would hunt me down no matter which home I was in, and he'd finish what he started. I believed him.'

'Not an idiot, love, just a scared kid. You don't have to be afraid any more. He can't touch you. I'd never let anyone touch you.'

Marlo let Ali hold her, resting her head on his shoulder.

'You're right,' she mumbled against him, 'it does feel better getting it out.'

'Told you so,' said Ali, kissing her on the head. 'Now that we are both about ten tons lighter though, I reckon it's time we got some more sleep. Bedroom?'

Marlo nodded, got to her feet and shyly held out her hand.

17th November, 0610 hours – Connor's Parent's residence, Sunderland

Fred parked his car outside the front of the house and rested his head on the steering wheel. He'd had a shit night; one of the girls had been found dead in the brothel – the fourth one in six weeks. This wasn't just an overdose though: one of the johns had been a little too kinky and she'd died in the throes of his orgasm. Needless to say he wouldn't be coming back to see Fred's girls. He'd left with a broken nose, bruised pride and an attitude that stunk to high heaven.

Fred wasn't too bothered about the girl, there was plenty more where she came from: it was more the fact he'd had to drive out to the moors in the dead of night to dump the body. Over the years he'd lost count of the number of bodies he'd dumped out there. Nature and the wildlife were great at disposing of bodies.

He rubbed his eyes. He felt too old for this shit today.

Pushing the front door open, he paused momentarily, confused by the silence. Normally Sheila was raging holy hell when he came round on a morning.

'James,' he yelled, cocking his head to one side and listening.

Hearing a whimper from upstairs, he made his way up to their bedroom.

It was the smell that hit him first. The central heating had kicked in a while ago from the stuffy temperature in the house, and the heat had exacerbated the stench.

Sheila was lying in bed with the duvet curled at her feet. Beneath and around her was a pool of her own piss and shit, and it had been there a while.

'Sheila, where's James?' he asked, crossing the room and trying not to wrinkle his nose in disgust.

Vacantly, she looked up. 'I made a mess,' she whispered forlornly.

'It's OK, let's get you cleaned up,' he sighed.

It took him a good fifteen minutes to get her cleaned down and seated in her chair with a cup of tea. He left the bed, though: there was no way he was taking care of that mess.

Leaving Sheila, he went searching for James. His clothes were in the wardrobe so he hadn't done a bunk.

He wasn't anywhere in the house and Fred realised the only place left was the shed. On his way down the path, he smiled to himself. His adopted brother was a sick fuck – they were cut from the same cloth, even if they didn't get on. He knew James had spent all their life savings on the girls from Fred's brothel. Hell, he even knew James had pilfered a couple of thousand from Marie's student account – she'd phoned Fred in tears, unable to pay her university fees. And like a dutiful dad, he'd handed over the money.

Connor had always been a little shit, but he had a soft spot for his little girl.

He didn't quite understand why he'd never confronted James about the money though, brotherly love maybe? *Not bloody likely.*

The shed door was unlocked – that was his first warning that something was wrong. Fred had some idea about what went on behind that door, and James always made sure it was locked.

Pushing, he realised something was behind the door, something heavy. Shoving hard, he squeezed through the gap and into the shed itself.

'Shit,' he gasped, jumping backwards as he came face to shoulder with a very dead James. His face had a bluey-grey hue, his tongue protruded from his mouth, and the rope round his neck had left deep grooves where it had taken the man's weight.

'What the fuck have you done, you dumb son of a bitch?' said Fred, kicking out at James' leg. Looking around, he quickly found the note and read it carefully. 'You snivelling little bastard, grassing me up to end your guilt? This note didn't exist,' he enunciated the last part of the sentence slowly. He felt anger burn at the attempted betrayal. 'If you weren't dead already I'd fucking kill you, you useless bastard.'

He was so busy cursing he didn't realise the door had opened until Connor squeezed through the gap. Fred couldn't help but grin at the way Connor's face paled as he saw the man he'd always believed to be his dad reduced to a lump of flesh swinging from a rope.

'Noooo!' cried Connor, taking his dad's weight and screaming at Fred to help him.

'That's not gunna happen, Son,' said Fred calmly, a recovery plan starting to unfold in his mind.

'Fred, please,' begged Connor, 'I don't care about all the other shit, please help him, he's your brother, please.' His voice broke as he continued, 'He's my dad, please, help me.' Connor dropped to his knees, tears coursing down his cheeks.

'He was my *adopted* brother, and one I never really cared for,' said Fred. 'He's a bloody coward, is what he is. Killing himself like this, leaving you all with nothing but a guilty plea.' He waved the note under Connor's nose. 'That's right, lad. Your dad was nothing but a sick fuck. It's all in here. But he's not taking me down with him. Quit your whining and look around, boy. Does this look like your typical shed?'

17th *November, 0645 hours – Connor's parent's house, Sunderland*

Connor stood and looked around, confusion settling on his features amidst the streaks on his cheeks. 'What the fuck is all this stuff?' he said quietly, as if whispering would make it all go away. 'Let me see the note,' he demanded, stepping towards Fred.

Fred handed it over watching as he read.

As he read, he felt himself detach from his body as a wave of dizziness overcame him. *My dad's a killer? He killed girls?*

Suddenly it clicked – the reservoir had been their favourite picnic spot when they were kids. They'd gone there several times a year; his dad loved it. Apparently so much that he'd decided to dump dead girls in the water there for Connor to fish out.

'Why, Dad?' he whispered, distraught.

''Cos he was a sick fucker, that's why,' said Fred. 'Doesn't matter anyway, you're gunna help me clean this mess up.'

'No, Fred. I'm not. I'm going to ring this in. Dad made his bed, he can lie in it. I'm not covering for him, and I'm certainly not covering for you.'

He pulled his mobile phone from his pocket and dialled 999.

'You put that phone down right now, lad, or so help me I'll –'

'You'll what? Shiv me like you threatened the other day? Kill me? Do what you want, Fred, I said I'm phoning this in.'

Connor pressed the dial key and put the phone to his ear.

The roar that came from Fred was guttural, as he viciously whacked the phone from Connor's grasp. Connor noticed the glint of the switch blade Fred had pulled from somewhere about his person as it arced towards him. Blocking the blow, Connor yelled out, 'Get the fuck away from me with that knife, Fred. My career is over anyway, I'm not taking any more of this shit. Get off me!' Fred brought his palm up to impact with the bottom of Connor's nose, almost blinding him with the blood that spurted forth. Connor stepped back and brought his knee into Fred's groin, propelling him backwards towards the door.

'You're not taking me down. I've built up too much to let a prick like you ruin it. Just die already you fucking twat!' As Fred spat the words in Connor's face, he brought the knife round and rammed it upwards, hard. Connor felt the blade slice into the soft flesh of his stomach, and just as he thought it couldn't go in any deeper, he felt the hilt split his skin even further apart. Then Fred twisted it sharply, grunting as he tried to push it in even farther.

Connor couldn't let it end like this. He couldn't let Fred get away. Blindly, he felt behind him and closed his hands round something with a wooden handle. Praying it was a hammer or something, he swung round and connected it with Fred's temple. Fred dropped like a tonne of bricks, the mallet more than sufficient to knock him unconscious. As he'd fallen, his hand had maintained its hold on the knife handle and the blade had slipped from Connor's stomach.

Connor vaguely heard the mallet clatter to the floor, and looked down as his fingers pressed against the gaping wound in his stomach. Blood poured steadily, rapidly soaking the waist band to his trousers. *Damn, this burns. I thought it would hurt more.*

Dropping to his knees, he noticed his mobile phone within reach. With blood soaked fingers, he picked the phone up and gabbled, 'The bastard fucking stabbed me. He stabbed me... I'm sorry. Jesus, this fucking hurts. Sorry. I'm at 22 East Lea in Ryhope in the shed. I might've killed him, but he stabbed me. With a fucking knife. And my dad's dead, swinging there like a fucking monkey in a tree.' Shock caused him to start giggling hysterically, and the phone fell to the floor with a clatter. Following suit, Connor slid to the floor with a soft sigh. 'Hurry,' he whispered as he passed out.

Chapter Twenty-Eight

'Guys, settle down. I've got stuff to pass over.' Sharpie's voice was stern and Marlo looked up expectantly, pausing from taking the Micky out of Doc's bed-hair.

'Where's Connor?' asked Mac, glancing around.

'That's what I need to tell you,' said Sharpie. 'This morning Connor rang 999 from his parent's address. I don't know the full circumstances yet, but Connor's currently in theatre after being stabbed in the stomach. It's touch-and-go at this stage: he'd lost a lot of blood. His dad was found dead, a presumed suicide. His uncle has a serious head injury and is in intensive care.'

Marlo, Mac and Doc sat back in their chairs, too shocked to speak.

'Obviously, we all wanna be at the hospital,' continued Sharpie, 'but with Bravo Team on rest days, we are already short. We've pulled poor Angelo in on overtime as it is – he's gunna be working with us today at the reservoir. We'll try and get wrapped up asap so anyone who wants to can visit the hospital. Alex is handling the case and he's promised to let us know as soon as there's any updates.'

Silently, the team filtered down to the wet room to get the gear together.

'I should've made him talk to me. He's been off for a couple of days now,' said
Marlo.

'There's a difference between being a bit off, and being mixed up in something so bad you end up getting stabbed. What the fuck was the kid into?' asked Mac, shaking his head.

'Come on, Mac, don't be judging,' said Doc, 'we all have shit at home we don't bring to work. When we speak to him we'll find out what's been going on. 'Til then

229

anything else is just gossip and hearsay, and you know how I feel about that. And Marlo, if Connor had wanted you to know, he'd have told you. Now, what say we crack on with this search? The sooner we get it done, the quicker we'll get to the hospital.' Doc's words were wise, and both Marlo and Mac nodded their agreement before focussing on gathering the kit they needed.

17th November, 0820 hours – Sunderland City Police HQ

Ali walked into the Major Incident Team office and momentarily thought he'd wandered into the wrong one. Every seat was taken, the bustle already loud, and Alex stood at a large whiteboard in the middle of the room.

'What's going on, bro?' Ali asked, looking at the paperwork pinned up already.

''You know Connor, the lad off the dive team? He's in critical condition in theatre – he was stabbed. It was like a bloody massacre site, Ali. His dad's dead – hung himself from the looks of it. Connor was next to another male, believed to be his uncle, Fred Rockingham. Fred had been clocked upside the head with a mallet. He's in ICU. It's touch and go for both of them. We're still trying to piece together what the heck happened.'

'Bloody hell, you'll have to keep me updated, and give me a shout if I can do anything. Has Marlo been... I mean, does the dive team know?' Ali had the grace to blush – his thoughts heading straight for Marlo rather than the team as a whole.

'It's OK, Mum's already brought me up to speed on the whole you and Marlo thing. It's about time. She seems canny. And yes, the team knows. Their sergeant, Sharp I think it is, has said they'll still be working your murder scene. They'll be heading out about now I think. I spoke to him like forty minutes ago. Charlie was in a bit ago: she's moving your case boards into the side office. Seven murders huh? I'm not the only one with my work cut out. Shout up if you need anything.'

'Will do. They're all kids, Alex, wee bairns can't be more than maybe seventeen or eighteen. Whoever did this is one sick fucker.'

'Sure it's the same guy?'

'Aye pretty sure, same MO for each. The PMs are today and tomorrow though so they should help confirm.'

Alex nodded, then turned his attention back to his own team.

17th November, 1100 hours – Crankle Reservoir, south of Sunderland

The temperature had risen slightly, and ominous looking white clouds floated in from the south, threatening snow. The whole region was on a yellow weather alert warning from the met office; severe winter storms and ice due any moment. The fresh scent of snow hung in the air and even the birds were quiet. It was never good when the birds hunkered down.

Days like this were tough at the best of times, let alone when they were worried about one of their own.

Sharpie had used a map to section off the reservoir, and the team was using the sonar to scan each section individually. So far they hadn't picked anything up that was of similar size and structure to that of the bodies recovered.

The radio burst to life in the bow of the RIB and Marlo picked it up and depressed the speech button, 'This is Buck, go ahead, over.'

'Marlo? It's Ali. Can you speak?'

'Yeah sure, Ali, what's up?' Her stomach had flipped over at the sound of his voice, and she smiled widely much to the amusement of Doc and Mac who happened to be sitting next to her.

'Just an update on Connor, love. He's out of surgery, still on a ventilator in intensive care, but doing as well as he can be. Alex said they're keeping him in a medically-induced

231

coma until at least tomorrow. His sister's on her way back up from university.'

'OK, thanks, Ali. Erm, I know his mum wasn't too good. Is she OK?'

'Yeah, Alex has taken care of it. She's in a respite home for the time being. We'll see what her daughter wants to do when she gets here, though it'll be primarily down to social services, I think. Alex said she's pretty far gone, doesn't have a clue what's going on.'

'I guess that's a good thing,' said Marlo, sadness tingeing her voice.

'Aye. I'll see you when you get back to shore.'

'OK, Buck out.'

She turned to see all eyes on her, and it didn't surprise her to see them as confused as she felt. What on earth had Connor been into?

'You guys heard that?' She raised her eyebrows in question.

'Yeah we heard – that and more,' Mac winked slyly at Doc, 'Marlo and the DI seem pretty pally there, like, what do you reckon?'

'Sure do, Mac. I'd almost bet my wages they were getting more than pally,' Doc smiled at Marlo and winked back at Mac.

'Come on guys, stop ribbing Marlo,' said Sharpie. 'The DI's alright, he is, and whether there's anything going on or not, it's no one's business but theirs.'

'We're only teasing, Marlo knows that, don't you, hon?' said Mac, elbowing Marlo gently in the arm. 'You tell him from me though, that if he hurts you we all know how to bury people underwater so they don't pop back up, and we know the best places to do such a thing.' His tone was light but Marlo knew he meant it. The team couldn't have been closer if they actually were family. Mac and Doc were the big, over-protective brothers she'd never had, and if she was brutally honest, she loved that they looked out for her. Not that she'd ever tell them that.

In truth, she didn't know what it was between her and Ali yet anyway. This morning hadn't been awkward; she'd thought it might be, but they'd sat drinking coffee and chatting like they did it every morning. It all still felt a little surreal.

Pulling herself back into the here and now, she focussed her gaze back on the sonar screen. Wouldn't do to miss anything.

17th November, 1245 hours – Mortuary, Sunderland Royal Hospital

'OK, guys, I think it's about time we broke for lunch,' said Nigel Evans, glancing around the mortuary examination room for confirmation.

So far, they'd done two of the six post mortems. They'd started in the order the girls had been pulled out of the water, so newest kill first. She'd only been in the water maybe twelve hours when she'd been found. Her injuries were marginally different from the second body he'd looked at; different broken bones, but strangulation the definitive cause of death.

Following the CSIs, he made his way to the wash room and cleaned down before stripping out of his protective clothing and heading to the kitchen.

'Hey, Nigel,' said Ali, 'your Earl Grey's on the side. I arrived half way through the second PM. Didn't want to disturb you so I stayed in the viewing room.'

'Anyone want owt from the canteen?' asked Deena, glancing round before standing with Johnny. 'We're heading over now. Didn't bring bait.'

'I wouldn't mind a sarnie please, love. Anything is fine, and a bottle of coke.' Ali pulled some coins out and handed them over. Deena and Johnny left, leaving Ali, Cass and Nigel sat together at the table.

'So what've we got, Nigel?' asked Ali.

'Both females examined so far are approximately 16-18 years old. Can't say much more than that I'm afraid. Even bone density tests will only give an approximate age. They're both of Southeast Asian ethnicity at a guess from the bone structure and features - I'd say possibly Filipino. Again the tests will confirm this. The first one pulled out was immersed no more than twenty-four hours prior to the body being located. Allowing for the water temperature's impact on body temperature, and the ambient outside the water, I'd say she was killed between 1800 and 2000 hours last night. There was no presence of diatoms in her lungs so she was dead before being dumped in the water. She had track marks to her arms, not fresh but obtained during the last two to three weeks. She was sexually active, though no trace was found inside the vaginal cavity. That said the UV light has shown several older bruises to her inner thighs so there is a possibility she was raped. I've done the required swabs and combs of the pubic area, though there was nothing obvious. We did find skin under her fingernails, and since her hands were protected by the plastic sheeting, I'd be hopeful of an ident.'

'OK, have those samples been sent as priority?' asked Ali.

Cass nodded, then Nigel continued.

'There was evidence that both of the girls have been tortured. They both had contusions, lacerations and broken bones. The second girl is a little harder to provide a time of death for, the water and the fish have done their jobs at degrading any evidence, but I'd estimate she was placed in the water around a month ago. She had fused breaks, so it's possible he held her for some time after she'd had the bones broken.' Nigel stopped and took a long drink of his tea.

Cass carried on in his stead. 'We've bagged the plastic and the rope from the exterior as well as the clothing and what not. Kev's going to arrange the examinations of those items with Faith and Jackson tonight – he's been drafted in from the south and they're due in on backshift. They'll check for trace, then submit the plastic to the chemical lab for examination.' Cass sighed, 'Poor kids. I wonder who they are. Have you checked missing persons?'

'Charlie's on doing it today. Looks like a slim chance of finding who they are to be honest, but you never know, right? I need to head back over to the reservoir shortly and speak to Andy. Did you hear about Connor?'

'The lad from the dive team? Yeah, Ben's out at the scene with Cath, one of the CSMs from the south. Awful business. They called in the blood spatter analyst. Never good when it's one of our own.'

17th November, 2250 hours – Ali's flat, Sunderland

Ali closed the door with a soft click. He was so tired today he could cry. It wasn't just him either; his whole team had that look of utter desolation mingled with defeat. What with the number of deaths the city had seen recently along with the number of serious assaults, and other crimes, his team had been run off their feet for weeks. Even the prospect of overtime pay for all the extra hours hadn't been enough to crack a smile today and it was pay day.

It was a good job he had a work vehicle – he'd done the rounds about ten times over today. His eyes were strained, his calves ached. It felt like he'd done a few hours in the gym, not just driven about the city.

How he'd remembered to ring immigration about Elvie was beyond him – they'd been curt on the phone, obviously sick of being messed about. He knew if they didn't sit down tomorrow, he'd be making things even worse for Elvie. He had to ensure the meeting took place this time.

His stomach grumbled loudly, reminding him he hadn't eaten since the sandwich Deena had picked up for him at lunchtime. He knew he should eat: it had been days since anything substantial had passed his lips, but in truth he couldn't be bothered. He wanted a cup of something hot and sweet, and his bed.

'Oh crap,' he muttered, realising that his mum had text earlier and told him she and Elvie were taking the bedroom. 'Can't even sleep in my own bloody bed, I so need a bigger flat.' Then he felt guilty: his mum being down had been a god-send with the whole Elvie thing. She'd taken the kid under her wing and made sure she didn't want for anything. Ali knew Alex was grateful their mum was visiting too. With him and Cass tied up with Connor and the murders, Izzy would have ended up with a multitude of babysitters.

The coffee-maker whirred to life just as he heard a soft knock at the door.

'You must be psychic,' he said to Marlo, grinning as confusion passed over her face. 'I just put the Tassimo on. Am having a chai latte, want one?'

'Please,' said Marlo. Frowning, Ali looked at her. She looked shattered, the kind of tired that seeps into your bones and makes you feel a hundred years old. Dark rings circled her eyes and her skin was pale and drawn.

Leaving the cup on the side, he crossed over to her in three steps and without speaking, he pulled her into his arms tightly. He didn't really know if she needed a hug, but it wouldn't hurt. And when her arms snaked around his waist, he knew they didn't need words. Suffice to say it had been a crap day.

They stood for what seemed like ages until Marlo pulled back slightly.

'I believe the offer of a latte was made,' she said, her voice gruff as she tried to keep the tears from spilling from her eyes.

'Sure was,' said Ali, putting the cup under the machine and hitting the pour button. 'I won't ask how your day went, it was obviously every bit as shit as mine. How's Connor? Have you been to the hospital?'

'Yeah, I popped in. They let me sit with him for a few minutes. He looks so small, Ali. It's scary. They were saying they're going to try and take him off the ventilator tomorrow so he can breathe on his own.'

'That's good. Maybe we'll get the full story then. Alex was saying there's a lot of unanswered questions, as well as a lot of supposition going on. Professional standards are already sniffing about, too, apparently. As it stands, it doesn't look good for him like.'

'I know. Alex told Sharpie about his dad's suicide note and the 999 call Connor made. He admitted hitting his uncle with the mallet. Could've been self-defence, like, but as you say, 'til he wakes up and we can all talk to him, we don't really know what happened.'

Ali took a sip of his latte – the sweetness was just what he needed. 'You heading out to the reservoir tomorrow?'

'Actually no, for the first time in I can't remember how long I'm having my rest days. Feels like I've not been off in months. Though to be fair, there's a good chance we might get called in to assist with any searches, but that'll depend on staffing and what comes in. Andy, the other dive team sergeant, has already said he'll consider calling in from out-of-area if anything comes in. We've got our hands pretty full at present. Think I'm owed about a year in rest days now like,' Marlo grinned at him ruefully.

'Yeah, me too. Living the dream, huh? Did you always wanna be a cop?'

They'd migrated naturally through to the living room, and Ali pulled his legs up under him as he faced Marlo, waiting for her to answer.

'Honestly, no. When I was younger I wanted to be a vet. I love animals, always have. But being a vet involves understanding when it's kinder to end an animal's life. I didn't think I'd be able to do that, so I found something else to do. Actually I found a lot of different things to do before I settled on being a cop. I was a DJ for a while; I worked for a glazing company, even worked on a construction site. Eventually I realised that I wanted to do something to help people. Nursing was out of the question 'cos of my issues with blood, so being a cop was the next best thing. How about you?'

'My Dad. He was a cop, Alex is a cop. Even my uncle Angus is a cop. It was kinda expected I guess.'

'Angus? Your uncle's called Angus and your mum is Agnes? Are they siblings?'

'Yeah,' grinned Ali. 'My pops thought it would be hilarious – Mum got the piss taken out of her for years. They're twins too.'

Marlo couldn't help but giggle. The sheer exhaustion helped, and Ali found himself laughing with her. When the laughter ebbed, there was a comfortable silence whilst they both drank. Marlo stood to leave when she'd finished.

'You're going?' asked Ali, trying his hardest not to sound disappointed, but failing miserably.

Marlo smiled as he stood. Surprising him, she leaned down and captured his lips with hers, kissing him deeply. 'I wish I could stay,' she said against his lips, 'But, your mum and Elvie are asleep in the bedroom, and if I stay, I'd be anything but quiet.' She winked at him and straightened.

She looked much more alive now, her cheeks flushed pink at her innuendo. Ali knew she was right, but he really didn't want her to go.

'I'll see you tomorrow, OK?' she asked, as she pulled open the front door.

Not trusting himself to speak, Ali nodded.

He clicked the latch behind her and tried to reason with himself. *She's right, you're knackered, she's knackered. You need sleep...*

'Aye and a cold shower' his mind argued back as he made for the bathroom.

17th November, 2330 hours – the landing outside Ali's flat, Sunderland

Marlo paused outside of his front door and tried to steady her breathing. She'd never acted so brazen, kissing him like that. Walking away had been one of the hardest things she'd ever had to do – she wondered if he was still stood at the other side, and contemplated knocking again and dragging him to her place. He'd been ready to take her there and then, she could feel it in the quiet urgency of his kiss.

And she'd wanted him to.

If he'd followed her out of the flat she'd have been lost.

She found it a little amusing to realise that she was still stood there contemplating going back inside.

Come on Marlo, get a grip. You're an adult not a horny bloody teenager.

The telling off did little to chasten her, though – *Home, now!*

Chapter Twenty-Nine

'Ali, great, you're early. We need coffee, well I do anyway. Izzy's teething again – think I've had about two hours' kip.' Alex greeted Ali with a pat on the arm, guided him to the kitchen, and poured two cups, handing one over.

'You OK, bro?' asked Ali, taking the mug.

'Yeah am OK, the super's office is free, we'll go in there.'

'What's up?' asked Ali, sitting down.

'I think our cases might be linked. Hear me out before you say anything. Maynard senior's suicide note says 'I never meant to hurt the girls'. The shed where Connor was found is… well, I'll call a spade a spade; it's a fucking torture chamber. There's a seat with wrist and ankle straps, a cage, and tools mounted on the wall.

'Other than the blood off Connor and his uncle, the place was spotlessly clean. Ben said it stunk of bleach, though all I could smell was the metal from the blood. There was even a video camera set up in the corner though we didn't find the memory card. Whatever Maynard senior was up to, it wasn't good.

'Then there's the uncle, Fred Rockingham, or Rocko as he's known to the local thugs. Intel have had a few bites come through. They were about to put an UC in place to build a case.' He referred to an undercover cop, someone sent into the organisation to gather evidence. 'Rocko has his fingers in a lot of pies, it appears, long record from years ago for being a pimp, and running drugs. This was down in the Midlands, like, but still.'

'Sounds like a lovely guy - not,' said Ali sarcastically.

'We're still looking for the memory card, but it's not a huge leap that the girls he refers to in the letter could be your girls from the reservoir, right? Maynard also states he got the girls off Rocko which ties in to the theory of the prostitution ring.'

'Not a huge leap no, but it still feels like we're missing something, though.'

'Yeah I know. Listen I'm about to head to the hospital to see Connor. They're taking him off the ventilator this morning and I wanna be there before professional standards stick their beaks in and rip this out from under me. Do you think he's dirty?'

'Dunno, bro. In all honesty, he seems like a canny lad, if a little hot-headed,' said Ali, recalling the comments Connor had made at their first meeting.

'Hmm, OK well I'll catch you later. Don't get too comfy in that chair, mind, the super'll be in any second,' Alex grinned and left the room.

The chair was comfortable, though. He was almost tempted to take it with him and use it in the office. But that would provoke a whole war he didn't want to be in the middle of.

18ᵗʰ November, 1900 hours – Sunderland City Police HQ, Sunderland

'So far we've searched the car park, the section of walkway leading to the tower and the path down to the beach area. Surprisingly, it's quite clean. We've picked up the usual suspects, cans, cigarette butts and what not, but nothing that points immediately towards a suspect. There was nothing on the wall by the tower but we did find a button right underneath the historic sign that was mounted, possibly from a coat or a cardigan. We're heading back out in the morning.' Tony Cartwright's explanation was short and sweet and Ali nodded in agreement.

'OK great, get yourself off home, Tony. We'll catch up when you get back in tomorrow,' said Ali.

'My turn,' said Cass, 'I need to get back for Izzy. The whole scene's been photographed – we've taken a couple of casts of footwear marks from the mud at the edge of the car park where the path meets. They've already been looked at by the footwear technician who hasn't got anything matching on the database. The fingernail scrapes from each victim have gone for DNA but I reckon the best chance of an ident is from the last girl to be dumped.

'All the usable plastic sheets have been sent for chemical after being dried, and I know Jeff's coming in early to do it tomorrow. It'll take him a while like, he has to cut them to fit in the superglue chamber and I know Andrea, the assistant lab tech there, is off on leave at the minute. From the looks of the trace, we've got a few hairs that don't match the vic's, doesn't look like there's any roots but mitochondrial might be usable if we have the killer's mum's DNA on file. The clothing the girls had on was pretty generic, Primarni's best, most of it. Just usual stuff kids of that age would wear. The rope has been retained but will probably be too contaminated to yield any evidence, best we'll get is manufacturer info and where the local sellers are.'

'OK, Cass, thanks. I haven't had my thumbnails from the PMs or the scene yet though. Can you chase up whomever you've got tasked and get them over to me asap so I can put them in the file?' He referred to the thumbnail-sized images of the photos taken by the CSIs.

'Yup, Johnny's doing them as we speak,' replied Cass with a grin.

'Just pop outside with me for a sec,' said Ali, needing to speak with Cass privately.

'Have you spoken to Alex today?'

'Yeah, briefly when we left the house and through a couple of texts. Why?'

'Has he mentioned his theory to you?'

'Oh you mean that his case possibly overlaps with yours? Yeah, we talked about it last night. I've mentioned to submissions to compare the nail scrapings to Connor's dad's DNA. His PM is scheduled for tomorrow, I think, but don't quote me on that. Kev's handling it. I'll mail him and ask him to update you as well as Alex if you like?'

'Yeah, if you don't mind. Is Mum at yours this evening?'

'Yeah, her and Elvie are having dinner with us. Then they're coming back to yours, so you'll have to go to Marlo's if you want to get your end away,' teased Cass crudely.

Ali couldn't stop the blush burning its way all the way from his neck to his forehead.

'It's a good thing, Ali. You're too nice a guy to be single and focussed on your career so much. Marlo brings out the smiles in you. Maybe it'll turn into something, maybe it won't – but it damn sure wouldn't hurt to give it a go.'

'Yes, *Mum*,' said Ali. He knew she was right though. He already had an inkling it, whatever it was, was going somewhere as opposed to nowhere. It had hit him last night as he'd held her in his arms.

'Go see my goddaughter,' he ordered, giving Cass a gentle push towards the stairs. 'I'll catch up with you tomorrow. Elvie's immigration meeting is at 10 a.m. so I'll let you know how that goes.'

Surprising him, Cass turned and kissed him on the cheek. 'You're a good guy Ali McKay: start believing it a little more.'

He didn't have chance to reply – she'd pushed the stairwell door open and disappeared before he could.

18th November, 2035 hours – Marlo's flat, Sunderland

For the first time in ages, Marlo had had a relatively lazy day. She'd offered to take Elvie shopping but the kid had looked so devastated at the thought of not seeing Cass and Alex's baby that she'd let her go with Agnes to the cottage. She knew they'd probably be back at Ali's flat by now, but hadn't yet gone round. Agnes had a way with

Elvie, had been getting her to open up and talk. Marlo knew it was doing the youngster good, teaching her to trust again.

She should have been nervous at the prospect of the immigration meeting Ali had told her about, but she wasn't. She just knew in her heart it would all go their way and Elvie would be allowed to stay. She'd been giving a lot of thought about what would happen. At only fifteen years, if Elvie was granted immigration status, it would mean she would be placed in a family home or with a foster parent. Marlo had experience of both, and in her opinion neither would be suitable. She needed to talk to Ali to see what she could do.

Marlo had been to visit Connor that afternoon. He was still unconscious but he was breathing on his own now which was good. She'd sat with him a while, reading the articles out of the newspaper and chatting about nothing. When his sister, Marie, had arrived, Marlo had made her exit. She'd checked on his uncle's welfare also – he was in a medically induced coma and hadn't been woken.

She didn't know what to think any more. She'd trusted Connor. He'd become part of the team rapidly even if he was surly at times. A small part of her doubted him, wondered how involved he was with his uncle, but then her heart was telling her he was a good man and that she ought to trust him. She sighed, something else to talk to Ali about, she supposed.

Marlo felt her cheeks colour, she was a little ashamed to admit she had practically been waiting for him to come home, jumping at every slight sound in the corridor then being bitterly disappointed every time it wasn't him. *Sad is what it is. You've not even been on one date and you're hankering after him like a lost puppy.*

But she managed to drown out her negative thoughts – it wasn't like she was falling in love with him or anything. She liked him. He was a nice guy. There was nothing wrong with that. *Aye if you say so, pet.*

As the knock she'd been waiting for finally sounded, she pulled the door open with a smile.

'Oh thank God you're home, I need wine!' said Deena, breezing inside and heading for the kitchen. 'You do have wine, right?'

'Yeah, there's a couple of bottles in the cupboard beside the sink – did we have plans for tonight?' asked Marlo, wondering if she'd forgotten.

'Nope, I've just had a shit day and needed wine and a whinge. You fancy pizza or Chinese for tea?'

Marlo took the glass offered by Deena. 'Shit day? Why?'

'Am sick to death of bloody post mortems, pardon the pun. Seem to have drawn the short straw this week. Had two today, both suicides. Heart-breaking it is. One of them was only a young lad. Had his whole life ahead of him.'

'Sorry, love. Are you back in tomorrow?'

'No it's finally my rest days – and this time I'm turning my mobile off. No way is work calling me in if something kicks off. I'm away the day after tomorrow – going to see my sister in Liverpool for a couple of days. She would absolutely have the biggest drama queen hissy fit if I cancelled again!'

Deena took a long swig of her wine, topped the glass up, then made her way back through the kitchen towards the living room. She was just about to plonk herself on the sofa when another knock sounded.

Darting to the door with a wide 'oh yes, who's this then' grin at Marlo, she flung the door open and smiled widely.

Ali stood in front of her, his mouth open in shock. It was almost comical and Marlo had to stifle the giggle that threatened to escape.

'Ah, a man to join our pity party,' said Deena dramatically, sweeping her arm across to invite Ali inside. 'Enter, kind sir, come drown your sorrows with us. Wine solves all problems, don't you know.'

Ali grinned. 'Why the hell not?'

Marlo handed him her glass – she hadn't even taken a sip yet – and nipped to the kitchen to pour herself another. Grabbing the second bottle while she was there, she put it on the table in front of the sofa and sat down next to Ali, much to the amusement of Deena.

'So,' said Marlo, 'you wanted to whinge?'

'Who me? No, no. No whinging. Just fancied a quick glass of vino to be honest. I've got plans tonight anyway, I'm meeting some of the traffic lads for a few drinkypoos down at The Old Nun. Didn't know you were expecting company, though.'

Lifting the glass to her lips, she downed the rest of her wine in one gulp.

'I'll be on my way, pet. Don't forget the tables booked tomorrow at Filoria's for 1 p.m. You can catch me up on all the bedroom gossip then. Unless I need to ring you to drag you kicking and screaming from your duvet and away from the wonderful Ali?'

'Jesus, Deena!' said Marlo, mortified.

'Not Jesus, pet, just little old me. I'll see you tomorrow.'

Deena planted a kiss on her forehead then flounced out of the room as energetically as she'd flounced in just minutes before.

'Sorry, did I interrupt something?' asked Ali.

'No, she's… well she's a little nuts if I'm honest. I'll catch up with her tomorrow.'

'Another day off, huh?' Ali teased, 'to be fair though, I'm off tomorrow, too. Going in for the immigration meeting then handing off to DI Caville for two whole days. I've not been off for seventeen days straight now – it'll be so nice not having to get out of bed if I don't want to. Or even just having the time to go to the gym or whatever.'

'Yeah know what you mean, resourcing think we're machines half the time. I bet they never get their rest days cancelled.'

'So, dunno about you but I'm starving. Chinese?'

Marlo nodded, and pulled a menu from the magazine rack beside the table. 'Sounds good.'

Chapter Thirty

18th November, 2240 hours – Ali's flat, Sunderland

Elvie suddenly sat bolt upright in bed, startled, the remnants of the nightmare still clear in her mind. She put a hand over her mouth to stifle the noise she knew she would make. She didn't want to wake Agnes who was asleep on a camp bed beside her.

Agnes had been wonderful to her, Elvie knew that and she appreciated it. But she was afraid. What if they sent her back to her village?

Silently, she left the bedroom and padded through to the sofa. She pulled her knees to her chest and hugged herself tightly, tears running down her cheeks. It was awful not knowing what would happen. Tonight was almost as bad as being in the container.

She didn't want to go back. She never wanted to go back where people could just take her from her bed and force her to go with them. Everyone kept telling her she would be OK, that they were petitioning and giving statements for her to stay in the UK. But she didn't really understand what it all meant. All she knew was that the immigration people could make her go back.

Guilt was another emotion she was feeling, so much so that it was giving her nightmares. Horrible dreams about Nita getting hurt and Elvie never going to get her despite knowing where she was. The trouble was that she didn't actually *know* where Nita was. The name of the street had gone from her mind, and now it only hovered on the perimeter, not quite letting her reach it.

And what if immigration said she could stay, and then Marlo didn't like her any more. Then what would happen? Elvie really liked Marlo, she'd saved her life and Elvie would always remember that, but that made her beholden to Marlo, not the other way around. What if Marlo didn't want a kid hanging around, especially a kid that wasn't a friend or relative. Did Marlo even have relatives?

She knew she should feel lucky. Things could have been so much worse for her: she could have ended up with the man that Yolanda wanted to sell her too, or Danny might not have turned out to be so nice, or she might not even have survived the container trip. But lucky wasn't something that she felt right now.

I tell tomorrow, I tell them about Nita and the horrid men in that house. She need my help, she my friend.

Elvie resumed the rocking motion, unable to stop the sobs this time. *What did I do? Why is this happening?*

But nobody answered.

18th November, 2250 hours – Ali's flat, Sunderland

Elvie didn't hear the front door open a few minutes later, or notice Ali step inside, see her crying then sneak back out to get Marlo. The first she knew of anyone being there was when Marlo's arms wrapped round her and pulled her close. She could feel Marlo stroking her hair, and it reminded her so much of Noni that the tears refused to stop.

'Shhh, it's OK, it's all going to be OK, baby. Shhh,' whispered Marlo.

Elvie wanted so much to believe her. Heaving great sobs shook her thin body, eventually petering out into hiccups and occasional shudders, and for the first time, she felt a little bit of hope. Maybe it would be OK.

19th November, 0910 hours – Sunderland City Police HQ

Ali walked into the office with Elvie and Marlo in tow, and it was every bit as busy as it had been the day before.

'Elvie, can you and Marlo go wait by my desk at the end? I just need to speak to Alex, and I'll be with you,' said Ali. Marlo showed Elvie where his desk was and started talking to one of the detectives as Ali made his way down to where Alex stood.

'Hey, bro. Anything on Connor or his uncle yet?'

'I've just had word from the hospital actually, Connor's come around. Nurse said he's still really groggy and the painkillers keep making him sleep, but he's awake. I'm heading over there shortly to speak with him. The uncle is still in a coma but they're bringing him out of it today.'

19th November, 0915 hours – Sunderland City Police HQ

Elvie watched as Ali spoke to his brother and Marlo chatted with a woman in the office. She felt really alone, and didn't know quite where to put herself. Her eyes were drawn to the open file on the desk, and she tried to tell herself she wasn't being nosy, but really she was. There was a picture on the front that looked familiar.

Glancing around to make sure no one was watching, she pulled the file towards her and focussed in properly. She couldn't stop the scream that escaped her mouth as she realised who the picture was of. It was a very dead Nita Thress. She stumbled backwards, crashing into the filing cabinet behind her, sending trays and paperwork flying.

In the back of her mind she could hear someone saying 'no' over and over. It took her a minute to realise that person was her. As Marlo reached her side, rapidly followed by Ali, she sank to the floor in a dead faint.

19th November, 0920 hours – Sunderland City Police HQ

'Easy, love,' said Ali softly as Elvie opened her eyes seconds after falling to the floor. 'You're OK. Take it easy.'

He had to grip her as she scrambled to her knees in panic, her eyes darting about wildly.

'Nita. I saw Nita,' sobbed the girl, falling forward into his arms and wrapping hers round his neck so tightly he thought she might actually stop the circulation. He gave her a few minutes to cry, then pulled back and looked at her.

'Where? Where did you see Nita?'

Elvie turned and pointed at his desk, her face bleak. 'In file.'

'Wait a minute, what? Which file?'

Marlo quickly scanned the file that was open and glanced at him – 'It's one of the reservoir girls, the first one we got out.'

'Elvie, listen to me. This is very important. Are you certain that the girl in that picture is your friend?'

Elvie nodded firmly. 'Nita dead. Is my fault, Nita dead. I forget the road, I forget to tell. My fault.' Elvie started crying again.

Ali knew the whole office was watching him. He was kneeling on the floor cuddling a girl who looked so much like the girls they'd pulled out of the reservoir.

'Do me a favour: phone Mum? Ask her to come down?' Ali asked Alex. 'She's now a witness in a murder investigation, I'm not handing her over to immigration, not yet.'

Elvie pulled away from Ali. 'You will find bad men, yes? Bad men do this. Rocko and Gaz they do this to Nita. I see them in house.'

Alex paused, his mobile in his hand, and looked up. 'Did you say Rocko?'

'Yes Elvie say Rocko. I think pronounce correct. He bad man.'

'Where did you see this Rocko?' Alex asked. Ali knew he was trying to keep the urgency out of his voice.

'Elvie not see. Elvie hear of Rocko. First at big house where Yolanda kept Elvie and Nita. Then at dirty house. Gaz hurt Nita, Rocko tell Gaz hurt Nita. Danny help Elvie, stop Gaz and bad man hurting Elvie. Gaz tell Danny Rocko will kill him.'

The words Elvie were saying made little sense to Ali, he knew he needed to try and structure her answers so that they made sense. Flashing Alex a look, he got to his feet.

'Elvie, come with me. I need to ask you some questions and write the answers down, OK? Marlo can come too. And Alex.'

Elvie nodded and clambered to her feet, wiped her tears on the back of her hand and stood there with a renewed look of determination.

'Elvie will help.'

Once they were seated in one of the old interview rooms, Ali took the lead.

'When you were brought here on the container, who got you out of it?'

'Danny and Gaz get Elvie and Nita out. Other girls too but Elvie not see them again.'

'Where did they take you?'

'Take Elvie and Nita in van to big house. Then we eat food and wake up much later.' Elvie's eyes dropped to her lap, 'We wake up in different clothes. Wet hair. Smell of soap.'

'So they cleaned you while you slept,' said Ali. He sidled a glance at Alex. *Drugged.* They didn't need to speak the word – they were both thinking the same thing.

'What happened then?' asked Ali, keeping his tone soft. He was almost afraid of the answer.

'Yolanda bad lady. She made Gaz and Danny take Nita, say Elvie will bring much money. Yolanda not know Elvie understand English. Noni teach Elvie English. Speak little, understand more. She say Elvie bring money because pure. Elvie not know what she mean but not like.'

'Where did they take Nita?'

Elvie thought for a minute, obviously trying to recall the exact details. Tears pricked her eyes as she couldn't remember. Determinedly, she closed her eyes and tried harder. 'Real Street, maybe? Real not right though, sound like real.'

'Do you mean Wear Street?' asked Alex, standing and putting his hands on the desk.

Elvie nodded swiftly, 'Yes Wear. They take Nita to Wear Street. Take Elvie too later. House dirty. Smell bad. Danny put Elvie in room but Elvie see Nita. Gaz hurting Nita.'

'Then what happened?' asked Ali.

'Danny tell Elvie not to be virgin. Say man no want if not virgin. He kiss me and man shout at Danny. Man punch Danny then leave.'

'Wait a minute, was Danny a dark haired lad, about 25 years old? Would you recognise him again?'

Elvie nodded, 'Yes. Elvie would know. He nice man. Help Elvie escape later. You know where Danny is?'

Her voice was so hopeful that Ali felt bad for having to tell her the truth. 'I think Danny was killed, possibly by Gaz and Rocko from what you've told me.'

Elvie started to cry again quietly.

'Think that's enough for now, bro,' said Alex softly, pulling a tissue from his pocket and handing it to Elvie. 'Here you go, pet.' Turning to look at Ali, he said firmly, 'I think it's safe to say our cases are now officially linked. Take care of her? I'll go brief the super and the teams upstairs.'

19th November, 1200 hours - High Dependency Ward, Sunderland Royal Hospital

Connor tried to fight waking up. He didn't want to, it felt good floating on the clouds that the morphine left him on. His throat felt sore, and his tongue felt like it was coated with a thick carpet. Groaning, he forced his eyes open a slit, but the room was blurry and he couldn't focus.

His memory of what had happened taunted him, just out of reach. He knew it had been bad, but that was all he knew. He wanted to go back to sleep and not remember at all.

He went to turn over and curl back into the covers, but his stomach protested. It was tight and pulled painfully, causing him to gasp.

Feeling around with his hand, he managed to find the button that released his morphine. He vaguely remembered an angel in white telling him about it the last time he'd woken up. He pressed it several times, not conscious enough to realise it was on timed release anyway so repeat pressing wouldn't affect the amount entering his body.

As his mind drifted again, he saw horrible flashes of things that could have been memories. His dad swinging from a rope, smiling eerily. His uncle cutting the rope with a rusty old knife and laughing evilly as his dad fell with an oomph. He couldn't decide which bits were real and which were made up by his drug-addled mind.

He felt something between his lips – the nurse had put a straw there. For a second he forgot what he was supposed to do, but then recalled and sucked hard as though his life depended on it. The cool orange juice slid down into his tummy smoothly and he welcomed it gladly. He hadn't even realised he was thirsty.

'Thank you,' he said, though it came out more as a muffled groan. The nurse knew what he meant though. She patted his arm gently and told him to rest.

Drifting again, he closed his eyes and fell back into slumber.

19th November, 1320 hours - Marlo's flat, Sunderland

Marlo didn't know what to do.

Agnes had gone to Cass's cottage, but Elvie hadn't wanted to go. Since they'd gotten back to the apartment, all the kid had done was sit on the sofa staring into space, her eyes so full of pain that Marlo wanted to gather her up into the biggest cuddle ever and never let her go. She felt wholly unqualified to deal with the situation, if she was honest. Agnes had told her that all Elvie needed to know was that Marlo was there, that she was safe and that she could talk if she wanted to.

Marlo trusted Agnes: she'd brought up eight kids practically on her own, so she obviously knew what she was on about. Besides, Marlo had no other point of comparison. Her growing up in and out of children's homes hadn't taught her how to handle kids. She'd generally just stayed out of the way absorbed in whatever book she was reading at the time.

Marlo had tried with Elvie, she really had. She'd tried talking but Elvie hadn't spoken back, listening but Elvie was just not open to replying. She'd tried interaction – asking Elvie to help her in the kitchen and with some chores – but the kid had just sat on the couch and shook her head. She looked small, and so very sad sitting there lost in her lonely world.

Deciding they needed to get out of the house, Marlo decided to try another tactic. She got to her feet and passed Elvie her shoes and one of Marlo's thick jackets. 'Come on, love. We're going out.' She kept her tone firm so Elvie knew she had to go, and Marlo had to stop herself grinning as Elvie reluctantly pulled the shoes on and stood.

The drive to Seaburn would have been completely silent if not for the music coming from the radio.

Marlo parked up the car, still not quite knowing what to say, but she'd felt the need to show Elvie the sea. When Marlo had been growing up, the ocean had been a constant. The care homes she'd spent most of her time in had been a stone's throw from the beach, and she'd become a frequent visitor, the soothing sound of the waves helping her cope with the crap she put up with at home.

On a whim, she bought two ice creams from the shop and led the way down to the sand. She didn't know if Elvie had ever seen the sea, or sat on the sand, but it had always helped her.

Feeling the soft sand beneath her shoes, she felt calmness wash over her. Finding a raised dune, she sat down and looked out towards the sea. Elvie took the offered ice cream with whispered thanks, and sat down beside Marlo. It was bitterly cold, the sea breeze mixing with the already low temperature for the time of year and Marlo was glad of the heavy coats they both wore. There were still people on the beach though, dog walkers, joggers, and even a bunch of teenagers larking about. She hoped the calming sound of the waves crashing on the sand was helping Elvie to relax.

When Elvie finished her ice cream, Marlo said, 'Talk to me. I can't help you if you don't tell me what's wrong.'

Elvie hung her head. It was almost as if she was too scared to speak.

'Whatever it is, sweetheart, I'm not going anywhere. No matter what happens you will always be able to talk to me.'

'Why Marlo nice to Elvie? Elvie not nice person.' She sounded devastated, and tears filled her eyes.

Carefully, Marlo asked, 'Why do you think you're not a nice person? From what I know of you, you're a lovely girl with a big heart. I think you're nice.'

'Elvie leave Nita, not help her. I leave her in house. I bad person. Why Marlo like Elvie when I bad person? You no want me to stay. Send me back.'

'Is that what you think? That I'd send you back because of what happened? Now you listen to me, young lady, I'll not have this self-pity. What happened to you and Nita was awful, but you couldn't help her, sweetheart, not then. You had to make sure you stayed alive. You told me and Ali about Nita as soon as you could. I don't want you to go back, not if you don't want to go. I've even been looking at bigger houses so you could stay with me. I don't want you in a children's home, love. If you have family at home and you want to go back, then I'll help you do that, but if you stay, I'd like you to stay with me.'

'Marlo really want Elvie to stay? I not want go back, only my aunt there and she not nice, always shout at Noni. She hate Elvie.'

'Yes I want you to stay. I want you to go to school and learn, and later do a job you really want to do. I want you to be happy.' Now Marlo felt her eyes fill with tears, she wanted Elvie to stay more than anything. But it had to be a decision made by Elvie.

Elvie didn't speak for a moment, but then moved suddenly and threw her arms around Marlo's neck and squeezed tightly.

'Thank you,' she whispered in Marlo's ear.

'From now on, missus, you tell me when something's bothering you, OK?' Marlo sounded gruff, she felt really emotional. Elvie just nodded, and kept hold of Marlo. They must have looked strange, sitting hugging on a freezing cold beach in the middle of winter, but Marlo didn't care. It felt right.

19th November, 1625 hours - Sunderland City Police HQ

Ali rubbed a hand over his face - so much for days off. He'd ended up being involved in searching the house on Wear Street with Alex and the NCA, National Crime Agency. His need to see the crime scene for himself was not that strange, though. The girls who'd been found were his cases, not Alex's. He had a responsibility to speak for them when they couldn't speak for themselves.

He'd never seen anything so dingy and horrible as the house, and he'd seen some shitholes. The whole place was damp, mould had covered the walls and ceiling corners, and any wallpaper that had been left behind was from the seventies, aged manky patterns peeling and hanging in the midst of cobwebs. The whole building had felt like it should have been condemned.

The attic room had been the most awful, he didn't think he'd forget it in a hurry. Sparsely furnished and decked out with a torture chair similar to the one Alex had described in the shed of Connor's dad. And the whole attic was fully soundproofed so the screams couldn't be heard outside. A large stash of liquid heroin and syringes had been found in a small fridge situated beside a small

K.A. Richardson

computer. The computer had gone to Jacob Tulley in the digital forensics lab for examination - Ali hoped Jacob would be able to get information off it that would aid the investigation.

They'd found six girls inside, all high as kites and out of it completely. The two men located engaging in sexual activity with the barely conscious girls had been arrested, and the girls removed to a specialist centre for people trafficked into the country. He didn't know what would happen to them yet, but they were safe.

The man Elvie had mentioned, Gaz, was in the wind. He hadn't been at the house with the girls. Unease settled in Ali's stomach: Gaz appeared to be Rocko's second-in-command. He needed to be found. As did the house containing the female, Yolanda, that Elvie had spoken of. The voter's roll checks had brought forth only two living in the force area, and intelligence on both of them had been sparse. Charlie was running down the addresses now.

Alex had returned to the hospital to see if Connor was ready for interview and to check on Rocko, leaving Ali to finish up the paperwork and handover. It had been a long day, but he had to admit it felt good too. Rescuing the girls had definitely been the positive outcome he had hoped for – it was too late for the girls in the reservoir but at least some had been saved.

Frowning, he knew there would be locations like that all over the UK in a similar state, filled with girls like those. All he could hope, though, was that the National Crime Agency would be able to piece together additional contacts and locations and use it all to locate and assist more of them. Funnily enough, he'd heard on the news earlier that a container filled with about forty people had been discovered. He'd once thought that human trafficking wouldn't affect him in his role but now it seemed suddenly to be coming to the forefront.

Before he took the files down to handover to the DI coming on duty, he hit send on the email to both his and

Alex's teams calling a joint strategy meeting the next day. He had no intention of being in that meeting. If he didn't take a day off he'd go insane. Besides, he had to visit immigration with Elvie. There was no getting out of it this time.

20th November, 1505 hours - High Dependency Unit, Sunderland Royal Hospital

Connor had sensed Alex sitting by the bed ages ago. He'd come round a little more over the course of the afternoon and the nurse had reduced his morphine dose. He no longer had the push button and had it administered intermittently instead. He'd been trying to pretend to be unconscious so Alex would just leave it all until the next day, but his tactic hadn't worked. He knew Alex was there for the duration.

Slowly he opened his eyes.

"Bout time you stopped pretending, mate,' said Alex, looking up from his newspaper, 'I get it, though, don't worry. Trouble is, professional standards are coming tomorrow, and I wanted to see you first, get your version of events.'

'You mean find out if I'm dirty,' said Connor.

'Aye, that too,' replied Alex with a nod. 'Are you?'

'Depends on your definition, I guess. You need to understand something, though; I did what I did because Fred would've hurt my whole family. He held every single card and he knew it. He would've put Mum and Dad out on the streets, forced Marie to leave uni. I didn't have the money to pay for her uni and their house as well as mine. I know it sounds cowardly, I know I shouldn't have done it. But I didn't feel like I had a choice.'

'What are we talking about here, Connor? What didn't you have a choice about?'

'I gave Fred intel. Nothing major, just dates of drugs busts and what not, and where I could I fabricated it. He told me he'd hurt us all if I didn't.'

K.A. Richardson

'OK, and you're gunna stick to that with standards. You tell them the whole truth, OK? No covering up, no lies, tell it like it was. Wanna tell me what happened in the shed now?'

'Dunno where to start. I just thought Dad was pottering down there. My mum has Alzheimer's and she was sitting in the window, quiet as a mouse. I just thought she was having a good day. I'd never been in his shed before. I didn't expect – I mean, I didn't know he –' Connor broke off, emotion clogging his throat.

'I'm sorry, Connor, I need to know what happened.'

'Dad had hung himself. I walked in the door and he was just swinging there. I knew he was dead, you know? But I still needed to try and help him, was going to give him CPR. But Fred wouldn't let me. He threw Dad's note at me. Laughed when I read it. He did it. He killed the girls we pulled out of the reservoir. My own dad. Though he's not really my dad, and that makes it even worse. Fred's my dad. I never had a chance. The man I thought was my dad is a killer, and the man I thought was my horrible criminal uncle is actually my dad. It's fucked up.'

'You just found this out? What happened then?'

'I pulled out my phone to call the control room – I couldn't do it anymore, couldn't cover for any of them. I know my job's over, there's no way prof standards will let me stay now. I dialled, and Fred lost it.' Connor closed his eyes for a minute then opened them again. 'He came at me with a knife. I pushed him away, tried to get him to stop. But he kept coming. It was like he was possessed. He didn't want me to tell, wanted me to help him cover it all up. I grabbed the only thing I could, didn't even know what it was. I hit him, and I killed him. Told you it was fucked up.'

'Killed him? Connor, Fred isn't dead. He's a few rooms along the corridor. And from the sounds of it, it was self-defence.'

The blood drained from Connor's face. 'Alive? But he can't be. He dropped like a stone. I hit him so hard.'

'Honestly, he's alive. I wouldn't lie, Connor.'

'Jesus. I'm fucked. He'll kill me. He ran it all. Gave the girls to Dad, knew everything that was going on. Marie can barely even look at me. She blames me. She's right. I could've stopped it years ago. I thought moving back up here from the Midlands would stop it, sever the ties once and for all. But Fred followed. Blackmailed me for info. I didn't know what to do.'

'You should've told someone, Connor, let us help you. As it stands, it'll be down to professional standards now. Everything will be taken into account though. Your mum's safe, by the way. She's in a council-run home over on the other side of the river. Marie's been staying at the Premier Inn. Make sure you pass all the information you know on Fred over: it will help your case. I shouldn't really be here, but I wanted you to know what was going on and I wanted your side of the story. That said I'd better make tracks. You did the right thing in the end, Connor. Try not to let all this eat you up.'

Alex left, and Connor realised he actually felt a little relieved. For the first time in a long time, he felt like a weight had been lifted. He wasn't being controlled like some puppet on a very short string. Whatever came of the professional standards investigation, he'd make sure he was OK. Him, Marie and his mum were all that mattered now.

20th November, 1835 hours – High Dependency Unit, Sunderland Royal Hospital

Marlo stuck her head around the door to Connor's room, finding him awake but staring vacantly out of the window.

'Hey,' she said softly, trying not to scare him. She wasn't sure he'd heard her come into the room. He jumped then winced as he turned to face her. 'Sorry, didn't mean to make you jump. How're you doing?'

Connor shrugged, 'OK, I guess. Just sitting here doing bugger all. They won't let me go home.'

'That's kind of understandable. You were stabbed, guess they need to monitor you.'

He looked really sad as he shrugged again and said, 'I know. Just hate hospitals is all.'

'Oh quit your whingeing, you're alive. That's what counts. Sitting there doing naff all for a few weeks beats being dead any day. You were lucky from the sounds of it.'

'Depends on your definition of luck,' grumbled Connor.

'Hey, enough already,' Marlo's voice was strict and she almost groaned as she realised how very 'school ma'am' she sounded. 'I don't care how much it hurts now, you're still here. Pull your head out of your arse and be grateful.'

Connor had the grace to look contrite, but didn't speak.

'Look,' she continued, softening her tone, 'I know you've got it tough at the minute. I don't know the ins and outs and you don't have to tell me if you don't want to, but you're not alone here, Connor. You have friends and family who care for you. Whatever your mistakes, you're a nice guy. If you need a friend, I'm here.'

Connor's eyes filled at her kind words, all the stress catching up on him suddenly. Tears fell, and embarrassed, he swiped at them with the back of his hand.

'Sorry, it's just – I can't –'

'We all cry, there's nothing to be ashamed of in that, Connor.' Marlo handed him a tissue.

She was so focussed on Connor that she didn't even register the door behind her had been pushed open.

She heard Connor cry out, and then everything seemed to start moving in slow motion. Marlo half-turned towards the door, and felt something hard hit the side of her head. Gravity defied her as she toppled forwards, not even having the time to put out her hands to stop herself from face-planting onto the floor.

Rivers of red ran through her eyes as she fought to stay conscious, and vaguely she heard Connor cry out again.

Forcing herself to her knees, she made out a blurred form through the blood covering her eyes. The figure had Connor by the throat, and somewhere in her mind, she thought he was wearing a hospital gown.

Knowing Connor needed her help, she pulled herself up using the bed rails. Her legs wobbled as she fought the wave of nausea that swept over her. Carefully she pulled herself round the bed to the side where the male grappled with Connor. Taking a deep breath to steady herself, she tried to focus.

The man definitely wore a hospital gown, and he had his hands around Connor's throat, squeezing hard, pure hatred shining in his eyes. He'd not even registered that Marlo had stood up. Which she knew worked to her advantage. She manoeuvred herself around the bed, and once behind the man, she used her training and quickly grabbed him in a choke-hold, kicking at the back of his knees to displace his weight.

His roar was primal and he let go of Connor and grabbed at Marlo's hands. Pushing himself back to his feet, he threw himself backwards in an effort to release her hold. Marlo's back smashed into the ledge around the base of the window and she grunted as pain burst across the base of her spine. She kept hold, though.

He bent double suddenly, trying to throw her over his head, but she was ready and had adjusted her own weight to compensate.

She heard him gurgle, his air supply cut off by the force of her arm against the front of his throat, and she knew he was starting to weaken. If she could just keep hold, then maybe he'd lose consciousness. Which was precisely what she couldn't do. Even now, the corners of her mind were screaming at her to stop, to give up and embrace the darkness that threatened, but she couldn't. Not yet.

He scratched at her arms, his too-long fingernails gouging welts into her skin, but still she held on. *Is he ever going to go down? What the hell is Connor doing?*

Marlo's hold slipped even before she realised she'd allowed herself to become distracted and her attacker was ready. He tried to spin round as her legs collapsed on her and she sank to the floor, but she somehow managed to land in a tangle of mixed arms and legs.

Realising he was free, he rose to his feet, and booted Marlo hard to the ribs. She was sure she felt one crack under the impact, and braced herself for another impact.

It didn't come.

She lifted her head and glanced up, but her vision was so blurred all she could see was a shadow sweep past her and slam the man into the wall at the back of the hospital room. Marlo shook her head, trying to rid herself of this incessant dizziness.

'That's blood on my arm... it's my blood... oh, crap...' the words had started with a hint of wonder but the second she realised it was her own blood, her head hit the floor as she fainted. Again.

Chapter Thirty-One

20th November, 1845 hours – High Dependency Unit, Sunderland Royal Hospital
The last thing Ali had expected to see on entering Connor's room was Connor gasping for breath, and a blood-covered Marlo grappling with Fred Rockingham on the floor. Panic almost knocked him for six, and he'd seen Marlo start to sink to the floor. The crack her ribs had made when Fred had kicked her had reverberated around the room, and he'd felt his breath catch.

Then the anger had arrived.

He'd all but flown around the bed and used his whole body weight to slam Rockingham into the wall behind the head of Connor's bed.

Now he stood with his arm jabbed up into the man's throat, practically daring him to fight back. 'Calm the fuck down,' he said. How he was managing to maintain control of his temper he didn't know, but he was doing his best. Fred struggled beneath his arm, and in one movement, Ali spun Fred around and shoved his face into the wall. 'In case you hadn't gathered,' he panted as he pushed Fred's arm up his back, 'You're nicked. Now calm the fuck down before I put you down,' said Ali firmly.

Fred was spent though. He sagged in his hospital gown beneath Ali's grip and whispered, 'It's over.' His head shook as though he couldn't quite believe it.

'What the…' Alex's astounded voice came from the doorway. 'I go for coffee and come back to… What the hell is all this?'

'Take him, Alex. Get him the hell out of my sight. I need to check on Marlo.'

'Bitch deserved it,' muttered Fred, his muscles tensing beneath Ali's grip.

'Don't bother yourself,' Alex's voice was calm as he took over his brother's hold on Fred and pushed him

265

towards the hospital room door. 'Like he said, you're nicked. You do not have to say anything but anything you do say…' Alex's voice faded as he took Fred down the corridor.

'A little help here,' shouted Ali, kneeling beside Marlo.

20th November, 1920 hours – Sunderland Royal Hospital

Marlo groaned and opened her eyes. Her head felt like it was splitting in two, and the light was as sharp as a pin.

'Christ,' she said, trying to sit up.

The movement caused the room to tilt sideways, and her head flopped back down to the pillow.

'Easy, Marlo. You took a helluva knock to the head. Doc says you've got concussion.' She cracked her eyes open again and glared at Ali, just because he was the nearest thing to her and was stating the obvious.

'Bloody bloke was huge. Was it Connor's uncle? Is Connor OK?'

'Aye, it was Rockingham, and yes Connor's going to be fine. Has some bruising to his neck and larynx but he'll be OK. He's a tough guy. Said you were like a thing possessed, pulling his uncle off him and putting him in a choke-hold. Little spitfire you are, love.'

Marlo knew Ali was teasing, 'Wish I'd just left him to it. My head's bloody killing me. Was it you who slammed him against the wall?'

She watched Ali's eyes darken with anger, and realised he'd been genuinely afraid for her. He nodded with a grim smile, and instantly she knew he'd wanted to do way more than slam the guy against the wall.

'How'd you know I was here?' It suddenly hit her that she'd arrived at the hospital alone.

'Elvie, she told me you'd left. I needed to see if Rockingham was awake so I could arrange the interview, and I figured I'd pop up and meet you before I went down. He knocked Harry Green out, you know? Harry had let his cop go back to the nick for change-over. He was just gunna wait for the replacement to arrive. Rockingham fooled everyone into thinking he was still out for the count, the sneaky bastard. He's cuffed to the bed now, like. The nurse didn't even know how he was conscious. Says he can be taken to court tomorrow, and my guess is, thanks to his behaviour, he'll be remanded without bail.'

'Should bloody hope so too. You'll need a statement off me?'

'Yeah, but tomorrow'll be soon enough. Only reason the doctor let me sit with you was 'cos I told him we were engaged. Don't think he believed me, like, not 'til Alex backed me up anyway.'

Marlo blushed, 'He probably thinks I'm a right slut then. I had to say the same thing to get him to let me in to see Connor.'

Ali smiled, his face lighting up. *I've never seen him smile so brightly – solving cases is good for him. I like him… oh, I like him!* The thought hit her like a ton of bricks and for a moment she couldn't speak.

When his hand reached over and brushed an errant strand of hair from the side of her face, she shivered at his touch. Seeing the look she gave him, he leant over the bed and kissed her.

Marlo kissed back, instantly wanting more. Nipping at his lip, she moaned as he pulled away.

'Bad girl,' he said gruffly, 'Keep kissing me like that and I'll take you right here and right now.'

Marlo blushed furiously. 'Who says I don't want you to?' she countered, her words bolder than she actually felt.

Ali made a strangled noise and purposefully stood and walked to the door. He went to flick the catch on the lock, when the door suddenly opened and Alex walked in.

Glancing first at Ali, then at Marlo, Alex put two and two together and guessed what he'd interrupted. 'You two are best keeping that kind of behaviour for home,' his voice dropped to a cheeky whisper, 'besides, the locks are shite. Me and Cass nearly got caught twice when she was in.'

A spurt of surprised laughter burst from Marlo, and Ali grinned.

'Anyhow, hormones aside, the super's on her way down so be prepared for a grilling. Your sergeant's on his way down too, Marlo. So,' he added with a wink, 'I'd try and control yourselves.'

21st November, 0940 hours, Sunderland City Police HQ

Ali sat at his desk, a little on edge as he waited for the interview with Fred Rockingham to conclude. He hadn't trusted himself not to leap over the desk and rip the guy's head from his shoulders after what he'd done to Marlo, so he'd sent Charlie in to interview him instead. His anger had been simmering since the night before, and he knew handing the reins to her had been the right decision.

It didn't stop him wondering, though. Would Fred give it up, provide them with the coveted information on the people behind the whole trafficking malarkey, or remain schtum and not give them the smallest of bites at the bigger fish. Wouldn't really matter either way, Ali knew. They had him bang to rights for attempted murder of Connor and for assaulting Marlo. He would go away for a good long time regardless.

'McKay,' he said absently, picking up the phone receiver as it rang beside him.

'Ali, it's Jacob Tulley from the digital lab. Have you got a sec?'

'Aye, go on, Jacob.'

'I'm trying to squeeze in the exam of the PC seized from the address on Wear Street the other day. Just wanted to make sure I have it in the condition it was seized in. The front cover of the base unit is separated and I need to be sure no one's messed with any of the interior components. Chain of command seems solid but I figured a quick question to the source would put me at ease.'

'As far as I know, that's how it was seized. If memory serves, the cover had been screwed to the table leg. They had to loosen it to remove the base unit. Double-check with Kev Lang - am sure he was the one dismantling. He's on duty now, saw his Romeo in the car park this morning. Talk about a mid-life crisis car, like,' Ali's tone was light: he knew Kevin's wife had died. Everyone did. He didn't blame him for spending his money on something a little flashier than your average car.

'Chance would be a fine thing,' said Jacob. 'Thanks, Ali. Catch you later.'

Ali hung up the phone just as Charlie pushed open the door to the office.

'Hey, boss. Well that was a complete waste of time. He made 'no comments' all the way through. Solicitor's paid for, decent company too. So whoever's pulling the strings is making sure he's not going to speak.'

'Yea I thought he might go that way. Did he react to any of the names you threw at him?'

'Not really. Glimmer of recognition at Yolanda but nothing substantial.'

'We any further forward on getting details for her?'

'There's six Yolandas registered on the voters roll across the north east. Two are in their eighties and live in care homes, the others either live so far north they're in Northumberland or so far south they're in Catterick. None live near to Sunderland at all. And the information doesn't lend to a large amount of time taken travelling. Elvie said she'd walked on foot to where she hitched a ride in the dive boat.'

'RIB,' correctly Ali absently, considering what she'd told him. 'How about Gaz? Any leads on him?'

'Sorry, boss. He's still in the wind. We're running down his known associates, but they were tight-lipped last time we dragged them in. Can't think their attitude will have changed that much between then and now.'

'Damn, NCA are already going to be pissed with the lateness of the intel. I can see a sit-down with the chief super in my not so distant future.'

'Did we get anything else from the dive lad? He must know something. This was his dad and uncle for God's sake. Bit hard to swallow like, him being a dirty cop.'

'Aye, well we don't know the full ins and outs yet. We've all been given gag orders though: no one but professional standards are allowed to speak with him. He's been suspended pending full investigation, but I doubt very much he'll be coming back.'

'There's always a choice,' said Charlie, 'he made the wrong ones.'

'Aye, I know, just a shame, is all. With his dad and uncle as relatives the lad never stood much chance really.'

'True enough, boss. I've got an interviewee coming in shortly so I'll need to go prep. Catch up with you later.'

21st November, 1420 hours - detached house, near Hetton-Le-Hole

Gaz glanced around furtively before slipping into the long driveway that led up to the big house. He didn't even know if the boss lady would still be there, but he was determined to find her if she was, tell her what he knew and leave with her. Since learning of Rocko's arrest, Gaz had harboured dreams that he would be the next boss; that he was next in line to bring the girls into the life for which they'd been brought to the country. He knew it would mean a different location, and he was fine with it. He had no ties to the north east.

He'd almost had a heart attack on the spot when he'd wandered down Wear Street the other day and found the brothel surrounded by cop cars. Ducking behind an old van for protection, he'd watched as the cops had marched all of the girls out of the premises and taken the computer from upstairs. And for the first time in a long time, he'd felt desperation.

This job was his only source of income, and already his meagre funds had run dry. He'd barely had enough for the petrol over here, let alone for anything else.

Reaching the front door, he tried the handle, not surprised to find it opened with ease. Stepping over the threshold he paused, listening for the slightest sound to indicate that anyone was inside.

He heard nothing, not even the whisper of a spider crossing the floorboards. It was as if the house itself was on edge.

He shivered, almost turning to leave, but something compelled him forward. And that something was the thought that maybe Yolanda would trust him and take him with her to wherever she was headed to set up shop.

Determination flooded through him - he deserved a break, he'd worked damn hard for Rocko, recently, doing all the crap that no-one else wanted to do. He deserved the money, the freedom to shag whichever girl he wanted whenever the need overtook him. He deserved to be part of the bigger picture.

Pushing open the door to the main reception room, he froze as he came face to face with the barrel of a gun.

He felt his stomach bottom out in shock. He knew violence, hell, he enjoyed violence, but never against himself. And this was the first time he'd ever been faced with a gun.

Gaz looked past the gun, up the man's arms, and straight into his steely, emotionless eyes. In that moment Gaz realised he knew nothing of violence. This man, standing in front of him with his hand raised steady, and his finger on the trigger, knew all about pain.

Belatedly, Gaz registered the tell-tale smell of metal in the air - metal from freshly spilled blood.

His eyes drifted to his left, and he saw the bodies of Yolanda and her two henchmen, a single bullet wound to the middle of each of their heads.

'Please, no...' begged Gaz, stumbling backwards in a feeble attempt to get away.

21st November, 1425 hours – detached house, near Hetton-Le-Hole

The man clicked his jaw twice, steadying himself as a soft pop emitted from the weapon in his hand. He felt the subtle jerk in his hand, comfortable in how it felt. The silencer deadened the noise that would have alerted every house in the vicinity, and he watched as Gaz toppled sideways, his eyes wide, his life already extinguished.

Such was the nature of the job.

Quickly, he progressed with a through sweep of the premises; his orders were clear. Make sure no-one was left standing: and he never failed to carry those orders out. He'd done it for years, was the best in the business.

Happy that the house was now void of life, he did a search and recover for any documentation that could potentially point to those he called 'the management'. What little he found was immediately destroyed in a flash of flame.

One last check of the reception room, and it was time to leave. He slipped down the driveway using the trees as cover, got into the non-descript ford focus that hovered near the driveway entrance – the false plates meant that even if it was seen it wouldn't be identifiable – turned the key in the ignition, and drove off.

Another job complete.

Epilogue

18th December, 1045 hours - Marlo's flat, Sunderland

Marlo's stomach hadn't stopped churning all morning. She knew it was just nerves, but it was unsettling.

Agent Kenton from the Border Force was due to ring before noon to let them know the status of Elvie's immigration request. She'd sought asylum, of the firm belief that if she returned to her village that she would be taken again and forced into the sex trade elsewhere. He'd already indicated there should be no problem, but one could never be sure.

Elvie was nervous, too. She hadn't moved from her perch on the sofa all morning, sitting in silence and chewing on her fingernails. Marlo would have been worried but for the fact Ali sat next to her, cradling the lukewarm coffee she'd made him almost an hour ago.

Marlo's head was filled with what if's and maybes. She was terrified something would come up at the last minute and Elvie would be returned to the Philippines.

They all jumped visibly as the phone rang.

Picking up the receiver, Marlo listened intently.

All she heard though were the words '... pleased to grant Elvie Aquino UK residency...'

She couldn't stop the smile that lit up her face, and when Elvie jumped off the couch and threw her arms around her, Marlo hugged back tightly, tears streaming down her face. Ali grabbed them both, wrapping his arms around them simultaneously and they just stood for a minute.

When they broke apart, Marlo decided it was time to tell Elvie something she hoped would make the child even happier.

'You remember you told me about your granddad, the Englishman your gran lost touch with? Elvie, he's not dead.

He had a stroke so couldn't write, but he's alive, and what's more he doesn't live far away. I spoke to his carers this morning, explained about you, and they think it would do him the world of good to see you. Would you like to go and see him?'

Elvie nodded, obviously not trusting herself to speak. Her eyes were filled with wonder.

I hope they never stop being filled with so much happiness. Marlo kept her thought to herself and held her hand out and took hold of Elvie's, turning to smile at Ali as they went to leave.

'You coming?'

'Can't,' he replied, his voice obviously disappointed. 'Have to go in for a meeting with the super. I believe her exact words to the whole team were 'be there or heads will roll' so I can't really bow out. She's practically blown a gasket over the deaths in Hetton - a professional hit in the north east, no viable leads. It's a certifiable shit storm.'

Marlo nodded, 'Sorry, love. If the leads aren't there, though, that's not your fault. Don't let her bully you. We'll see you when we get back.'

'OK, love. Then we'll talk about looking for a place to live. Together,' he said meaningfully.

Marlo blushed. Moving in together after only a few weeks was rash, impulsive, and a completely out-of-character decision.

But it also felt completely right, she acknowledged as she left the flat with Elvie.

18th December, 1045 hours – a care home, Sunderland

Across town, Connor sat in the green, leatherette chair, staring out of the window at the fields beyond.

He'd received his marching orders from the police before he'd even been discharged from hospital. He'd known it would happen but it still stung. They couldn't let him keep his job when he'd been swayed into giving intel to a criminal, whether said criminal had blackmailed him or not. Most of the people he'd considered friends, had slowly backed away, not wanting to be associated with a dirty cop, which was what he essentially was.

He'd managed to avoid criminal charges: the Crown Prosecution Service happy that he'd acted in self-defence where Fred had been concerned, and happy that the information he'd provided on Fred was sufficient that the issue of him passing intel over was lessened to a non-chargeable offence. Not that it mattered now anyway. Fred was locked up in a tiny cell with no release imminent. The judge had ruled he would serve life, no parole.

Connor was still jobless though. And in a few short months when he couldn't pay the mortgage on his flat any more, he'd be homeless.

Marie hadn't spoken to him at all since she'd blown her top at the hospital. She'd accused him of being in with Fred, saying only a partner would pass him information that wasn't supposed to be shared. She'd already gone back to her perfect uni life, requesting additional financial aid, and had every intention of carrying on without Connor in her life at all, blaming him for the death of their dad, for Fred being a criminal and for their mother being placed in the home.

Sheila lay on the bed near the window, her head turned towards the window permanently. The nurses said it was shock from the change to her living arrangements. They didn't know if she would improve. It was guilt that drove him to sit with her every day for hours on end. Guilt and the knowledge that he'd finally got his way: his mum was in the home like he'd wanted, so in essence everything that had happened was indeed, his fault.

Gently, he rubbed his thumb over the razor blade in his jacket pocket, feeling the sharp edge cut through the top layers of skin as though they were nothing more than hot butter. He felt the smallest amount of blood well to the surface, and he smiled. This he could control, when everything else around was falling to shit, he could feel this.

Closing his eyes, he laid his head back and rested against the chair.

Life sucked. It was, in fact, a complete load of bollocks.

His stomach pulled as he shifted position, reminding him he still hadn't healed. The doctor had said it would take months to heal properly – when Fred had twisted the blade it had caused bad muscle damage.

He didn't know what he was going to do now. Nothing was any clearer now than it had been a week ago.

Sighing he laid his head against the back of the chair and closed his eyes.

The shit would still be there tomorrow.

THE END

Acknowledgments

Bloodhound Books make getting published an absolute pleasure – the whole team from Betsy and Fred to my lovely editor Claire, and the fab designer are just brilliant. I couldn't do this without you.

This book is based around the dive team – and a massive thank you goes to Steve Howe who is a police diver, a sergeant, and has been instrumental in helping me get this novel into shape. My unending questions about where to submerge a body, and would *this* reservoir be deep enough to hide the body etc, were answered rapidly without him even batting an eye lid. The dive team headquarters and the equipment room were fab in helping me paint a picture to use in my mind.

I couldn't write this novel without thinking of those trafficked into the country illegally and the things they have to go through – it was part of my research but as it progressed I came to understand more and more about how much these folk go through and how very hard it is for them. If I could have one wish come from this book, it would be to raise awareness – human trafficking is real, it's dangerous and it's close to home.

To all my crime scene investigator friends who are always there with answers when I need them – you're fabulous. Thank you. As always the lovely Inspector Caz has been on hand for my police related questions and as always she's been fab.

My whole family are so supportive - without them writing just wouldn't be possible. The support and patience they provide is unwavering and constant. They all make me so proud every single day.

My close friends are my rocks – constant support through good and bad, and not being too shy to tell me when I'm doing something I shouldn't be! You know who you are – but to mention a few names (by no means all) Claire,

Angela, Dionne, Rachel, Vicky, Eileen, Michelle and Char. Keep shining like the stars you are.

Finally, I'd like to thank *YOU*, the reader. Writing really wouldn't be as pleasurable without each and every one of you, whether I know you or not, you make my dreams a reality. It makes me very proud to admit I'm a member of THE Book Club, UK Crime Book Club, Crime Book Club and Crime Fiction Addict on Facebook – these clubs make speaking to readers simple and I thoroughly enjoy the interaction, banter, and suggestions for books to read, characters and plots to write. I look forward to meeting more of you at the various events planned in the near future.

Glossary of terms:

Brown Sugar – Heroin
CSI – Crime Scene Investigator
CSM – Crime Scene Manager
DCI – Detective Chief Inspector
DI – Detective Inspector
DNA – deoxyribonucleic acid
Fed – federation (police union)
Gov – governor (used by lower ranks to address higher ranks)
HOLMES – UK database for logging major crime
HQ – Headquarters
ID – identification
LV – force terminology used by the force to describe themselves (i.e LV refers to North East Police)
MIT – Major Incident Team
NCA – National Crime Agency
PADI – Professional Association of Diving Instructors
PNC – police national computer
PM – Post Mortem
POLSA – police search advisor
QT – quiet (you're not allowed to say quiet or it jinxes the day!)
RIB – Rigid Inflatable Boat
RVP – Rendezvous Point
SOCARD – database for logging crime scene information
Super – superintendent